My Real Life
A REMADE MAN

Books by the same author

For adults:

Sun on Distant Hills

For children:

*Darcy, the Farm Foxie — How a little dog
helped his family in the drought.*

My Real Life
A REMADE MAN

ELIZABETH EGAN

My Real Life by Elizabeth Egan

Published by Elizabeth Egan © All rights reserved

1st Edition 2019, paperback.
ISBN: 9781925999143

Ebook version
ISBN: 9780648499992

Publishing services by: PublishMyBook.Online
Book design and layout done by James Munro and Julia Lefik

Font: Minion Pro 12pt on 15pt leading.

Printed by Top Shot Photographics and Prints, Goulburn NSW on 80gsm Supreme Uncoated paper manufactured under ISO 14001 Environmental Management System using elemental free chlorine pulp sourced from well-managed forests.

NATIONAL LIBRARY OF AUSTRALIA

A catalogue record for this book is available from the National Library of Australia

Thank you to my husband and friends who helped bring this story into existence and to the people who inspired it.

Chapter One

'Just leave it, Mum.' Andy flicks his head aside as Mrs Contopoulos reaches to stroke hair from his forehead. 'That's how I want it. And I dunno if I'll be here for dinner. Probably not. Just leave something you can heat up for me when I get home.'

Mrs Contopoulos fusses around her son. If she hadn't rushed to the foyer from the kitchen when he called goodbye she would have missed him altogether.

'Such a handsome boy! You should not let hair fall over your face. And you should come home to eat with us because your Aunty Zoe will be here. She comes to see you, I think, more than to see me. Do not forget she is your godmother. I am cooking your favourite tonight—moussaka! If you are not here, I will save you some.

'But you should be here. And remember, your father says you must do some study each night.'

'Yeah. I know what Dad thinks. I get told every day, and I wish he'd stop trying to run my life. Why do you think I don't get up to have breakfast with him before he goes to the hospital? It's always the same. He never lets up. I do plenty of study. I got to have a life as well... see friends, take girls out.'

'Your father only wants what is best for you. You know

he loves you very much, Andy. If you are successful, you will be happy. That is all he wants for you.'

Mrs Contopoulos softens when Andy calls her 'Mama' and puts an arm around her. He says, 'There's more to happiness than being a famous doctor.' Andy steps back and strikes an heroic pose. 'This Adonis must scour the land for a woman beautiful enough to be his wife. That means I have to meet every chick at every pub and nightclub. It's hard work and takes time. That's my job, starting now. It's huge but I'm willing to try. Besides, if you and Dad want to be a Yiayia and Papou then it's up to me. Right?'

Mrs Contopoulos blanches and grimaces. In silence she scoops his leather jacket off the visitor settee and holds it for Andy to slip both arms into the sleeves. Her hands linger on his shoulders. He turns to peck her on the cheek and stays bent for the return kiss. Instead, she flings her arms around him and sobs, only once, before pulling back and presenting a bright face.

'Sorry, Mum. That was a stupid thing to say. I miss her, too.'

Mrs Contopoulos pats Andy's arm to reassure and forgive as she opens the front door for him. 'Take care, my boy.'

●———————●

As Andy remotely closes the garage door, he gives a fleeting thought to this morning's class: physiology. He'd be late even if he went straight there. Anyway, it's the sort of stuff that's easy to catch up on. He turns west to the outer suburbs and heads to meet the guys at a workshop that belongs to a cousin's friend. Half a dozen young blokes run the shed, but a circle of car enthusiasts trickles by to admire the vehicles that come in, and to be awed at how their identities are transformed. They get a kick from the sheer size of the operation and the expertise of the guys who run it. The fact that it's illegal and covert is an extra buzz.

Andy hasn't mentioned car rebirthing at home. He knows it's unlawful, and something about it strikes him as immoral, but it's what his friends are in to, so he goes along with the crowd. The friends are an amorphous group of between twelve and twenty, mainly of Greek heritage, and with a common interest in parties, girls and fast cars. Andy's Lotus is considered a chick-magnet so he's first choice for a lift to a party, and a 'must-come' when they're cruising for women.

Some of the group are uni students like Andy, although he's the only one enrolled in Medicine. The other students are doing courses with fewer face-to-face lecture hours so they have more free time. The Demetriadis brothers work in their family's restaurant at night and can only party in the day time. A few are in long-term limbo as would-be entrepreneurs or as failed students, or are admittedly unemployed. The set-up suits all the guys because it means there's like-minded company any time of the day or night. They are as a group of brothers.

No two identify as best mates except that Andy and Chris have a lot in common: Chris likes to party but he's not wild, and they talk about things the others aren't interested in. If Andy had a real brother, he would want him to be like Chris. He and Andy are each prepared to, and have in the past helped the other out in difficult circumstances.

Chris isn't coming to the workshop this morning but he'll be at the pub this afternoon. Friday night is party time and kicks off with a big session at The Royal on Parramatta Road opposite the university. It's a student hotel but the whole crowd likes to drink there because of the good bands and chicks in abundance: adventurous, sociable college girls from up the road, and others who rent locally but socialise at The Royal. He's looking forward to it.

Andy pulls up at a neat bungalow. It's unpretentious and far from homely. He walks around the side and down the long yard, bare except for closely mown grass, to the huge shed at the back. There's a back lane and he can see some of his friends' cars through gaps in the paling fence. Andy slips in a side door and registers his usual reaction: admiration and trepidation. He respects their skill and audacity, he's amazed at the scale of what they do, and he's burdened by the guilt of knowing about it. He shouldn't even be here. If the police ever tied him in with this business, he'd be history. Doctors can't have a criminal record.

A semi with a 'shipment' pulls up in the lane and the shed wall slides open. It's all hands on deck as goods are whipped inside, the door is slid shut and the truck waved off: it barely had to stop. Andy helps move and stack boxes but his adrenalin fuelled high evaporates as he looks around: all the gear is there; hoists for lifting engines, drills to grind off engine numbers, even a sealed compartment for spray-painting. The reassembled cars are a marvel... and very profitable. Just being there makes him an associate of a criminal organisation, and an accessory before and after the fact. He's feeling bad vibes about sharing something illicit, even with mates.

Andy says, 'Gotta go. Just remembered something. See you tonight at the pub.'

'Okay,' says one. 'Thanks for the help.'

They shrug off Andy's sudden departure. He's never entirely fitted in.

●————————●

'Skol! Skol! Skol!' The sound rings through The Royal.

The boys are back into the beer and the boat races, urging each other to chug-a-lug schooners. They started on beer, then the mixers and wine, and now it's back to beer.

'Reckon it's time, Larry?' queries the barmaid.

Larry, the publican, doesn't like cleaning up after Friday night drinkers, but nor does he want to stop serving earlier than necessary. It's the best night for business, but it's also the night most likely for licensing police to check he's serving alcohol responsibly.

'Let them go a bit more. I'll keep an eye on them.'

Across the room in Andy's group one of the girls pulls her T-shirt and bra up high under her chin. She exposes her breasts and invites Spiros to snog her but as soon as he attempts to bury his nose, she pushes him off. Others hoot and howl.

'Debbie, that's cruelty to a dumb animal!'

'Go on! Don't be mean. You gotta share!'

The guys clamber over each other to reach Debbie for the chance of a snog. She covers herself and stands up, swaying as she signals for quiet.

'Tell you what,' she slurs. 'You gotta win it. Whoever wins a chicken race gets a go. And who ever snogs the best gets to walk me home. And I live... just down the road.' Her theatrical wink is undone with giggles and a hiccough.

They surge out onto the footpath. Spiros demands to be in the first pair to run. Eddy wants a chance with Debbie but he hasn't come to the pub with the boys before so Debbie explains the rules.

'It's called 'traffic chicken' 'cos you're playing chicken with the traffic. When the lights down the road go green you run to the island in the middle of the road and turn round and run back before the cars get here. The first one back gets a bit of this!'

Debbie hoicks her clothes up again and shimmies for five seconds. She's got a great set. The guys start pairing up for a run. Spiros and Eddy line up on the edge of the footpath and when the lights change, they charge. It's the main road between the western suburbs and the city so there's always traffic, and late on a Friday night people are still streaming in.

The first pair do it easily. Traffic dawdles down from the lights about one hundred and fifty metres away. Maybe there's a police car amongst them. Eddy is declared the winner and there's a melee around him and Debbie as he collects his winnings.

Andy lived at college for his first year of uni and then

moved home so he could study with fewer distractions. A lot of the guys he socialises with still live on campus and the warden at college still spouts warnings about dangerous things students do and how many have been killed or injured over the years while playing the fool. The traffic chicken game has killed two young men in the last ten years. College boys laugh at the warden.

The more they drink, the more daring they are, the worse their judgement becomes, and the slower they run. Right now, the whole group is paralytic. Some of the girls start up a chant: *Heaven and hell! Heaven and hell!* That's what the boys must go through. It's hell outrunning the traffic, but heaven when they get back. Two more girls on the footpath flash their tits as the boys turn. If they time it well, and are brave enough to *walk* the return leg, the snogging is extra-long—that's more heaven.

Andy and Chris leap forward to be the next pair and line up, howling down other would-be strutters. Traffic streams past and clears because of the red lights up the road. The lights change and two cars roar off. They've been dragging each other since Strathfield—it's the highlight of their Friday night. Andy and Chris jump, sort of, from the kerb amidst sooling and hooting and it's all fun as they canter to the island. They turn to look at the crowd outside the pub: the blokes are yelling and the girls are shrieking. Andy and Chris ogle Debbie and another girl who are trying to outdo each other with their shimmy. The boy who dares to walk back will get the prize.

They begin to saunter without looking at what's

coming. Someone shrieks a warning to hurry. Andy is too drunk to hear Chris shouting at him to get out of the way. He feels Chris grab his arm, then pull and push him, but it's too late—the cars are there. There's a bang as one hits Chris and then clips Andy. Andy spins as Chris flies past—close enough, but too fast for Andy to grab him in mid-air—and thuds metres away into a power pole at ground level. Andy bounces off the second vehicle like a rag doll, arms and legs flailing as he falls in a tangle. Brakes screech only after the boys are hit. The squeal of tyres, the screams of onlookers, the bangs and thuds are a hellish symphony.

———•———

DR AND MRS Contopoulos rush to the hospital to find Andy is in a coma. He has head injuries and several fractures and may not live. Dad grits his teeth and tells the staff that if Andy is alive he can be saved: if his son dies, he'll have their hides. Dad is just hanging on inside: he sobs against the wall in the men's toilet, almost dropping to his knees. Mum sits, rocking and mumbling in shock. They are sent home at dawn when Andy is declared stable, although still critical. Out of habit she opens the fridge and sees Andy's plate of moussaka, ready for the microwave. That's when she collapses.

Of course they can't sleep. Dr Contopoulos returns to the hospital mid-morning and Aunty Zoe comes around to be with her sister. Mrs Contopoulos has an unlikely request: she wants to visit the accident scene before going back to Andy's side.

They find flowers tied to the power pole where Chris

died. An accident investigation team has sprayed a white outline of his body where it landed: his head, arms and torso were on the footpath bent around the pole, his legs trailed onto the road. It's a bit like street art. Mrs Contopoulos stares. Is this all that remains of her son's friend? Andy's body could fit in the same outline. At least his heart still beats in his body.

Chapter Two

Eighteen months later Andy is at the Great Southern Pub in Greta, in the Lower Hunter Valley, staring at ice cubes in the bottom of his glass. It's past closing time and all the tables are empty.

The barman says, 'They've gone, mate. Vamoosed, skedaddled, left! They ain't coming back and you can't stay here. I'm shutting up. Get your gear and get on your way.'

Andy thought he and the boys had been having a good time. A general belly laugh broke out when a bloke from the local abattoir stuck an ox tail under Andy's belt at the back and his weird walk made it wag like a dog's tail. Andy tried to see who was making a fool of themselves so he could share in the fun, but they were laughing at him. At first, he wasn't happy to look like an idiot but then he thought they'd like him if he amused them. It hurts when people poke fun at him, but he's getting used to it.

Andy asks where his mates went.

'I ain't their mother! They didn't say.' Nor does the barman repeat what he heard the boys say about Andy; *friggin' nuisance... boring as... bloody millstone... changed heaps.* 'And get over here where I can see you.'

Andy shuffles into the light. 'What should I do?' he whimpers.

The barman clangs the last tray of glasses into the dishwasher and mutters about lunatics at closing time. He thumps the bar and says, 'Look, if you're short on cash go to Fat Leo's and sort something out tomorrow. It's the dump on the next block. He's always got an empty van, but don't stay too long. Your rucksack's over there. Now, get!'

Andy drags his backpack out the door and stands on the footpath. It takes a few seconds to register he's on his own. It's the first time since the accident he's had to fend for himself, let alone find his way to an unknown place. He feels as a lone astronaut might, still collecting lunar rocks on the moon's surface when he looks up to see the rocket ship leave for Earth.

Feels good in some ways, but he's scared, too. He promised Mum and Dad he would stay with the guys, but he's got no choice. They've abandoned him. He swings the pack onto one shoulder and shambles off. It's Sunday night, almost eleven o'clock, and the streets are empty. Good. No one will see him jerk and haul down the street, forcing one leg forward with a flick and a push, then dragging the other one to meet it with an extra twist from the weight of the pack. Flick, push, drag, roll, flick, push, drag, roll. That bastard right leg never cooperates. He looks down to tell it to move, he looks up to see where he's going: he looks down, he looks up, he looks down, he looks up—there's slowly acquired vertigo to deal with as well.

The good left arm clutches to his chest the one that looks like a snapped stick with its bent elbow and frozen, cocked wrist. It must be restrained when he walks or it will wave like a semaphore. This altered body is so much harder to control when he's tired or confused, and right now, he's both. The song phrase, *Walk Like an Egyptian*, loops in his head as it does whenever he's on the move. He used to deride spastics with that phrase. *Spastics...* before his accident that's what he called people with cerebral palsy. It wasn't meant hurtfully but he doesn't like that name applied to himself now. He once talked the talk, now he must walk the walk, but he can't laugh at himself the way he laughed at others. It's still a matter of gritting the teeth and trying not to be a spectacle.

He finds the van park and stumbles to the only light showing. It hangs off a van on blocks beneath a tattered canvas awning. Everything else is lumps and shadows. Rotting garbage, burnt cooking oil and motor grease waft on the warm air oozing from inside. Smells tell Andy more than they used to.

He climbs one step to knock, and again, louder. A light comes on inside, there's a grunt and snort followed by, 'Yeah? Who is it? Whadaya want?'

'Is this Fat Leo's?' Andy enquires.

'This is Leo's Hunter Holiday Park,' a voice barks back.

'Sorry to trouble you so late. Do you have a van for the night?'

'Wait there!'

Andy steps down and away as Leo squeezes sideways out the door. Once he stands still and faces forward, his huge outline obliterates the silhouetting light. Andy's definitions of *morbid obesity* are inadequate. The man is monstrous—he's well over six feet tall, and smooth: his globular expansion begins at the ears and tapers about the knees, with the peak diameter somewhere around the hips. A full, unshaped beard obscures any narrowing at the neck. Tracksuit pants of unimaginable size and a plain singlet coat him like a second skin, ready to disintegrate in a single, explosive moment. The bad odours intensify. He shines a torch in Andy's face, up and down him, then around about to check for company.

'You after a van, son?'

The friendly manner seems genuine so Andy hopes he won't be refused because of his oddness. 'Just for tonight,' he says.

'All right, we'll see. Got money? Yeah? Follow me.'

Andy follows the dim flicker of Leo's torch past rusting car bodies, derelict vans, gaunt machinery wrecks and the startling remnants of sideshow rides. The arms of an ancient octopus ride soar off at bizarre angles into the darkness, and shabby riverboat gondolas sit grounded in a strangely ordered line. A streetlight's faint glow gives opalescent life to a dozen clown heads that once sat in a row and turned in unison, casting identical, open-mouthed smiles at fair-goers. Now they lie in random piles, grinning at each other nose to nose, smooching the dirt against their cheek or gaping at the blackness above. Mist wafts ghostlike from the ground through the torchlight into a black night.

Andy trails the waddling gargantuan past skeletal

Hills Hoist clotheslines, old fridges and the warped grills of a cage that may have once held a wild man from Borneo in a travelling circus, but is now filled with objects of terror from a ghost train: skeletons long ceased jangling, and monsters that gave screaming girls an excuse to jump into their boyfriends' arms.

When Leo stops for a breather he turns and sees Andy's ungainly walk. He says, 'What's wrong with you, boy? Why are you walking like a banged-up mongrel dog? You tell me if you've been fightin'. I don't want cops round 'ere. Not for nothin'.'

Andy says he hasn't been fighting. There was an accident and this is the way he walks now.

'What do you mean, *now*? What 'appened?'

Andy doesn't answer so Leo says, 'Aw, tell me later. Just keep up or you'll get lost and end up in the wrong cubby 'ole.' His chuckle degenerates to a wheeze. 'You don't want to go to Silo's. He's partial to young men. Ate one once, or so 'e says. Then there's old Mrs Curry and young Miss Curry. Young Miss Curry is sixty-five but her mum still reckons Prince Charming will come along for 'er lovely daughter. They might both fancy a young fellow like you, so watch out. There's danger everywhere for innocents. Believe me!

'ere we are. The power's off so take this torch to find your way inside. The path to the crapper's two vans back. Just piss out the door to save yourself a walk. Bring the torch back in the morning. Sleep tight.'

Leo lumbers off into the darkness. The step creaks and the door sticks but Andy manages to get inside.

There's a ragged blanket in a heap on the bed, no sheets or pillow, and the mattress is a thin, hard wad. It's marginally softer but no cleaner than the ground he'd be sleeping on if camping. He remembers to pee out the door before lying down. At least that goes right.

Even though Andy is bushed from working out what happened today and from wondering what will happen tomorrow, he can't sleep. The place is rat central and his van must be the convention hall: there's squeaking and scratching all night. When he does drift off, he has the same weird dreams that often flood his sleep; smell of beer, taste of vomit, bright headlights, the world upside down and his life falling off it.

The next day when he returns Leo's torch, Andy asks can he stay till the end of the week. That way, he can get a lift back to Sydney with his friends, and Mum and Dad won't ask questions about how or why he separated from the group. Besides, he has no idea how to get home.

'Course you can,' Leo booms. 'But you better pay me for the lot by tomorrow.' To Andy's shuffling back he adds, 'In the mornin' I'll run you to the shops. There's one of them ATM machines there.'

———•———

ANDY SLEEPS THROUGH the afternoon and night, and wakes on the second day ready for a big effort. His mantra of the last few months has been *Think straight, be calm.* The inside of the van still freaks him out but not as badly as it did the first morning when he opened his eyes to what looked like a bombed operating theatre.

He closed his eyes tight against that first daylit view. Memories surged of hospital rooms, clean yet monstrous. Time spent there inverted his life: anxiety greeted him at the door; pain flickered like electricity around the walls and gashed his body with lightning barbs. Those rooms were hellish places. The images still come to him again and again, asleep or awake: they make his body twitch and his mind heave.

He lies on the bed pondering last night's dream in which he passed through a door from the fluoro-lit hospital into the van, from ubiquitous dazzling glare into a dull box daubed with neglect. In shadowy, early light the original colours of the van's linoleum are undecipherable, and mould, dark and thick as lichen, coats the inside of the tiny window.

The van's tap doesn't run and the naked bulb barely flickers when Leo turns on the power. Nausea rises as bad vibes multiply. Andy can smell his own fear.

He reassures himself the van is a temporary refuge— somewhere to lay his head. He can put up with it till his mates come back through town and pick him up. They must have had a good reason for leaving him. Andy knows he's not as much fun to be around as he used to be, and the guys have made it clear he's an oddball. He can live with that. Besides, how could he make new friends the way he is now? He faintly remembers the guys joshing him at the pub: running him down and giving him a hard time. But blokes do that to each other, so it's okay.

Whatever they said is already fading. Uncomfortable thoughts and memories do that. He doesn't know if he should try harder to remember, or if he should let them evaporate so his mind will be clearer and happier. Even though he can shed negative thoughts, he can't say he's any happier for losing them.

Perhaps his mates thought the campsite would be too rough for him, or too cold, or too anything. They're his mates and they've always looked out for each other. They'll be back, for sure.

The van makes him think of home. Of course, it's nothing like home: it's the contrast. He looks forward to being back in his own room with its king-sized bed, ensuite, balcony over the pool, and recalls wistfully the tiled floors throughout the house that are dust-mopped every day. Occasionally, Mum cleans the house herself because no one does the job to her standard. And her cooking! She used to bring stuff to the hospital to encourage him to eat; moussaka (the best!), meat balls, mince and rice in vine leaves. Memory of the aromas makes his mouth water.

A few years ago Andy was embarrassed by their mansion. It's so Greek. It stood out in the street like the Parthenon in a row of tenements: there was no yard to play in, just paving and pot plants. Now there are houses like that up and down both sides: bigger and better than the Contopoulos house, with more columns and bigger statues. Some even have fountains but Andy's dad can't work out where to fit one in.

Andy loves his dad but likes home best when Dad is out. Then it is soothing: quiet, still and glistening, but electricity walks in the door with Dad. It's like he brings a swarm of bees with him: the air buzzes; he laughs out loud, shouts, demands, razzes. He wants the family to shine, to be better, and often better isn't good enough, even best isn't good enough unless it's best by a long way.

Andy has no doubt his dad is a great man. He came from Greece with parents whose tiny, rocky farm couldn't grow enough potatoes, or feed enough goats to keep the family alive. He won a scholarship to uni, became a doctor and brought up his family in luxury. He's not a big guy himself—only about one hundred and sixty-five centimetres tall because he was malnourished as a kid—but he wants Andy to have the same experience of success. He wants his son to be the best he can be, to have an even bigger house and to be a more famous doctor. That's the best way to be happy and do good for the community.

Dad only ever hit Andy once, with a cane, when he was ten, and it was the pits. That's a bad memory he hasn't been able to let go. Mum went ballistic. She threatened Dad with a carving knife and screamed at him. Andy had never seen her like that before. She was a madwoman. Dad never hit him again but from time to time he would get the cane out, wave it around then whack a pile of papers for effect.

His father's high expectations give Andy a goal, but Dad loves too hard, and he pushes too much. Sure, Andy is happy his parents care, but that amount of love is a burden to lug around. Responsibility for the dad's happiness wears the son down, and Andy is uncomfortable being the focus of his father's attention.

There used to be a sister but she died four years ago. That was the worst time in their lives. She was a lot like Andy but a better student. When he was still in high school and she was steaming through Medicine at uni, she fell in with some slimy high-flyers. She wasn't into drugs herself but some of them were. One night, after a big session at the casino they went to a private gambling hangout where things got ugly: the Greeks, Asians and Lebanese all at each other because of their different hang-ups. There was carnage—blood everywhere the reports said. No guns, just knives, and three dead, including Lydia. She could have run off but stayed to help someone else—that would be just like her, and she was stabbed too.

Lydia and Andy were close. He could talk things through with her more easily than with his parents. He feels sorry for them now: they lost their daughter and their son has come a cropper and may never have the life they planned for him. Dad never was partial to gambling but now he despises anything to do with it; the races, casinos, lotteries, lucky door prizes, scratchies— he won't even buy a raffle ticket. It's all to do with greed, he says, and without that his Lydia would still be alive. Andy agrees.

Andy can remember everything that happened before his accident, even what he learnt at uni. Because his memory was intact when he woke up from the coma, they thought he'd recover and after six months of rehab he was back at uni. Everyone hoped he would have to cope only with the changes to his body caused by head injury and fractures, but as Andy went through the year, he worked out for himself that his short-term memory was stuffed. New information didn't stick.

The short-term memory problem is why he's worried about imminent exam results. Work from the first two years of the course is still in his head, but nothing he studied since the accident has found the right niche. It made sense in lectures so he thought it had sunk in, but by the next day he couldn't even remember the topic. He can nut out problems if the criteria are written down and in front of him, but at other times he reaches the end of a train of thought and has forgotten where he started. Andy hopes he can improve this with time.

Old memory is different. All the words he learnt early in life are the ones he mostly uses now. Simple words. The further back in time he learnt them, the easier they are to recall. It's as if his memory is stored in layers, each year's thought and knowledge on top of the one before, and if a tornado rips through the brain it's the top layers, the fresh, growing tips of the memory that are blown off and they never come back. The capacity to put down new layers has been shaved off.

The damage goes into the layers beneath, too, like dieback on a tree, but diminishes as the layers get deeper. His Greek is still good because he learnt that before English. Andy is proud he's worked all this out. For the same reason, recent daily life blurs. But because images of people have more impact than information, he can, with considerable effort, recount the recent past.

Out of the massive trauma there have been gains.

Since the accident, intuitive responses to people are so strong they exclude social niceties and, at times, rob him of words. He must deal with escalating, tangled emotions before he can respond using speech. And he's just getting used to the visible vibes that float like disjointed rainbows around bodies. Initially, during recovery, he ignored the colours, thinking they were caused by medication or eye damage. Now he pays them the attention he would a companionable friend. The colours don't appear around everyone and not always straight away: they vary between people and may change for a single person depending on their mood. He believes it's a picture of their mind but he hasn't fully worked out what the images mean, or how to best use this new skill. Sometimes the interpretation makes no sense or is blatantly wrong, but increasingly, he senses a pattern. The colours relate to character and emotion and energy: they show strength and weakness, stability or deceit—things worth knowing about people that in normal interaction can take a long time to become clear. Trouble is, even if it's a new way to suss out what people are about, he must still look dumb in the same way he used to think a person stupid if they couldn't remember a name. He has trouble with names now.

Another by-product of the accident sitting in Andy's consciousness like a boulder under snow is a lump of guilt over his own near death. It upset the family so much. Aunt Zoe told him later that his mum and dad were alternately crazies or zombies: Dad harangued medical staff, insisted on different treatments, and scoured every test result. While Dad was around, Mum was withdrawn and white under her olive skin, but at other times, with her sisters, she wailed and sobbed and prayed for God to look after her golden boy, her one remaining child. Andy is sad to have caused his parents so much grief. He hopes for a time when his and their world will be righted.

When Andy woke up after two weeks and came out of intensive care, Mum and Dad thought the worst was over. Mum had her boy back and that was enough. Dad kept quiet about the effects of head injury. They would have to wait and see, he told the family, wait and see. If there was a problem, he could help. He was a doctor, after all, and knew what to do. There would be more operations and months of rehabilitation. Andy would be behind his peers but that was all right. The study of medicine is a long road and success is a matter of hard work. He, Dad, knew that.

Andy had facio-maxillary (and was chuffed to remember the word from first year anatomy) surgery to rebuild his jaw, he had physiotherapy, counselling, and tutoring. He looked at the previous year's texts and most of it was still in his head. He expected to be rusty so gaps didn't faze him. He went back to uni, attended lectures, tutes, pracs and clinical work. All seemed well.

Andy's friends welcomed him back with open arms, but it wasn't the same as before, for them or for him. Andy couldn't get into the stupid things they did, and that he used to do with them. They couldn't accept his disabilities, especially the strange walk, and the way his arm sticks out like a sign announcing *Damaged Goods*, or how he speaks slowly. They said he'd scare girls away.

They still laughed at what they said to each other, but Andy didn't catch on. They used to behave like clones but now he was different. They told him to go and get another bang on the head to make him like he used to be. He thought that was funny.

Andy didn't go to the post-exam parties because he's too tired to go out at night, let alone drink beer and stay out late. That happens with head injuries, Dad warned him. In the car on the way up to Greta the guys told him how they'd gone to see Cynthia, one of their girlfriends, whose parents were overseas and due back next morning. She wanted her boyfriend there for one more night but six of them went over with alcohol and pills. They told Andy what happened and he said it was wrong.

They called him a loser and yelled at him in the car, 'Hey, what's the matter, Andy? We had a good time and Cynthia loved the pizza!'

They laughed so hard the car rocked, but he couldn't see the humour in five spewing men having group sex with a drugged girl. She was still out to it the next morning when her parents came home. There was vomit all over the place, broken glass and greasy pizza boxes. Before the accident he would have been with them at Cynthia's, but what's the point in doing that to someone?

•———————•

ANDY GETS UP. He scours his memory for where he is and how he got there. Now he thinks about what he must do for the next few days. He puts on clean clothes, eats a muesli bar and a bruised apple from his backpack and steps outside. He finds his way to Leo's for a lift downtown. The man confuses him. Andy's gut feeling and Leo's auras are inconsistent. Sure, Leo wants his rent, but it's still a favour to give a lift. Andy would have trouble walking to town, let alone carrying back enough food for the rest of the week. All in all, Andy decides, Leo is being a friend.

Leo is poking around outside his van when Andy gets there. The big man plods to and fro, achieving nothing in particular, but chats to Andy, who finds something to lean on while he's not in motion.

'How are you today, sonny?' Leo asks. He pauses as if interested in Andy's reply, but Andy only nods. 'What do you think of my little kingdom, then?'

Andy feels he should make a suitable response but can't think of one. His eyes roam over a wall of car bodies, two high and two wide. It's a miniature Great Wall of China, an auto wall of cannibalised, rusted, crushed and discarded metal.

Leo continues. 'Over where you are, outside this divide, them three vans, they're for *salts*, like you—visitors who shoot through. All these other vans, they're for *lifers*—my 'appy, long-term tenants. Word gets round. Some 'ave been 'ere for years and others 'ave come when they're down and out. I don't advertise, but the needy ones manage to find me. If they stay a while, they stay forever. Seems they're comfortable with their own type, not to mention their great landlord.' Leo rubs his belly. 'But don't you go wandering round the lifers because they don't 'preciate intruders. Best leave that lot to me.'

Leo's people-mover van tilts alarmingly when the big man gets in but doesn't register Andy's weight. At the shops Leo drops Andy in front of the ATM machine and gives him an hour to do what he needs. Andy keeps two wallets: one has PINs in it because he can't remember them and the other has the cards. That way, if a thief steals a wallet there's a chance of preserving his money.

The little grocery store also does light food and coffee. After Andy has bought supplies he hopes will get him through the week he sits down to eat. It's nowhere near as good as home but it fills him up. As he finishes eating, he notices off in a corner a sign *Free Internet Access* and a terminal. Exam results! They're out this week. Mum and Dad will look them up for him. They have his codes and passwords as they've been doing it while he wasn't up to it. He searches frantically through the numbers wallet and finds the codes there.

Andy has been trying not to think about results but has to know sooner or later. He reckons he's done enough to pass but he doesn't expect anything great. Pass results would be acceptable to him, but probably not enough for Dad. He thinks ahead: if he can just get home, apologise for mediocre results and get on with the rest of the course, he can improve as he goes.

Andy sits at the terminal, waits for it to boot up, wishes hard. He keys in the numbers one at a time, presses *Enter*. All his results are *Fail*. At first he thinks it's a mistake, or results withheld, or someone else's marks, but it's all *Fails*. Mum and Dad will have looked them up at home by now, too. He can hear Dad already: *How did this happen? I tell you how this happened! Not enough work and too much time with your friends. I told you it would be harder since the accident but you don't believe me. You know better. You've wasted time. All your friends will get ahead of you now,* and more.

Andy is not sure how it happened either. He worked hard and understood everything but none of it stayed in his head. All the anatomy, pharmacology, physiology, endocrinology—the stuff he learnt before the accident— is still there, but all the new work he was sure he knew must have evaporated from his brain before he reached the exam room. Nothing stuck. He can't hang on to new facts, let alone learn new ways of thinking or doing.

If his brain can't cope with uni then he's not the guy he was or thought he knew. He expected study to be difficult but these results are a complete stuff up. It's one thing to lose the use of an arm and half the use of a leg: it's altogether different for a brain, the brain, to decide it's going to do some things and not others, especially without letting him know which will be done and which won't.

Feels like there's three of him now: the Andy he thought he was, the one with the different body, and the one with the strange brain. Can he roll the three into one whole person again and how will he turn out? He might not know or like himself.

Chapter Three

Andy stares out the window on the drive back. He puts the exam results out of his mind because they're too upsetting to contemplate. Then he wonders why he feels so bad and the answer comes straight back to him. *I failed everything!* The cycle goes around a few times. The scenery and the route don't register. He vaguely hears Leo asking if he's okay and did the ATM transaction go through.

Leo pulls up near his van and they get out. Andy asks how much he owes and pays Leo who grunts a thank you and fires at him, 'What's up with you then? Cat got your tongue? You're a shockin' colour. Sit yer arse 'ere and unburden yerself.' He directs Andy to an upturned milk crate.

Leo sits under the sagging tarpaulin beside his van in a chunky, throne-like chair. It's roughly hewn from planks and logs, and built to be sturdy enough for his great bulk. It's the sort of thing you'd expect a king of the axe men to have in their yard. A stained pillow belches sideways from under him. Andy is struck by the shifting mix of strong colours that float around Leo but can't guess what it means. There's a lot of red but parts of it deepen to the colour of old blood, and some blue, but that also muddies.

Another man, young yet derelict, sits a bit away. Before the accident Andy wouldn't have acknowledged his existence, but that was then, when he was different, and deros didn't matter. Andy would have called him a low-life or a feral. Now he feels they have a lot in common. It makes no difference to Andy that the fellow is scrawny, hollow-cheeked, and has stringy hair on one side of his head combed across a bald pate. Even the strands that haven't made it across his head and hang to his shoulders like black wet worms seem normal for this place.

Leo does the introductions. 'Andy, meet Goob, Goob Spittall, my right-hand man. Goob's good with motors.'

Goob puffs out a pigeon chest and grins at an imaginary multitude like he's an award-winning apprentice. Andy's exam results briefly recede.

'Pleased to meet you, Goob. I wish I could do all that stuff,' Andy says, thrusting forward his good hand.

Goob hesitates and returns a limp, grease-stained paw.

Leo's eyes shift between them and he lets the silence settle. He waves a hand at the mountains of junk and asks Andy again what he thinks of the fine establishment.

'It's okay. It's good.' Andy's head nods unbidden and Leo takes it as enthusiasm.

Leo gazes at the broken rides. He sighs. 'Was a good life, travellin' round country shows. Had a few whirly gigs, them clowns, a kiddies' ghost train. Lotsa stuff. Stopped 'ere one time for the off-season and ran out of puff. Never got going again. I got no complaints. Things have worked out okay.'

Andy is still nodding.

Leo shifts forward in the throne to ask, 'So did you used to talk more than you do now, eh? You said there was an accident. What 'appened? Pity for something to 'appen to a nice young fella. Maybe we can 'elp each other.'

The caring enquiry draws Andy out. Goob is alternately counting something on his fingers and gazing at cars on the other side of the yard, but it doesn't matter if he hears.

Andy tells Leo how he was hit by a car and nearly died, that he had a fractured skull and a broken jaw and shoulder and a few other things. And how his brain was damaged and that's why he's different to how he used to be.

Leo wants more, so Andy tells him that he and his friends thought what they were doing was fun, but it was stupid. He describes the drinking, the game of *heaven and hell*, and what happened to him and Chris. Andy is leaning forward on the crate, rubbing his face as he talks. Leo mumbles sympathy.

Andy explains that he was in a coma for a while, and in hospital a long time after that. There's lots of things still wrong with him. Sometimes he wishes it was him who died, not Chris. He can't walk right, his arm's spastic, he can't drink, and people are different. He knows he must now come across as, well, less than what he was to people who knew him before.

Andy tells Leo about the disastrous exam results and how furious his father will be. Andy hopes Dad will calm down by the time he, Andy, gets home. Andy is sure he worked hard and doesn't know what else he can do to pass. He'll just have to work harder.

Leo looks at him intently and asks, 'What were you learning, matey?'

Andy tells him, 'Medicine. I've done a bit in hospitals and I'm in the last semester at uni.'

Leo pretends he's found the answer. 'Look on the bright side: even if you don't get any further and you remember everything up to the accident, you're all trained up to be an ambulance officer!'

'Yeah, like Dad would be happy with a paramedic for a son. He's hanging out to see what specialisation I'll go for. I do want to make him proud, but I'm not sure any more that I have to be the famous, rich doctor he thought I'd be. Or that I can be. I just want to be a proper person.'

Andy slumps and wonders what he's just said. Since he started his course, he hasn't considered any life other than medicine. The notion of being a 'proper person' just popped out. He's shocked himself. His face spasms and his lips turn to limp rubber. Leo watches Andy rock and nod.

'Well,' says Leo, 'you got a few days to figure out what to say at home.' He thrusts on the log-like arms of the chair to launch himself upright, belly first, and plods to his van. He heaves up the steps one at a time and disappears like a soft-bodied sea creature morphing through the small opening of a shell.

———•———

ANDY ROUSES HIMSELF and sets off back to his van. As he weaves through a maze of junk and around puddles, staring at the ground to select each footfall, he hears a scratchy voice.

'Hey, sonny, watcha doin' here? What's Fartso got his claws into you for?'

An old woman, dried up and sparrow-like, stands mid-path on the boggy ground behind the shower block. Her thin, frizzy hair and Roadrunner smile give her a crazy look. The Looney Tunes cartoon theme romps along behind Andy's eyes, as it often does when he meets a weirdo. She's clutching a bathroom bag to her bony chest, and wriggles her shoulders forwards and backwards, chortling like a mouse with emphysema. He can see in the spaces between the buttons of her housecoat that she's got nothing else on, but there's no towel over her shoulder.

Andy doesn't know who she's talking about and says nothing.

'Fartso, Fatso, Gasbag Leo, whatever you want to call him. Him up there.' She gestures coarsely in the direction of Leo's van.

Andy is still lost for words.

Lola looks at him in exasperation and asks, 'What struck you dumb? All right, all right. We'll do things formal like. I'm Lola. I live here,' she croaks. 'What's keeping you here?'

'Nothing. I can go whenever I want. I'm waiting for someone to pick me. And I'm Andy. Hello.'

Lola cackles and slaps her thigh. 'That cracks me up! If you've got something Fartso wants, he'll find a way to keep you here in the pound with us strays. We all start off like you... *just for a few days... just till things sort themselves out.* I did the rounds of other places like this and landed here fourteen years ago. Still ain't sorted. Can't see it's going to happen, neither, the way me mind's going. I have to write things down so's I don't forget them, but remembering to write them down in the first place is the problem. Leo helps me a bit, but I still have my elusive moments, enough to keep him wondering how much money I got stashed away.'

'So why do you stay here?'

'Oh, a long time ago I was in a house when someone died.' Lola looks around while she talks. 'Leo reckons I good as killed him with me own hands and I'd go straight to gaol if the law catched up to me. It wasn't really like that... we was drinking, there was a fire and I got out but me old man didn't. There was no way I could lug that bugger down stairs. It was an accident, but I ain't sorry what 'appened. He deserved to die. I had to fight the rotten bastard with every inch of my being just to stay alive. *What are you getting on your hind horse about?* he'd ask if I told him to stop hitting me. Well, he's gone and I'm still here.

'So, how old do you think I am?' Lola asks.

'Eighty,' Andy blurts out.

'Sixty-six,' Lola hacks with laughter. 'I know I've gone downhill in the looks department, but I didn't think medopause did that to me! Here, look at this. What do you think?'

She fishes a photo in a clip-top plastic bag from between the soap and comb.

'I keep it to remind meself that life wasn't always bad. What do you think? Quite the looker, eh?'

The fading photo shows a voluptuous, perky showgirl in dance costume—not much more than clinging swimmers with frills, but plenty of uplift. She dazzles through the milky, scratched plastic: a spunky pose in high heels, hair softly curled around the sides of a pixie face, with a pouting smile and sexy wink.

'Aaah, that's lovely, Lola. You were beautiful.'

Lola sighs as she replaces the picture. 'Yeah, times change. Life lingers but beauty fades. Double ammonia didn't used to keep me from a party when I was young, but now I'm 'appy just to get to the john in time. Reckon I'll see you 'round, young fella.'

Humming a racy tune, Lola skips with a geriatric swivel into the shower block.

Chapter Four

Three more days at Leo's Hunter Holiday Park drag by. Andy passes the time in the study of bark on a stunted tree, a weed's tiny flowers and columns of ants coursing to and fro along well-worn tracks. In the van walls at night the scratching of mice and rats is like radio static which he reimagines as music or voices. Each morning he checks with Leo what day it is as he can't remember what day it was yesterday, and he can't afford to miss Saturday. That's when his mates are due back through Greta. He keeps the paltry items he brought camping packed and ready to go.

Today is Saturday, Leo told him a few minutes ago and already Andy is on the roadside opposite the pub, staring in the direction from which his mates should come. They won't arrive earlier than midday but he's there hours earlier, just in case. He doesn't want to delay them looking for him and they're his only chance to get back to Sydney because train and bus timetables are as useful as hieroglyphics, and his pack is heavy. The security and comfort of home are an irresistible lure even though there'll be big problems when he gets there: anticipation of Dad's tough talking registers like body blows. All those *Fail* results. It's hard to believe.

He sits on the ground at the edge of an unofficial

truck layby. Drivers stop there to go across to the pub for a feed and a toilet break. He'd rather wait up or down the road, toward Maitland or back into Greta, under the tall, graceful eucalypts that line the roadside: their trunks soar twenty feet before branching out, and great ribbons of bark hang down like fraying tentacles. He should have left the van one day to lie under them and stare up. Perhaps he'd find what he needs if he gazed at the sky for long enough. He chooses the truck stop to wait because it's an exposed patch on the verge and the boys can't miss seeing him.

Andy scrutinises the ground between his feet—pebbles, grains of sand, dust, leaf litter, grass stems, but looks up when he feels eyes upon him. There, in front of a tumbledown pioneer cottage lurks a sorry excuse for a dog: it's part bull terrier, part shepherd and who knows what else? He's a dirty grey colour and looks moth-eaten because of patchy, dark pigmentation under thin hair; he's ribby and ragged-eared from fighting. As the dog moves, a bung back leg that's possibly been broken and healed crookedly affects his gait. Perhaps he fell off a truck weeks ago and is hanging around hoping his owner will come back. Andy names him Casper straight off, after the cartoon ghost, because with his colouring he's more not there than there.

Casper and Andy lock eyes: they have a lot in common — they're two damaged rejects living on the edge. Casper won't come when Andy beckons, outstares him and is gone when Andy looks up.

The warm sun makes him dopey so he flops back on

the grass hoping that a token gesture of one arm over his backpack will deter thieves. If someone does a runner with his pack they'll be gone before he's vertical. He dozes off and slips into the nightmarish parallel world that plagues him: young men leaping like drunken satyrs, beer slops and bright lights.

An empty semitrailer with a clanging bogey rattles past and scatters his dreams. Immediately after that, a pumping car horn jolts him alert and he sits up to see a hoon machine coming straight at him. There's no kerb, just a wide gravel verge then the grass where he's camped. Andy can't move to avoid the impact but at the last minute the car swerves away, spraying him with dirt and stones. Two of his friends are hanging out the passenger-side windows up to their waists, waving and shouting over each other and the throbbing boom box. *Yeah, Andy! Did that take ya back? We had a great time camping. You shouldn't have waited. We've got a chick in here so there's no room. See you in Sydney,* and they're gone.

He waits for them to enjoy the joke and come back around the block: he stays there long enough for them to reach the next town. That's when the thought registers—they're not coming back. A new perception that makes it okay to laugh at disaster settles on him: if every new idea takes that long to tick over, life will be in slow motion from here on.

◆————————◆

ANDY DRAGS HIMSELF back to the van park and finds Leo with a newspaper and beer on his Thunderthrone (that's the name Andy's mind spontaneously created for the seat). Leo doesn't seem surprised to see him and asks about the friend he's brought back. That's news to Andy till he turns and sees Casper skulking in the gateway. Leo yells abuse but gives up when Casper lowers his head and stands his ground.

Leo consoles Andy after he hears how the guys shot through.

'That's too bad, matey. Can't say I'm surprised. They sound like arseholes for dumpin' you in the first place. Why were you hangin' out with them?'

Andy asks himself the same question, and says, 'I used to be one of them.'

'Well, who are you now?' Leo quizzes.

Andy has no answer.

Leo says, 'Things will turn out, you'll see. And good news already: there's a spare van over here with us lifers, so you'll have a roof over your head, but you've got to toe the line. Comprendez? These are the rules, sonny; no job in town, no phone, no TV, no socialisin' with the others. You talk to me and anyone I send to see you. Electricity goes off at nine o'clock. You pay your rent with cash or by helpin' out with what you know how to do... or both. That's how we stay one big 'appy family... by doin' what I say. All right?'

While Leo is talking a tsunami of fear swamps Andy. Suddenly he's desperate to talk to Mum and Dad to tell them where he is and to work out how to get home. If they think he's gone they might also disappear off the face of the earth and then he'd have nobody. Andy will agree to anything Leo says to hear his mum's voice again.

'All right, Leo, whatever you say. Can I use your phone, please? I have to ring home.'

There's only one phone in Leo's Hunter Holiday Park, and it's in Leo's van.

'Sure, go right in.'

It's a weird place. There's crap everywhere and Andy has to pick his way in order not to trip and slide. Mum would spew from the smell and it almost has the same effect on him. Finding the phone isn't easy. Andy can't imagine how Leo exists in there, let alone turns around, gets dressed and cooks. There's a threadbare coat with worn elbows hanging off a wall and a few pairs of semi-inflated track pants in a pile. They could have been blown up with farts and tied at the legs and waist—that would account for the smell.

He finds the phone among a jumble of paperwork and porn magazines, and gets the piece of paper out of his wallet with the home phone number. He shouldn't have to carry it written down because it's *old* knowledge, but he can't remember numbers when he's stressed. That, and trying to remember, makes him more likely to forget.

Before Andy dials he plans what to say: how to fob off Dad's explosive reaction to the results; how to apologise for them; how to tell Mum he's looking forward to seeing her, and how he's missed her cooking. He recites the address of where he is so they can come and collect him. It will be so good to see them again. When everything is sorted in his head, he dials. Mum answers. Just hearing her say hello is a huge relief.

'Is that you, Andy? What have you done to us? Your father is furious. We are disgraced. He says we have children no more. He will not speak to you, even to hear what you have to say. I am to tell you not to come home until you can be different.'

Dad is ranting behind her about other things Andy should know or do, and he's glad Mum doesn't pass them on. All she says is, 'I am not allowed to speak with you, only to give these messages. Please God he will change his mind. I must hang up now.' The phone is still pressed to his ear and he thinks he hears her sob, 'I love you, my boy. Take care!' as she hangs up.

Andy stands staring at the phone till Leo bellows, 'Oi, don't use all your friggin' credit in one hit. Catch up on your family history some other time.'

Somehow Andy reels out of Leo's van before he vomits. He's like a puppet that's had its strings cut: his head lolls and his eyes roll; the unrestrained weak arm bobs and jerks as if he's communicating in a new sign language. Leo can see he's about to fall in a heap so Goob steers him to his new home: a slightly less beat-up van among the lifers.

Chapter Five

A ndy must have passed out because when he wakes up in the lifer's van it's dark and Leo's yard is jumping. The enclosure is made up of vans in a circle like a wagon train camp, with scrap and wrecks filling the gaps on the outer edge. Leo's own spot is just outside the main opening of the ring. From there he can keep tabs on the lifers and see out to the street, but passers-by can't see in.

The diesel exhaust that soaked into Andy's brain as he slept, the guffaws and curses, the cranking chains and banging doors that he half-heard in his sleep, are real. It's two in the morning. He peers out onto a floodlit, soupy brew of fumes, cigarette smoke and mist. The air glows and wafts in the yellow light, and swirls when stirred. Leo and Goob are there, and eight other men, only two of whom he's seen before. The engine of a semitrailer ticks over while men swarm on and off with assorted car parts. A late model Falcon that had been parked in the enclosure is already aboard, together with various car doors and bonnets.

Andy doesn't want to think ill of Leo, but he's reminded of the car-rebirthing operation in Sydney. It's highly suspicious. He contemplates repaying Leo's good turns by helping to load but remembers he can't do physical work anymore.

Something else holds him back. To step out the door would be more than a physical move. When Armstrong stepped onto the moon he said, *One small step for man, one giant leap for mankind.* Andy is excited how instinct kicks in. Moral and legal question marks hang over what's happening out there and a voice in the back of his mind warns him not to go. From inside he watches as parts of a carousel are loaded: just enough poles, facia slabs, and roof panels to make it appear to be the main load, and to cover up what's underneath.

When the tarp is rolled down and tied off Leo summons the driver and the off-sider: he issues instructions with waving arms and Andy hears some words emphasised—*Leichhardt, no piss, plates on that car.* Leo looks around and moves closer to the two men, puts a fist under the driver's chin and growls at him, 'I'll know what ya get, and I want the cash, pronto.'

The guy droops. Leo stands back and waves the truck out. He trudges back to his van with Goob shuffling behind. Other men melt away to their holes or out to the dark road.

The truck is gone and the show is over. Andy is left looking at nothing. The lights go out and he's thinking this is a bit like his life: bright lights then nothing, plenty of action then it's gone. The truck is going to Leichhardt and could have given him a lift. He knows how to get home from there. He wonders why Leo didn't think of that. He goes back to bed wondering about what else Leo does but can't sleep because of one black thought after another: failed uni, rejected by Mum and Dad, no sister to confide in, abandoned by friends (and were they friends at all?), and now he's fallen in with thieves. It's a downhill slide.

Eventually, when Andy does get some shut-eye, one of Dad's favourite lines resonates in his head, *You can tell a lot about a man from the company he keeps.* Then Mum's words bubble up like sulphur in hot mud, *We have children no more... not to come home... different.* He dreams about the beginning of the end of the world.

Chapter Six

When Andy wakes up mid-morning on Sunday he wonders if he dreamed what happened last night. He looks out the window—it was no dream: the car has gone and there are cigarette butts where the men stood. If only Mum's words were a dream, too, but they ring in his ears and he knows he heard them on the phone: *We are disgraced... we have children no more.* He perceives that new information will stick in his memory when strong emotion is attached, but he shuts out her words because they're painful.

Andy decides to look around the lifers' vans. Leo was emphatic about people minding their own business, but there can't be harm in checking the immediate layout. Before Andy moves away, he sees Casper lying under his stairs. The dog gets up and retreats out of sight. Andy hunts around for a container, fills it with water at the shower block and leaves it under the van. He's never had a pet but feels a connection with this dog that lingers near him. Maybe Andy is the only person who's never shooed him off.

Andy strolls around the inner yard then picks his way between the outer edge of the van ring and the second barricade of junk. Through a space he sees Leo approach a slim, middle-aged woman: she's attractive in a refined, out-of-place way, but appears strained and her sharp features are accentuated by tightly drawn-back hair streaked with grey. She and Leo speak briefly and Andy picks up an accent but no words. Leo gives her something and she sets off slowly, head down and basket in hand. He enters the van she's left, turns to see if anyone is about, and shuts the door. Andy sneaks closer and finds that by standing on a car battery he can see in the window.

Perhaps he'll find out something else about Leo's work. Watching what people do and working out why they do it is far more interesting than the principles of psychiatry in a lecture. Maybe, despite Leo's shady side, he does some sort of counselling work with these 'lifer' people. The ones Andy has met seem to have problems.

From his shaky perch Andy sees Leo standing inside the door. Then he sees a sylph-like girl of perhaps seventeen sitting at the table, head down, shoulders hunched, hands clasped on her lap. She's wearing a sleeveless, loose, floral dress and her skin is startlingly white against the dark hair that hangs in curls and hides her face. Even from this partial view Andy thinks she's the most beautiful girl he's ever come across. Intriguing colours move and glow around her. Until now the rainbow luminosity and tendrils of colour he has seen around some people have confused him but looking at this girl he knows what they mean. It is an amazing, full-on, glowing aura! He reads courage, intelligence, and distress.

Leo moves closer to the girl but he's too large for the other bench-seat at the table and remains standing, planted squarely before her.

Andy hears Leo clearly. 'This can't go on, love. Everyone what lives 'ere kicks in some 'ow and this is what you can do to 'elp you and your mum. It's a very nice lady in town runs the place and you'd be well looked after and well paid. I've explained it all to your mum and she wants you to go there.'

The girl raises her head to glare at Leo and says resolutely, 'It is not her wish. It is not my wish. You are trying to force this on us and I will not do it.' She can't maintain the defiant tone. Her voice grows tremulous and her shoulders begin to heave as she repeats, 'I will not do it. I will not do it.' She shuts her eyes as if to block his reply.

Leo's tone changes. 'There's no more free lunches, Esther. The rent's gotta be paid. Your mum's too old and I reckon she's not all that well and you know what'll 'appen if the authorities find out you're both 'ere. People like you ain't supposed to be 'ere, bludging on this country. Yeah, that's right. She'd be back off to Naziland or you'd both be in some reffo camp and things'd be worse wherever you went. Get m' drift?'

As if suddenly aware of being watched, the girl opens her eyes and looks past Leo straight at Andy. They hold an unblinking gaze for several seconds and it's long enough for ribbons of space and time and a thousand words to flow between them. His feet are welded to the battery and his eyes are riveted on the girl. Tears course down her face but her mouth is clamped shut. Andy drops to the ground breathing heavily. Parts of his body pound violently and he can't think. He's not sure what he's seen or what it means, and why is he shaking?

There's a pause and Andy can tell Leo's smiling when he says, 'My other income streams ain't all that flash right now and I've got some unforeseen expenses, so your rent's goin' up. It was gunna be two nights a week in town on the job but now I'm sayin' three.'

Andy hoists himself up because Leo sounds as if he might take a swipe at her.

'I will not do it! I will not do it!' the girl wails.

Leo throws his hands in the air and backs out of the van.

Andy stays hidden till his head clears, then creeps away. At least he knows her name. Esther! Esther! He will find her later and surely will look into her eyes again and talk to her without words. He keeps clear of Leo for the rest of the day, trying to rationalise what he's seen and how it sits with Leo's friendship. Maybe *friendship* is too big a word, but he has been a friend in need.

Andy is only just getting to know the person he has become and his new self might be more likeable. If the old self was similar to the so-called mates who abandoned him then the new him might be different and a shift in the right direction.

Leo's threatening behaviour toward Esther can't be right and Andy cares that she's unhappy with what Leo's planning for her, whatever that might be. If Esther is prepared to get to know him while he works out his new self, something good might come of it. Andy thinks he knows her well already because of that amazing glow. Perhaps she'll overlook his awkward body. Her name floats like a flower in his mind, wafting between heart and head.

Chapter Seven

Andy passes the afternoon and evening alone in his van, and wakes up ravenous on Monday morning. There's nothing left to eat from the supplies he bought last week. He reckons he can remember the way to the mini-mart and it's only a few blocks off. He decides to hoof it rather than ask Leo for a lift.

That looks like a mistake before he's half way there—much of the route is a gravel track and he stumbles more than once. There's no one around to care if he comes a cropper. Andy is pleasantly surprised by the village-like atmosphere when he gets to the town centre, but access to the cluster of shops is blocked by a display. The actual council chambers are in Maitland, but councillors visit Greta for exhibitions and community chat-ups. There's a dudey character in a flashy suit poncing around, but up close, his face is tough.

The guy leaps in front of Andy as if it's a hold-up and thrusts a hand forward. 'Good afternoon, sir. I'm Councillor Oscar Twigold, Mayor of Maitland. Pleased to meet you.'

He doesn't blink when Andy uses his left arm to push a limp right hand at him. The mayor takes hold and shakes too vigorously. Andy identifies himself and hopes the mayor will get out of the way, but he doesn't, so Andy tells him about the dangers of what passes for a footpath in places. The mayor apologises and assures Andy he'll look in to it. He still doesn't move.

'Andy, do you live in Greta or are you visiting?' the mayor asks.

The mayor is pleased to hear Andy is a visitor, but Andy thinks he'd act the same if Andy said he was Saint Peter checking out councillors for the next uplift of souls. Andy hasn't met anyone on a local council before, but the man behaves a lot like a politician friend of his dad's.

'That's good, Andy, that's good! I'm sure you're having a fine time.' He talks loudly and Andy is uncomfortable with how close he stands. Mayor Twigold doesn't let up. 'Everyone's opinion matters. It's good to have the thoughts of someone from further afield. So, what do you think about the proposal to build a casino here? It's just a proposal at this stage, but we want the best outcome for everyone. It would bring jobs to the area and attract patrons from all over to this very town and to the glorious Hunter Valley generally. What do you think?'

Andy is against casinos, mainly because Mum and Dad hate them. He doesn't mind gambling as such, but he doesn't like the crime that can come with it. Mum and Dad blame gambling criminals for his sister's death.

While Andy is thinking what to say, Councillor Twigold steers him to the display. There are artistic impressions of a swank building with sophisticated people who are smiling so hard you'd think they'd just cleaned out the bank. There's also a map showing the proposed sight of the casino. Andy is not good with maps but he can see it's on the highway.

'What's on the site now?' Andy asks.

'It's Leo's Hunter Holiday Park, and it's an eyesore, and council is in the process of acquiring the land.'

'But there's no *For Sale* sign. What's the go?'

'It's a legal matter,' the mayor says.

'Well, good luck with it,' Andy adds as a twitch sets in.

The mayor is about to ask him something more but Andy wobbles backwards and the mayor turns away.

The café serves meals; the lasagne in the bain-marie is tired but he can't resist and orders it with chips and salad. Appearances were correct: it's leathery and tasteless, and makes him more homesick. Not a whiff of garlic. Andy sets off with his groceries.

As he struggles along, Andy wonders why Leo hasn't mentioned the sale, and hopes things are sorted out at home so he'll have somewhere to go when Leo's place closes down. And then there's Esther, and probably her mother. He wants to get to know Esther, and if she's in a fix, he'd like to help. He can hardly help himself, but hey, a mouse freed a lion in *Aesop's Tales*. Mum used to read him all the Greek stuff when he was little.

And the other lifers, people like Lola and Goob, where could they go if Leo sold up? They aren't mad or criminal: well, maybe, maybe not, but they wouldn't make it if left to themselves in the big world. Not that they're any help to each other in the park. They don't act like neighbours who invite each other to barbecues, yet they're quick to jump when Leo calls. He's like a circus ringmaster who releases different beasts from cages to perform their special tricks, then coerces them back into their holes till next time: Goob till more cars need work, Esther till... whatever... and Lola... he doesn't know what she's got that Leo wants, and who else? What can he do for them?

Before the accident these down-and-outers would have been below his radar. They're all defective but in different ways. Andy too, at the moment is flawed, but he hopes in time not to be. He understands more about people than he used to, and that's a gift, but only if he can get back to normal. Otherwise, it's a compensation to help him survive. Sometimes personality has shape, words have a look, and he can touch a smell. Andy was embarrassed talking about those sensations to a counsellor because it sounds so weird, but she understood straight away. She said it was called synaesthesia. That, and the auras, give him a new way of looking at the world. It doesn't happen all the time and he needs to fine tune its use.

The inside of Andy's head is so different to what it used to be. He's realised that formulas and numbers don't get past his eyes, which is probably why he failed his exams. He's adjusting to losing old skills, but these new ones are a different ball game. It's as if he's passed into another dimension with different rules and senses. Some auras are clear as daylight and steady, so the person is predictable, and that's a big help, but others, like Leo's, change with mood or time of day, or what they're talking about. Leo confuses him.

Andy had told his mum about the new skills. She'd listened, and been interested, but then told him not to tell anyone else about it. Too late—he'd told the counsellor. Mum was worried people would think Andy was somehow different because of the head injuries and it's a short hop to being considered mentally deficient. That's the last thing Andy needs. He mulls that over now. It must be the worst thing in the world that could happen to anyone: to be sane but different, and for the little bit of common ground to be ignored, or not obvious. Andy has come to think that many people only hang on by a thread and to have that cut would be even worse than his accident.

There must be other people who see auras as he does. He needs to spend time with that girl because she might see them too. He can remember her name—Esther— because he talks to her in his head on and off all day.

Andy is deep in thought as he lugs his groceries up the road... van park, somewhere to live, auras, Esther, and his mind runs on: *how to get home, whether to try uni again,* and the most difficult—*what to say to his parents if he doesn't.*

Being at Leo's has taught him one thing: if some days all he can do is plan the rest of the day, and perhaps tomorrow, that's enough. It's not a momentous achievement but Andy is gratified he's been able to learn anything.

His head pounds with these thoughts as he walks. He sees two kids and their mother crack up laughing as they walk toward him. After they've passed, he looks behind to see what's so funny because he needs a laugh but there's nothing there. They're laughing at him. He expects their mother to rouse on them but she sniggers louder. Skanky bitch! He'd like to bang their heads together and kick her up the arse but he'd fall flat on his face if he tried. It's infuriating not to be able to stand up for himself.

He should be mature enough to tolerate their ignorance and help them get over it, but he wants to lash out. It's difficult to be reasonable when he's the victim. Andy used to laugh at spasos before he was one. It seems there were two of him back then: the dutiful, medical student son, and the guy who wanted to be liked by his mates.

It's a slow walk up the street but it gives him time to think, or what passes for thinking these days, and something amazing occurs. He used to work things out fast—more easily about science than people—and once facts went in, they stayed put. Now it's the other way around: people and emotional events charge straight into his brain and stick there.

One bonus is that impressions of people brew in a backwater of his brain. Then, they defrag, and an insight pops up to say, *Well, hi there, Andy. Here I am, a new idea.* He has a mind-blowing revelation right there, on the street.

There was a guy at college called Stan who was born with huge problems. He had dwarfism and ended up in a wheelchair when he was still a kid because operations on his spine went wrong. Smart as a button, nice to the core and a total charmer: worked like a Trojan to boot. Stan told Andy how when he was at school, he'd see other kids running around, playing sport and having fun, while he was in pain most of the time and saw more of doctors and hospitals than movies or the beach. Stan said he used to wonder when his real life would begin, when he'd be a normal kid and have a normal kid's life. Andy keeps saying the words to make it sink in... *wonder when his real life would begin*. How big is that... *wonder when his real life would begin*?

A mega realisation fills Andy's head to bursting. *He* used to have a *real* life, the sort of *real life* Stan was talking about, and it's gone. It couldn't have been any more real. It had everything: comfort, family, health, wealth, education, a future, but not anymore. It's evaporated! Phooff! Gone! What does he have now? An *unreal* life? Will it ever be *real* again? Ever since he got out of hospital, he's been thinking that one day he will get his old life back, but it's just sunk in that's not going to happen. He's damaged all right, but it's not for the moment, it's forever.

When that last thought bottoms out he puts his shopping bags down and leans against a fence. This is his *new real life*. Talk about an effing change of direction! Jesus! There's no going back to what used to be. Maybe in time he'll be less unco and learn new stuff, but his body will *never* be the same. He will *never* be able to make both arms and legs do what he wants them to, and certainly not like before. He will *never* be the sexy, cool guy he used to think he was. Women will either laugh at him or be disgusted. He will *never* be the wealthy, handsome, successful doctor with the mansion and his own pin-up family. He will be the Greeky, freaky, spastic guy who dropped out of uni and had no friends or family. This is his *new, very real life*.

The realisation hits him like a demolisher's lead ball. His old, *really REAL life* is gone; his new *REALLY UNREAL life* is what he's stuck with. It is the *new real life*. Crap! He will *never* be a man standing tall, *never* move like an athlete, *never* be normal.

Andy slides to the ground against the picket fence of a weatherboard house. It's one in a street of attractive homes with a well-formed footpath running its length. On the way to the shops he'd noticed its verdant garden and straight-edged lawn, with petunias peeking through the freshly-painted uprights, and pots of murraya trimmed to balls. Mum likes murraya because it doesn't drop much. The rest of it would be too much for her.

There's an outburst of expletives behind Andy and he wonders what else can happen. He turns to sees an old man, baggy trousers up to his armpits and sagging braces over a threadbare undervest, hobble like an enraged garden gnome down the steps from the veranda. He waves a stick at Andy while hanging on to the railing with his other hand.

'Go on! Get out of here, you bum! Take your drugs and booze and be off. Don't leave none of them needles on my lawn, neither!'

Andy understands he looks weird: twitching and moaning, and frothing at the mouth for all he knows.

But now he's an alcoholic, druggie dero as well as a spastic clown. What a town to be stuck in: criminals and bigots, and now they can pick on him.

'Sorry, sir,' Andy puffs. 'I'm going. I'm not drunk and I'm not on drugs so you can put your stick down. I had to rest.'

The old man lowers the stick and shuffles closer. Apparently, the fact that Andy can communicate sensibly, or even speak clearly, reassures him.

'Sorry, young fella. There's plenty in town I don't care to have parked on my front lawn dropping all sorts of trash. My grandchildren come here and I won't take risks with them.'

He leans over the fence and hoists up one of the bags with the crook of his stick. 'Come and rest on the veranda,' he says.

It's a kind offer, and nor does Andy want to see his shopping disappear into the house, so he supports himself along the fence to the gate and follows the old man, who pulls himself up the steep, concrete steps, with stick and a bag in one hand. Andy hangs the other bags off his cocked right arm and grasps the railing with his left hand.

The old fellow wheezes as he plonks the shopping down and directs Andy to one of two curvaceous cane chairs with faded, moulded cushions. He disappears into the house and returns with two glasses, stacked, and an iced-water container, all in one arm. He sits, pours, and hands Andy a glass.

Andy sucks it in, like a horse at a trough. He's amazed

how sweet water is at the right time.

'Gee, that's good. Thank you, sir. That's good water.'

'Yeah, natural's best, unless it's got a drop of best malt in it,' the man says. 'We'd better introduce ourselves. My name's Bert, Bert Foster. I've lived in Greta all my life: been a miner, footballer, one-time councillor, one-time RSL President. Haven't seen you round here, so what brings you to these parts?'

'I'm Andy Contopoulos. I'm a uni student and I'm on holidays.'

Bert nods and says nothing.

To fill the silence Andy adds, 'I had an accident and I'm getting better.'

'Right,' says Bert. They watch the stream of traffic for a few minutes.

Bert grumbles, 'Suppose you saw the bloody politicians up the street? Full of self-interest and greedy as graft! Did Shinypants Twigold shove his casino plans in your face? And where it would be? Yeah? They want that casino so bad they can smell the money. I wish the ground would open up and swallow the lot of them.'

'Yes, I saw the mayor,' Andy says. 'He says it will be good for the town. Why don't you want the casino?'

'Much as I'd like to see that dump down the road disappear and the rest of Leo's dogs go with him, I don't want a piece of the French Riviera or part of Darling Harbour plonked into the middle of our town. Think of the types it would bring; la-di-das from all over, and loud, flashy, wine freaks from the vineyards. They'd be worse than what's at Leo's now. His good-for-nothings steal cars and anything else that's not bolted down. He must be into drugs because the local motorbike gang is in there regular, and what else would they have in common? The police never touch them. I shudder to think why.

'Nobody round here wants the casino. We want Greta to stay the way it is, except for the undesirables, and we sure don't want those grubby politician types getting rich by exploiting this town. There might be more local jobs but others who've lived here all their lives could lose their jobs, and homes for that matter. There's been changes all right, sometimes good ones, but a casino would end the town as we know it.

'They say they're *consulting the community* but that's been done plenty of times before on a dozen different issues, and no notice taken. It will come down to self-interest. It always does. I know how it works because I've been on the council and seen what happens.

Forty years ago my missus—she's gone now, God rest her soul—got sick of my whinging about the council, and told me to put up or shut up, so I went for it, and got in. Worst bloody years of my life. Too many meetings and too much sucking up. Most of the councillors were there to advance their own cause, not to serve the community.

'So, believe me, I know what they're up to. Council will sell Leo's land for non-payment of rates, some of the boys will buy it, their mates on council will get it rezoned, and bingo, they'll all be millionaires when they build a casino. None of them gives a rat's about the people who live hereabouts. And that sleazebag, Twigold, up the road pumping hands like they were poker machine arms, is the worst. He runs the development company that would be sure to get the tender, and would negotiate to keep a share of the profits when it's up and running. I may look like an old codger, but I've had all the more years to work out the difference between velvet and slime.

'Far as I can tell, it's a race to get hold of Leo's, which would be their cheapest option, or they'll have to pay a motzer for a spot up the valley. Someone else might already be doing that. Gees, I hope they get done like a dinner, right down to their last razoo. Leo's not stupid and he must know what's going on so surely he's got something in reserve to keep council at bay.'

Bert finishes his set piece and sits with knees apart, hands resting on the stick planted between them, staring fixedly across the road at the hillside in the distance. Unformed words rumble in his throat.

Andy is tempted to tell him how helpful Leo has been but no one has said a good word about him, so he just says he's been there a few days but plans to move on soon.

Bert grunts and says coolly, 'Take care, young fellow. The price of staying there is more than the rent.'

Bert's house is on the high side of the street and Andy can see over the roofs across the road to green fields and low hills in the distance. He's tempted to sit and soak it in but he doesn't want to outstay his welcome.

'Thank you for the water, Mr Foster, and...' Andy trails off, unsure of what Bert has actually given him.

'Just 'Bert' will do, Andy.'

They get the bags to the front gate together and Andy loads up. Bert pats Andy on the shoulder and invites him to call in for a chat any time he's going past.

'I enjoyed meeting you,' says Bert.

'Thanks,' is all Andy says, so surprised is he at an affirmation.

The bags are heavy—could be the tins of dog food for Casper—and *Walk Like an Egyptian* plays on a loop in his mind, again. It's nice to have company, even if it's only in his head, and he gets a buzz that he remembered to buy a can opener as well as Casper's dinner.

As Andy heads for the gate at Leo's, he sees through gaps in the fence that Casper, inside the barricade, is keeping level with him. Warmth for another living thing floods through him.

Chapter Eight

There's more nocturnal action at Leo's than at a party after free booze and drugs are advertised on social media. One night it's a truck loading car parts and tonight it's a bikie invasion. The power is off and Andy is in bed in the dark at ten o'clock listening to the battery-powered radio—down low because he's not supposed to have one—when a hullabaloo breaks out. A pack of motorbikes—loud, throaty Harleys, roars up to Leo's van. They rev in unison to announce their arrival then all cut out at the same time. After the motors stop thrumming in Andy's ears, he can hear voices but they're not sociable. It's more interesting than the corny talkback radio program so he sneaks out and gets up close till there's just one van between him and Leo's callers.

There's a fire burning in a large drum out the front of Leo's van, and close by, the man himself fills his timber throne like a slouching hippo. Ten or so bikies loom like prowling bears: they could be midgets for all Andy knows but in the dim shadows they're huge, hairy and menacing. Their battered faces, full beards, tatts and muscular arms remind Andy of the Orc army from *Lord of the Rings*. It's too dark to see auras but the air is tense.

Goob twitches from side to side, making feints at a

body on the ground and whimpering *Fiddle! Fiddle!* to the prone figure. Each time Goob inches forward a bikie snarls and spineless Goob scuttles back behind Leo. Whenever the lying form groans and rolls a bikie heaves a kick into his guts. Goob gasps and Leo smiles. Andy gags.

The bikie leader is making pronouncements about being business partners, about trusting each other, about how Leo's dogs better stay out of the bikies' yards and quit thieving. If he catches Fiddle on his turf again he'll come back in pieces. Leo hasn't moved except to stroke his chin with one hand and massage a pendulous man boob with the other. He lets the visitors rant till they run out of steam then he tries to mend fences.

'Yeah, Fiddle's a bad little shit. I'll see he gets what's coming to him,' Leo says. 'Why don't you guys take a seat and Goob'll break out a few beers. Soon as you've done that, Goob, go and rouse out our new recruit to take care of this mongrel. Andy, ya dumb ass!' he adds when Goob swivels his head in query.

At the mention of his name Andy scurries away. He all but collides with Lola as she disappears into an old food vending van with a dented door and faded pink *Fairy Floss* sign along the top edge. He's barely closed his door before Goob thumps on the outside.

'Yeah, what?' Andy pretends Goob has woken him.

'Fiddle's hurt and Leo wants you to fix him.'

'So, who's Fiddle and what's wrong with him?'

'He's me mate and he fell over.'

'What am I supposed to do? I haven't got a first aid kit and I can only use one hand. Take him to hospital.'

'We don't do that round here. We look after ourselves. You better remember that... an' you better come when Leo says.'

Andy can't tell if this is friendly advice or a veiled threat. Goob has a torch that helps them reach the van that Goob and Fiddle share. Goob turns on his Fat Boy LED lamp. It deals with the darkness but can't overcome the stale sourness of the air.

Fiddle is a scabby runt with a mighty lump on his head, a squashed nose, a broken tooth with the nerve exposed, and probably some cracked ribs. He'll recover as long as there's nothing too bad Andy can't see. He finds unexpected satisfaction from tending to Fiddle and easing the little bloke's pain.

'Hey, Goob, I could hear those guys from my van. Who are they?' Andy asks.

'They're friends of Leo's. That's all you need to know.'

Andy nods.

'Smart answer, wog boy. You're a fast learner. You should be at college.'

After the kid is made comfortable, they go to where Leo and the bikies are piling up empty beer cans in the middle of their circle. It's a still night and the smell of pot lingers among the men. Its acrid sharpness appeals to Andy but he tries to avoid a contact high because he'd go arse over tit if his balance was affected.

Leo laughs at a joke, but it's only covering noise while his eyes scan. His mouth is doing one thing and his eyes and ears are doing something else. The bikies are further gone than Leo, but they're just as shifty.

'Oi, Andy,' Leo calls. 'Got another job for ya. Spider 'ere's got a dog at 'ome with a busted leg. It's his favourite little mutt and I said you'd strap 'er up for 'im. He'll whiz you over there on 'is bike and you'll be back 'ere no time.'

The bikies twig that Andy is not keen. Spider pretends to be a puppy and crawls across the dirt to plead with him. Some of the gang hoot and bay at his yipping and leg lifting while others topple off boxes, incapacitated by hilarity.

Andy hisses at Leo that he's not the man for the job, but Leo eases himself in his chair so Andy can see a handgun wedged in the corner of the seat. That puts a whole new dimension on his veterinary skills. They need to get on with these guys. Andy nods to Spider, hoping he's sober enough to ride. Spider looks Andy up and down, sneers, and agrees to travel slowly.

Andy is terrified yet exhilarated powering through the dark town. He's not embarrassed to align his body tightly against Spider's back and link his arms around Spider's waist. Andy's right arm has no strength but by clasping his right wrist with his left hand he ties himself on. It's a matter of survival. He presses his head against the back of Spider's neck: the creak of leather and the smell of engine grease, pot and beer glut his senses. Spider's beard is so long it whips Andy's face. As they lean into corners and roar up hills, Andy feels safe but fragile, like a fly riding on the outside of a jumbo jet. This is the most physical thing he's done since the last time he ran across a road. Andy wobbles off the bike when they stop but feels like he's climbed Everest.

The 'little' mutt is a pain-enraged pit-bull crossed with the Devil and she has a mutant, double set of canines. She's the size of a Rottweiler and is chained up in an old chook pen that's reinforced with weldmesh. She's earned Spider a lot of money and he wants her fixed up to fight again. Spider says Sweetie Pie took on the Hilux in the yard.

'Stupid bitch! It's her own effing fault. She's brave, or mad, give her that, but there's no future in trying to bite the tyre off a truck while it's going round. I reckon it's a clean break in her right front. Strap it up or something. If it don't mend she's no good to me.'

The only veterinary training Andy has had was when Mum had Dr Harry on TV. He insists on Sweetie Pie being muzzled with a belt and her back legs trussed. Spider takes a deep breath and flexes before entering the coop to tie her up. He slings off at her but she stands her ground, hackles up, teeth bared to the gum line, and shaking with fury. It's bluff on both sides but the dog has more to back it up.

Spider retreats and hollers at the house: an outside light comes on and woman in her late thirties reels out onto the landing. Her tight jeans are half-unzipped to accommodate a little belly, and a lime lycra halter-neck top clings around small undulations of fat above and below her bra strap. She stops under the light and swivels from right to left without moving her feet. Dried, blond tips are swept up onto the top of her head but slip out at the back. There's a sizable tattoo on one bare shoulder: it's a Harley nestled in roses with the words underneath *Jimmy rides forever.* Andy finds the package not unpleasant, although the infection around her belly ring is a downer.

'Whatcha doin' at this hour, darl?' She drags hard on a cigarette.

Spider tells Crystal, 'Andy here's from Leo's and he's gunna fix the brindle bitch. Get the boy out.'

A lad straggles out. He's about twelve and not happy. It's unclear why—a dozen reasons cross Andy's mind: maybe he doesn't like Sweetie Pie; maybe he doesn't like his dad, if Spider is his dad; or maybe he's just tired, although he's still up and dressed.

'Yeah, what?' the boy announces.

'Get one of them dried things she likes and help me truss 'er up.' Spider keeps his eyes on the dog while he instructs River, the boy.

River's demeanour shifts to the high alertness required for self-preservation around Sweetie Pie. While he distracts her with a dried pig foot, Spider whips a belt around her muzzle. They tie her back legs together and hoist the beast into a wheelbarrow to bring her into the light. There's no way to soothe Sweetie Pie—she's mad as hell, crazed with pain, and bred to kill.

Andy is mustering common sense and first aid training, and hoping inspiration will kick in. He lines up the bone and secures splints; a wooden spoon handle, River's ruler, clean sticks, and exhausts Crystal's supply of bandages. He checks that nothing will stick into Sweetie Pie when she walks.

All the while in the barrow she's been building up

internal pressure like a plugged volcano. Her nose wrinkles and strains against the belt. Her piggy eyes flit around their faces, sussing out the enemy, checking their strength, then, despite the closed jaws, a throaty growl seeps out. Like a didgeridoo player, she can breathe in her nose and keep the noise coming out her mouth. Bubbles of saliva ooze on her outward breath, adding musical notes as they splutter and pop.

It's bizarrely entertaining till a louder noise, like a peel of thunder rolling down a valley, resounds in her belly and comes out through her skin. Sweetie-Pie stiffens and her body trembles: she explodes out of the wheelbarrow with enraged shrieks. Her smooth body thrashes and rolls like a giant, voracious garden slug: the muzzle begins to unravel, she gains her feet and bounds in unpredictable directions, pulling on her front legs and propelled by joined back legs. It's a modern gladiatorial combat: weaponless man versus wild beast.

'Get the gun,' Spider bawls at River.

River baulks, then runs inside as Sweetie Pie crashes through a cage of sleeping guinea pigs toward the men. The little rodents squeal in panic and scatter into the darkness. Sweetie Pie's muzzle slips off, and she's slowed, but not enough, by having one conjoined back leg.

Crystal is on the roof of the Commodore in the yard and Andy is on the ground beside Spider. It's hard to know which of the men Sweetie Pie hates more: either way, she has them both lined up. They separate and she follows Spider. River emerges from the back door with the gun, stuffing a bullet in. He snaps it shut, gets a line on Sweetie Pie as she closes on Spider, and fires. The bullet hits a metal pole in front of River and ricochets. There's a hideous racket as River falls down the steps, screaming, and the gun clatters down beside him.

Sweetie Pie disappears down the side of the house after Spider. Crystal slithers off the top of the car across the boot and she and Andy fall over each other getting to River who's clutching his thigh and howling obscenities. There's blood everywhere and Andy yells at Crystal to get clean cloths to stop the bleeding while he puts pressure on the wound.

'Move the car closer and we'll take him to hospital,' Andy tells her.

It's as if she doesn't hear. He says it again and she says, 'Nup. We don't go to hospital. We got problems enough already without the police coming round.'

'But your son's got a great big hole in his leg. He needs stitches, antibiotics and maybe a blood transfusion.'

'Yeah, Mum, and I want to play in the pre-season comp,' River gasps.

'Nup!'

Andy can't think what else to say. He doesn't know if it's a continuation of his own nightmare, or if he's slipped into someone else's.

Chapter Nine

Spider climbs a fence three houses away to give Sweetie Pie the slip and comes home from a different direction. He steals along the side of the house and peers warily around the back in case the dog has returned. Andy helped Crystal take River inside, and on his way back outside, he bumps into Spider at the door.

'The kid needs a doctor,' Andy says. 'He got shot. He lost a lot of blood.'

Spider barges past Andy and he's back in less than a minute.

'Nah, it's just a flesh wound. He'll be right. Teach him a lesson. Come on if ya want a lift back.'

The return trip is slower but no less exhilarating and for a few minutes Andy forgets about River. Spider drops him at the entrance to the van park and the place is quiet and dark as Andy shuffles down the driveway. He sits on the bed pondering the best thing to do—best for River, best for himself. Disasters are piling up: his mates have vanished; he's failed exams; Dad has told him not to come home; and he'll be in worse trouble if he breaks Leo's rules and the bikies' code of silence. They'll all be after him but he doesn't care anymore because nothing could be worse than what's already happened.

Triple zero is one number Andy can remember. As he sneaks out of the park Casper appears beside him. They stick to the shadows and Andy tries to breathe without gasping. The phone on the corner is trashed, so he struggles on a kilometre to the twenty-four-hour servo. Casper stays close, stopping when Andy stops and padding between patches of darkness with him.

Spider and Crystal were going to let River take his chances but without medical intervention the poor little bastard could lose a leg, and even with help he still might. Andy has to give his name or the authorities won't take any notice, so he asks them to say it's a neighbour reporting the gunshot. The police need to go as well, he says, because Spider might not let the ambulance in.

Andy hopes what he does helps River because it won't help him... except for the good feeling he has for doing the right thing. He and Casper barely make it back by dawn but at least with a doggy companion the trek is more boys' adventure than dangerous quest.

It's been a big day and a long night. Andy entices Casper into his van. The dog is safer there, and hearing another creature breathe is comforting. Andy sinks into an exhausted sleep, heady with the satisfaction of achievement. There's a memory, too, of a beautiful girl, a dream-charmer who floats through his sleep. Thoughts of her lull him to a place long denied: it begins with the lowering of his weary body into a warm bath, but it gets much, much better.

ANDY WAKES IN the early afternoon with a single, reverberating thought. *Esther! Must see Esther!* She shines into his troubles like salvation personified.

He plans to wander around the enclosure so she'll see him, but he must take care not to look like an aimless idiot or a peeping Tom, then he'll drift to an out of the way corner and hope she follows. Leo's might be called a holiday park but it's not the sort of place where you can rock up to the girl next door and say hello. The 'aimless idiot' aspect of Andy's appearance weighs heavily on his mind. He knows a lot of society still call people with cerebral palsy spastics, and think they're stupid as well as disabled, but *he* also knows their brain is the same as anyone else's: they just have trouble co-ordinating their body—even talking can be beyond them. Andy also knows he's unusual because parts of his body have become spastic in his twenties, whereas most people with the condition are born that way. What's more, his brain *is* affected because it was bashed around.

If only she'll come and talk to him. He so wants her to understand.

There's nothing to look at in the enclosure, so he strolls as if exercising, and tries to look normal and contemplative: both hands locked behind his back; the crook leg on the inside of the circle so it doesn't have to move as much. It's as close to normal-looking as he can get. After each circuit Andy moves out of sight, but not far off, and waits for a few minutes. After four laps he's about to give it away when Esther glides out from behind a shabby ticket booth. On its counter sits a solitary clown head seeming to imitate a dwarf, red-faced ticket seller.

Esther is so ethereal she could vaporise at any moment. Except for the dark eyes nothing else about her has any substance: her charcoal hair falls in soft curls that sway in the lightest movement of air and her limbs waft more than move. She even blinks slowly and tilts her head a little to one side, but says nothing. Andy stays still to look his best. It's a sort of Mexican stand-off while they soak each other up until Esther starts to talk as if they meet like this every day.

She has a slight European accent which is a lighter version of her mother's, and her words hover like honeyed petals. 'I had to wait for Mother to go to the shower. I will have to go as soon as I see her coming back. Mr Leo does not like any one of us talking to another.'

She keeps her gaze fixed over his shoulder toward the shower block and glances intermittently at Andy.

'What's Leo got over your mother?' he asks. Esther frowns at the terminology and he rephrases the question. Direct conversation feels entirely natural. Their time is limited and they already know each other well, having exchanged so much in that short, intense stare through the caravan window.

'In the early 1970s, when she was twelve, Mother escaped with her parents from East Germany. When they reached Australia, the government found fault with the passports of her mother and father, and alleged their politics were not acceptable here, so they were deported. They managed for Mother to stay by telling the authorities she had run away but they secretly sent her to live with German friends in Queensland. She never saw any papers giving her the right to stay and was told by that family she was not a legal migrant.

'Mother stayed with those people for many years. They were academics, like her own parents, and educated her at home: they continued on with the languages and music and literature that my grandparents had begun. Those people were good to her in that way, although she had to work hard in the house and was never treated as well as their own children. Those children went to expensive schools and then to university, but Mother was not permitted. However, she did have access to all the books in the house and kept studying alone. She lived there till she was twenty-three.

'The man was not nice. He took advantage of her and... anyway, he is my father. When his wife found out, she evicted Mother, even though she was pregnant with her husband's child. She also gave Mother a bundle of letters her parents had sent to her over the years—letters they had kept from her.

'Mother was put on a train and came to Singleton, nearby here. Someone brought her to Mr Leo's because it is cheap. I was born here, in our caravan. Mr Leo helped Mother at that time. She has never dared move because she is afraid if the authorities find out who she is they will send her back to Germany and perhaps keep me here. We have only each other.'

Without knowing anything about the process, Andy

reassures her she wouldn't be deported. 'It's so long ago and you were born here. You're Australian, and your father might have been an Australian citizen.'

Esther is not sure. 'Mr Leo tells Mother we would certainly be sent away and it is just as bad in Germany as it used to be. People like us are punished. If we were not returned to Germany, then we could be sent to a *Reffo Camp* in Australia, whatever that might be. They sound most undesirable places. Mr Leo says it is his humanitarian duty to let us stay here for as long as we like. Of course, he wants to be compensated for his costs and we have no money, so he has worked out something else for us... as you heard, and he gives us a little money to buy what we need. Mother says we should be grateful to him for protecting us from a worse fate.

'He was kind to us in the past. When I was four years old, he took us to the circus. I remember everything. It was amazing. He also gave me a doll when I was small. He promised other excursions but they have not come to pass. From time to time he will bring a box of fruit.'

Andy is lost for words. What part of the twenty-first century should he begin to tell her about?

'Did you go to school?' he asks.

'No, we are hardly allowed out. Mother has taught me everything she knows. She says I would be considered well-educated in society. Of course, we have had no books or musical instruments but there is much to be learnt by talking and listening. She sings to me and we write down the music. She has told me all the stories she ever knew.

'How else could we spend our time? We have radio but cannot listen often as batteries are expensive. I have heard about television but never seen it. I would like to visit the library but Mr Leo says it is not safe for us to be known in town.'

Esther scans the shower block every few seconds. 'Mother would not think it right to be telling so much to someone I have not been introduced to, so, quickly, tell me your name,' she giggles. 'We will say Mr Red Hat introduced us.' She hugs the clown head.

Andy wonders if she has told him a load of bull and is crazier than he is, but he's in no position to criticise.

'I'm Andy Contos. I'm only here till I work out...'

Esther interrupts. 'Mother is coming. I must get back before she returns. Meet me here tomorrow when you see her leave for the shower.'

'Wait! What's the rest of your name?' Andy presses.

'I am Esther Schönburg. That is the name Mother was born to. It is not my father's name.' She vanishes like a will-o'-the-wisp.

Goob appears nearby, grins inanely and heads for Leo's. Andy is unconcerned. He's met Esther and that's worth a heap of trouble. Already she intrigues him.

———•———

ANDY LOLLS ABOUT in his caravan for the rest of the day. This is the first time he's not had Mum and Dad or friends to chat with about important events, and although he enjoys talking to Casper, he's yet to receive useful advice in return. But the dog's company has been a solace.

He told Esther he was there till he worked things out:

now he can't work out what he is supposed to be working out. Is it somewhere to go, given that he's not welcome at home? What about his studies? How will he travel alone? The problems are intertwined and he can't make the smallest inroad into any of them. Some decisions in life are obvious and some things we are driven to do, but many choices need a sounding board. Right now he's in a pickle—it's life on the edge with none of the usual backup: he doesn't understand how his mind works; his brain behaves in unexpected ways; his body is disabled and weary; and everyone around him is crazy or mean, or worse. He's struggling to discover anything positive, except for meeting Esther, and he's not even sure that thought is logical. Is she a suitable counterbalance for his thoughts? If she mirrors his craziness, they may delude themselves into sanity; if she is different from him, who is sane, Esther or Andy?

———•———

THEY MEET ON each of the next three days when Esther's mother, whose name is Adeline, showers. They exchange life stories in fifteen-minute instalments—from wondrous moments to ten years of sameness. He tells Esther about the two Andys—one before the accident and the other, after. Grief for the loss of a perfect life pitches Andy into silence and he slumps in dejection. Recollection of poor choices made when he was whole, for the sake of peer esteem, have evaporated: be those actions irresponsible, cringeworthy, illegal, or harmful to others. For him there is only *The Lost* and *The Now*. And *The Now* is second rate.

Esther dismisses his first life with a puffy breath. 'It

is gone,' she says. 'Now you are a butterfly with bent wings, but that is better than a grub in a cocoon. This change has given you understanding. University study can give you a degree, but only life can give insight. You are already ahead of your friends and your family: it is they who are the losers if they exclude you.

'It is not necessary to die to lose your life. My mother lost what should have been her life and now she has a different one. Soldiers who return from war are still alive yet they can be so changed they are totally unlike their former selves. Mother told me these things. You did not die in the accident but you lost your previous life. Now you have a new one.'

Andy concludes Adeline is a good teacher and looks forward to meeting her. He tells Esther what a fine education she's had and that her mother has achieved a balance between the cultural and the humanitarian. He does not add *except for human rights*. But he does ask gently if they understand how much they're being taken advantage of? Leo is attempting to force her into a line of work that she doesn't want to do. That's illegal and Leo would be prosecuted for his part in it. While he reassures Esther there's a better life for her and Adeline away from Leo's, he's praying that he doesn't lose her to the legal system and deportation. A faint voice whispers that Dad would like what he's saying.

•———————•

AFTER FOUR SHORT meetings Andy knows Esther better than he knows himself. She has lived at Leo's all her life;

Adeline is her only family; she has never been to school, to a doctor or dentist, hairdresser, library or the movies, yet she is more complete than any girl he's ever known. And he's in love.

Esther tells her mother about Andy, and Adeline becomes upset because she doesn't want to antagonise Mr Leo. They have nowhere else to go and what will happen if Mr Leo reports them to the authorities or evicts them? Esther calms Adeline by recounting some of Andy's beliefs: notions that may sow in her the seeds of assertion, bravery, independence—all the strengths he aspires to. The ideas must touch a deeper, tougher chord in Adeline because the next day she lets them meet for a whole half-hour. That's so much better than fifteen stolen minutes of shower time.

Andy and Esther like to think no one can see them as they talk but the wall of wrecked machinery they sit behind affords many peep holes. Andy sits to Esther's right because when they want to hold hands his left one can do the job, and feeling Esther beside him is the best rehabilitation Andy has had. Her presence makes him feel whole, even energetic. If they look into each other's eyes up close Andy almost passes out. He has to kiss her soon and he's sure, from the way she looks into his eyes, that she wants him to.

Toward the end of their first half-hour meeting when they're sitting close, his arms find their way around her and he shapes up to kiss. Esther surprises him by pulling back but it's only to say, 'My lips are for whom I chose, and I chose you, Andy.'

He goes into meltdown: he's trembling but it's not the palsy, he's almost falling apart with desire for Esther. Her mouth is raised and her lips are demanding to be kissed. He must make it good—not a smashing pashing, nor a lip-smacking, face contorting merging of mouths—he will awaken her parted lips with a whispering brush, the barest touch of his eager mouth. His hot breath will make her lips buzz, she will lick and purse them, pucker and plump them, wanting more, yearning to taste his touch. This will be no mere joining of lips; their mouths will hunt each other.

THE NEXT DAY they search for a more private place but there's nowhere to hide at Leo's, only places they are less likely to be seen. They find a refuge of sorts—a place with the scent of freedom. The back edge of Leo's block dips down a weedy slope to a cyclone and barbed wire fence. Unseen from the vans, they can look across an empty house block to the banks of a creek that was the town's first water supply. There are grassy mounds with waddling ducks, reeds, a willow tree and a glimpse of water. Dogs chase ducks and children dip for guppies. Esther and Andy hang off the fence and stare at an alien but desirable world, a birth right denied. They kiss again, as if christening a new home.

They discuss how life might be for them far away from Leo's. Esther's eyes glow but she's like a bird whose wings have been strapped to its body since hatching and have atrophied. She has never bolted through hot sand to the summer surf or, with popcorn and choc-top ice-cream in hand, settled into a movie theatre armchair to watch an adventure epic. He wants to shape their two lives into one. He also needs her help to travel home.

He looks into her eyes and says, 'Let's run away, just you and me.'

The light in Esther's eyes flares then dims, ebbs and dies. She draws back and lets loose a single sob as she leaps up and runs off.

Chapter Ten

The day after Andy's impulsive proposal Esther fails to appear at their trysting spot. And again the next day. After each abortive rendezvous he returns to his van and collapses on the meagre bed. He's failed again. Panic sets in. He was in her arms one day, and each day since has trudged alone between the ticket booth and their sanctuary overlooking the waterhole.

Andy lurches between self-loathing and the memory of euphoric love. He must have grossly offended her if she won't even see him. Of course, she wouldn't run off with such a useless bastard as him when in a free life, if she gets one, she could have her pick. She's been amusing herself because he's all that's available: practising her feminine wiles on a harmless idiot. Most likely he's repulsive in her eyes, and how stupid is he to think she'd abandon her mother? She's not that sort of girl.

With eyes closed Andy relives their first kiss in an orgy of adoration: her face, colouring, vibrations and scent expand within his head and exude through eyes, ears and mouth till he's enveloped in Estherness. She has become his world. Then the illusion of Andy and Esther as a couple disintegrates like cloud sucked into space.

The glory of her kisses suffuses Andy again: how warm and full of love they were, how restrained yet potent. He calms himself with excuses for her: perhaps she tries to meet with him but her mother has forbidden it. It's preferable that she's been confined, not that she's avoiding him. He imagines her voice, *Andy, help me, help us.*

It's torture speculating if she's sick or imprisoned or indifferent.

Andy encounters Goob on every foray from the van: around a corner, during a rare trip for provisions, in the toilet block. Goob offers a conspiratorial smile but no friendship. He says things like: *Leo wants to know how you're going* and *Leo says not to stick your nose in where it don't belong.* Goob's own contribution is, 'Leo's been busy last couple of weeks. He's got problems to sort out so he don't want you starting up any new ones.'

Andy slips into a dark place. He's exhausted by life in this nether world and has new woes in addition to the earlier insurmountables. Now he also hankers for a thwarted love yet is not brave enough to go to Esther's van, fearing both Leo and confirmation of abandonment. Even Casper has stopped coming into the van, lingering outside, and when Andy ventures out the dog keeps a wary distance, watching with soulful eyes. When Andy goes to the shops, he takes a different route to avoid Bert's house because he's too embarrassed to be seen like this. He knocks on Lola's door twice but she's not there. He'd be comfortable talking to her—she's a fellow crazy.

Knowing Esther gave Andy heart to keeping going, but that lifeline has vanished. Reality is suspended.

Meaning dissolves like a fresh watercolour portrait left in the rain. The colours of his existence are diluted: they form muddy rivulets that drip into the grass and trickle away. He sinks and rolls in a murky world like a body in surf at night—pummelled by waves, dragged back to the depths, and trounced again. He cannot imagine hope or a future, or begin any constructive process.

The one recurring thought is to end his life. First an inkling, but he's too scatty to hold it for more than a second. It recurs and lasts two seconds. It returns and lasts for three seconds. It impregnates his brain. Decisions are difficult, but this one appeals. He's almost happy to know what the future holds. There's brief euphoria that a decision is made—no more causing pain to others and himself, no more confusion, no more.

Small signs of life annoy him: a spider scurrying to safety with an egg sack, a lizard basking in sun, a butterfly sucking nectar. Their satisfaction confronts his shrivelling. Anger stirs other thoughts, other hatreds. Probably Leo has forbidden Esther to come outside; perhaps he has locked her in. Maybe Andy can rescue her and it doesn't matter what happens to him. He could end his life in a blaze of glory and achieve something meaningful in the process. Setting Esther and Adeline free is worth dying for.

The next day an altered obsession takes hold: he'll talk Esther and Adeline into leaving with him, maybe moving into Newcastle or Maitland. He can read forms and think what to say, although he'd get lost in the street unless it's straight there and back. He practised independence skills after the accident. If Esther and Adeline help him get about, he can guide them through applications for emergency housing, citizenship, social security, pension applications. Maybe Dad was right, and it is just a matter of application and diligence.

Perhaps he could work as a counsellor: their role seems to entail empathy and common sense. Esther says he has insight, and it is a profession of helping people. Certainly not with the glamour and pay of a doctor, but counselling is a job and Dad might get used to the idea.

Andy's highs lift him to optimism but the lows feel like truth. He can't escape the idea that he needs to die to feel better.

***

WHO WOULD IMAGINE that a few small pieces of coloured paper could turn a man from despair to elation? Later that day Andy gets closer to Esther's van than he has recently dared and spies on the window some pieces of coloured paper glued to the glass. One patch is blue and white; the other is black, red and yellow. They are facsimiles of the Greek and German flags, and they touch. She is still there and she thinks of him!

The flags rocket Andy from despair to sky-high optimism.

***

THAT NIGHT THERE'S another used car bonanza in the enclosure. Overladen utes and one-tonners arrive and their freight is reloaded onto a bigger truck. Leo runs the operation like a generalissimo and Goob scurries about like a crazed rodent.

Andy has never been asked to help handle the suspect goods so while everyone is distracted it's a chance to visit Esther and find out why she hasn't been out to see him. Leo wouldn't approve but he doesn't care.

Esther must have been peering out because she opens the door before he knocks. Out of sight of her mother she hugs him as he slips in. He's so relieved she's pleased to see him that he can't speak.

'Thank you for the flags,' he whispers.

The van's immaculate interior is a surprise—it's elegant, but it's homely, too. It's amazing how they've managed it with no money.

Esther is agitated. 'Andy, I have been praying for you to come. I told Mother how you could help and she is willing to listen but will make no promises. At first, she thought you were a spy for Mr Leo, like that Goob person, but one I would speak with. She does not think that now, not since Mr Leo found out we have been talking. He has forbidden it and Mother and I are allowed out only for ablutions.'

Adeline is sitting at the tiny dining table and stares at Andy's awkwardness. He's not embarrassed because it's an observation, not a judgement. She assigns him a seat like the Queen granting an audience. Andy glimpses strong colours around her: violets and purples that suggest compassion and neediness. The colours fluctuate.

He reassesses her age now he is closer. She may only be in her early forties but deprivation and ill-health have aged her—she's greying, both in her hair and in the silken skin drawn over fine features. Her dark eyes are intense and wary.

'Esther has told me of you. I was not happy at the beginning but she has convinced me you are a worthy man. I must believe her because it is I who taught her how to judge such things. The people in this place are not good to each other and have doubtful habits so we do not associate with them. It is best that way.'

After a break she adds, as if trying to convince them all, 'Except for Mr Leo, who helps us. So, tell me how you come to be here.'

Despite her incongruous refinement, Andy enjoys talking to Adeline. He tells her about himself and his family and what appears to be his new life. She's curious about Sydney but responds to the information as if it relates to another planet. Andy suggests they could have a better life in a nearby town but Adeline's eyes glaze over as if to say they might as well try to reach that other planet. He knows she wants better things for Esther and it's frustrating she won't consider the plan. Andy feels this is a rare chance to advance his prospects. Being blunt doesn't seem rash so he ups the ante and tells Adeline some hard truths in a calm, explanatory way.

'World War II is over, the Cold War is over, the Berlin Wall has come down and the Soviet Republic has collapsed. Germany is a democratic state and Australia is a democratic state with social security to support people who need help but you choose to condemn yourself and Esther to a life of serfdom!'

Andy has clearly overstepped the mark. Adeline sinks into her chair and fans herself frantically. There's no stopping now because there may not be another opportunity.

'You both live in this caravan park as if it's your row of huts in a concentration camp. Greta is at the limit of the camp but Esther never, and you rarely get that far. The rest of the world is there for the taking. Leo's been fooling you for years. If you went back to Germany nothing would be as bad as this and it's even sadder because you could walk away from this if you want to. Leo is vile! We could have him arrested for exploitation! All you have to do is get up and walk out. He can't stop you!'

Adeline is gasping and speechless. She waves Andy away and turns her back as she sobs into her hands. Esther rushes to her mother in panic.

After Adeline settles Esther hisses, 'Your harshness upsets Mother. She gets chest pains whenever she is worried and what could we do if she has a heart attack? You cannot come here if it has such an effect on her. I owe Mother everything. She has sacrificed herself to save me.'

Andy stares in disbelief. 'Save you from what? She needs a doctor to save herself, and this place is worse than if you were both deported.'

Esther says icily, 'Go now. I must look after Mother.' Her tears are welling as she hustles Andy out.

He says he's sorry Adeline is upset but she had to be confronted with the truth. Simple persuasion was never going to work. As Andy sneaks away trying not to trip, panic rises at the thought of losing Esther again. He hears a gluggy hawking near Mr Red Hat. It's Goob. He's slobbering over the clown head and jerking his slimy tongue across its face. Both pairs of goitrous eyes gleam. The degenerate pretends to be surprised to see Andy.

Goob has become viler by the day. Andy had first taken him as a down-and-outer making the best of things, like himself. They had something in common, but as Andy worked out his auras, he understood why Goob confused him. He's a weird fusion of Gollum from *Lord of the Rings,* and Rumpelstiltskin, the evil, self-serving fairy tale dwarf.

'Oi, Andy, is this where ya practise to get yer aim straight? How do spasos do it, anyway? Y'know, line 'er up? Ya must need the light on to see where 'er lips are! By the way, thanks for fixin' up Fiddle. He's come good—back in tune, ya might say. Reckon I'll take this little fella home to make a threesome. Ya don't need him no more, do ya? Eh?'

Andy wants to smash Goob's face in but he can hardly see him, let alone swing a punch.

Goob knows he's scored, and adds, 'By the way, Leo's got another job for ya. Come round 'bout eleven, after the truck leaves. See ya.' He lopes off like the feral dog he is.

That's the tipping point for sending Andy into another decline: Adeline won't budge; Esther pushed him away and Leo's onto him. A little voice starts up in his head, *Give up. There's no point in putting yourself through more failures. End the pain now.*

Chapter Eleven

A ndy doesn't want to see Leo but there's no way out. When the truck goes, he drags himself over, hoping Leo will just bawl him out but the big man is frostily civil, which is frightening. Leo doesn't look or sound drunk, but there's a pile of cans beside the throne. His low centre of gravity keeps him stable and he's so huge it probably takes a keg of beer to affect his speech. The air is acrid.

'Bit worried 'bout you, Andy,' Leo says. 'Looks like you're gettin' involved in other people's business because you got too much spare time. I can fix that. Our friend, Spider, is out of town for a few days. The whole gang's gone to some sort of bikie hoedown. Spider owes me heaps on a business deal and he don't look like comin' good in time. You and Goob get on over there and leave a message in 'is shed—bit of a hurry-up, somethin' he can't miss.

'It's a new line of work for you, Andy, but Goob knows the ropes, so watch what he does and you'll be schooled up for next time. This is the easy way, sonny. Easy for you, that is.'

Leo's pale eyes pierce Andy like shards of ice.

GOOB DAWDLES THE ute with the lights off for the last block to Spider's house, and backs up the driveway. He forces the shed door, flashes a torch around, selects a few portable objects and stashes them on the ute. No dogs are barking. They haven't heard whether Sweetie Pie was recaptured or came home—more fool her if she did. Andy can't feel her piggy eyes on him so she's not there. He's beginning to trust his intuition.

While Goob sets the fire bomb beside Spider's very schmick, second-best Harley, Andy keeps lookout. He notices a faint light inside the house. Guys like Spider have a sixth sense even when they are drunk or stoned so if he and Crystal are inside, which is unlikely, they must be out to it. Andy is unsure exactly what he's registering but it feels like pulsating pain, quite nearby. It's not so much an aura as oozing desolation and sadness. He tells Goob he's going to take a look, but the greasy ferret doesn't hear: his tongue is out the side of his mouth and his bulbous eyes are fixed on the fire bomb.

Andy surprises himself by how quietly he can sidle up the stairs, then sneak right into the kitchen and through to the lounge room. This is insanity but an irresistible magnet draws him on. The first tendrils of a stomach-turning stench barb his insides.

The television glows soundlessly and there's faint lamp light at one end of the couch. Biscuit and chip packets cover the floor and empty soft drink bottles are wedged under the couch. The figure on the lounge breathes in, stops and starts: it mutters and whimpers, attempts movement then groans.

It's River and he's very sick. Andy touches him but

he's past waking up. He turns on the light, lifts the blanket to see the injured leg, and nearly throws up at the suppurating wound. Then he sees the unexpected babysitter, a hand gun, beside the boy. Guns are a mystery to Andy but he'll need this one to make Goob cooperate. Without knowing if it's loaded or the safety is on or off, he goes to Goob in the shed.

'Hell, Andy,' Goob says. 'Don't sneak up on a bloke like that. It's enough to make me drop the fag in the petrol.'

Goob must be able to hear Andy's heart pounding and almost does drop his cigarette when he aims the torch at Andy and sees the shaking gun pointing at him.

'Bloody hell! What's that? Get it out of here!'

Andy surprises himself by saying, 'Listen, chicken shit. I've got a job for you now. Those cretins, Spider and Crystal, have left River inside in a real bad way. Before you start this fire load the boy into the back of the ute and I'll ride with him. We're taking him to the hospital. Yeah, you and me, to the hospital, because otherwise he'll die. He might die anyway, but I'm not leaving him the way he is. Drag a mattress out, then carry the boy. I'll be pointing this gun at you all the way, including through the back window at your head. If you make me cranky by going the wrong way my hand will shake more and it will go off.

'Just before we leave you can set your friggin' fire if you want, and we can say River dragged himself out and started it to get attention. We just happened to be passing, saw the fire and found him.'

Gutless Goob is persuaded by the gun and scampers to get River. He whines the whole time. 'Aw, 'e stinks!' then, 'Leo's gunna 'ave your arse. He don't want us gettin' involved in stuff like this. The cops have already been round askin' 'bout River and Leo fobbed 'em off.'

Now Andy knows why earlier calls to the police and ambulance didn't work. If they asked for Andy by name Leo probably told them Andy is the local half-wit. He's not wrong.

With River loaded, Goob lights the fuse so the fire will start when they're safely away. They set off to Maitland Hospital with Andy beside River in the back, still holding the gun on Goob's mangy head so he can see it in the rear vision mirror. Goob's a dead-set coward but cunning as all hell, and Andy half expects him to roll the ute on purpose.

As soon as they pull up at the emergency entrance, Goob leaps out with the engine running, undoes the back, drags the mattress out and lets it flop onto the concrete driveway with River on top. Andy drops the gun among the rubbish on the back tray and clambers down.

Goob yells, 'Get in! Get in! Leo'll do 'is block if ya don't come back with me. Come on! It'll be bad for all of us.'

Andy ignores the bleating and flops down beside River. A nurse comes out and Goob burns rubber. Andy is amazed at what he's done but is already turning numb thinking about what's inside those swishing doors; bright lights, monotone conversations, probing instruments and searching eyes.

Chapter Twelve

A ndy regains consciousness one piece at a time as if he's taking up someone else's life. He knows that he's in hospital, but there's no single, incontestable point of reality to grasp—not even who he is. There's no safe place in his mind from which to send out feelers to ascertain exactly where he is, or how long he's been there, or why he's there, or how he got there. Has he been abducted by aliens and is now the subject of experiments?

Everyone is kind but he's scared in a primeval, core-twisting way. The room is bright, white and clean—a hospital for sure, but which one? Has he gone back in time to the accident? His body is weak and twisted, but not banged up, so he hasn't been hit by a car in the last few days. That's a plus, but the rest is a mystery.

There are five other patients in the room. Some wear confining jackets and most have rails around their bed. The staff talk in tight whispers, or in a forced, jolly way.

'And how are we today?' they ask, not expecting an answer.

Andy wants to know how long he's been there, and where he is. He asks what's wrong with him, and are his mum and dad there? They fob him off with *A doctor will explain everything soon* or *Just rest for now.*

Pieces of the puzzle reassemble over days and he's unsure how much is fantasy. His dreams are drug-induced hallucinations; his waking hours are searches for reality. He dozes and starts awake from a sordid delirium in which a beautiful girl is in bondage to a troll. The dream merges into reality because beside him, next time his eyes open, is Leo, huge and hideous, leering at him. Even sedated, Andy rockets to the far side of the bed.

'Steady, sonny,' Leo cautions. 'You need to take it easy. You've given everyone a big scare, but you're in good 'ands, here in the psych ward. Seems you 'ad one of them schizoid attacks. They found you out the front raving and hurling yourself about, reliving your accident, I imagine. It was quite a scene—what, with you yelling and screaming, demanding help for some lad who turned up at the same time. They had to give you a jab to calm you down.'

Leo has shaved and is wearing clean tracksuit pants and a Tahitian print shirt the size of a carnival tent. He's a solicitous visitor, soothing Andy with familiar behaviour; mild-mannered small talk, pats on his shoulder and banal cheerfulness. It would be easy for Leo's words to wash over him unheeded and, at best, he's about three sentences behind what Leo is saying, but two chilling words leap out at him from the jumbled message. *Psych. Ward.* Why the eff is he here? He's not crazy! Is he? Has Leo pulled a swifty? He's already said ten more things Andy hasn't taken in.

'Goob told me you felt a wobbly comin' on at Greta, and you made him bring you to hospital. Said you'd been through this sort of thing before, and you had to get to a doctor or you'd be uncontrollable. You are one sick young fellow and you should thank Goob for saving your bacon. You know what they say... *a friend in need...* As far as the doctors are concerned, you're off your rocker. I told them about the other weird stuff you been doing, but for your own good, sonny. They got my joint as your address, so when you get out you can come back there, but I gotta agree, see? Mummy and Daddy ain't comin'. They don't know you're 'ere. So it's up to me to say if I'm prepared to 'ave you. Think of it this way, Andy, your life is in my hands. It'll take my signature to get you out of this psych ward.'

Leo emphasises the words again—*psych ward*. They drive like blunt needles into Andy's brain: his heart pounds; his breath catches and stalls. He understands everything Leo says but can't reply. Thoughts of love and loss, control and helplessness, action and submission bounce around inside his head like beams of light inside a mirror ball, but he can only lie still with eyes wide and mouth gaping. He sees Esther, Adeline and Casper sitting on the grass overlooking the waterhole, waiting for him so they can all slide through the fence to another life, but his face remains blank and his mouth silent.

'That's a good lad,' Leo says. 'You rest easy and as soon as you're well enough you can come back to my place, but only if you be'ave. If you're too much to 'andle, I'll sign you over to some other place, not so 'omely. This 'ere psych ward's for the loonies and nutters—next down the line is for the crazies. You see, Andy, no one knows you're 'ere, and I'm the only soul in the world can get you out.

'Think about that. I'll call by in a couple of days. You mightn't understand everything I've told you, so when I come back, I'll tell you again, just so's you understand what's what.'

———•———

LEO VISITS EVERY two days. It's hard to judge the passing of time but Andy tries to remember how many meal trays have arrived and lain untouched. Leo tells the same story every time: how crazy Andy was when he came in; how erratic he was at the caravan park; how Leo will take care of him; how Leo is the only one who can get him out; how Andy will end up in an asylum if he looks the wrong way.

After a few visits Leo outlines how Andy could earn his place with the lifers: not much expected and nothing against the grain... just first aid and helping Goob, like he was asked to do before. Leo's Hunter Holiday Park begins to sound like heaven; no mind-numbing injections, no pills, no washing rituals, no bright lights, no people in uniform, no sham questions. He could wake and sleep in his own time, there would fresh air and sunlight, and perhaps someone who accepted him once before when he was less than perfect, might do so again, even though he's more damaged now. Her arms around him would make the world right again.

The balance tilts in Leo's favour and, the more the ward becomes a prison, the more Andy looks forward to Leo's visits. He's the only visitor and he's the best chance at a normal life. Well, maybe not normal, but

95

better than this, better than the psych ward, and far better than where it might lead.

Andy observes conversations between two other versions of himself: Standing Andy, the man he was before the accident, loiters around the bed; Recumbent Andy is the one lying down around whom the nurses and doctors hover. From his perch on the bed head, Invisible Andy Number Three listens to their banter. Andy Number Three is sure he knows which one he really is—he's the crazy, disabled one lying down, but Standing Andy insists he's Andy who can do anything he wants, who still has the world at his feet, and so the debate continues. Invisible Andy Number Three sometimes wants to shout down One or Two but keeps his mouth firmly closed. Andy lying on the bed has seen what happens to patients who rave.

On the days he knows which one he is, Andy believes he would recover more quickly in a different ward. Confinement to the psych ward erodes every footing he finds on the treacherous climb to saneness. Once pigeon-holed with 'loonies and nutters' he sees what he has in common with them, and wonders if, maybe, he does belong there. Perhaps the patients are sane and the rest of the world is off-kilter. The more Andy works to convince himself he doesn't belong in the ward, the more tantalising and distant the notion of sanity becomes.

For there to be so many versions of himself is cruelly confusing. A faint recollection of internal conflict long ago flows into more recent times—as best he can tell. There was the whole him, but even that was fragmented, then the recovering him—who never quite made it—and whatever, whoever he is now. So many choices. Too many decisions.

Whose logic is logical? Whose reality is delusional? When does preference become an obsession? How does indifference slip into depression? The analysis is agony. Asleep or awake, his mind dissects the quandary. In circles, in tangents, in dizzy spirals, in inescapable mazes he pursues a beacon of reason that will be a rock in a sea of uncertainty. Standing Andy confuses him more and more.

Leo throws a lifeline. 'You can come 'ome with me tomorrow as long as you take the tablets,' he says.

Andy eyes him suspiciously while his heart leaps. He agrees to give it a go.

A sister hovers to witness the undertaking. She must have seen less likely carers than Leo and squints at him as she remoulds her mouth, then smiles sympathetically at Andy. She's the same sister he asked to find out about River, describing him as the boy who was dumped out the front at the same time as he himself arrived. She came back this morning to say the boy's holding his own: they think they've saved the leg, but no family has been to see him, only social workers.

———•———

ANDY STARES OUT the window in silence all the way to Greta. The world is as he remembers it, and would have been just the same if he had died and never come back along this road again. His passing would have changed nothing.

Leo makes his conditions clear: if Andy leaves it's because Leo is taking him to the psych ward. If Andy wants to stay, he toes the clearly-drawn line. Leo adds more restrictions: Andy must keep away from everyone, especially Esther; and he can only leave the park for supplies. Andy agrees, of course, because the alternative is too horrible. Half his being, the active, healthy body, has gone. He cannot afford to let the other half, a partly reasoning mind, go too.

At the least provocation Leo will hand him back to the doctors who could put him in a closed ward—that is one step removed from the old-style asylum. With a hint of amusement, which he knows is a healthy sign, Andy understands the caravan park imitates an asylum. It's a shadowy non-life peopled by crazies, where the partly sane people risk losing what sanity remains: Lola, ever fearful of arrest; Adeline, hiding from deportation into slavery; the truck driver who shrinks before Leo; Goob and Fiddle, corrupted agents of a stronger evil. Andy does not want to become *and Andy, consigned to an institution.*

He's relieved and glad to be back in his van, and surprised to be glad. He has no idea if it's because he's out of hospital, or because Esther is closer, or because he has an iota more control over life.

Casper reappears and is the only respite from loneliness. After talking to himself and the dog for a few days, Andy's hope for sanity dims. The mirage of normalcy that buoyed his return has vaporised and he recognises the gathering gloom. Depression is building like a tropical storm. Despondency drains him and wherever he looks, something irritates.

Dark disproportion envelops him like a toxic cloud. Food is tasteless, and not stars, not breeze, nor sunlight can stir his spirit, but he flogs himself to outward normality so Leo won't doubt he's fallen into line. He carries out mundane acts robotically: he eats, talks and walks a little, but the rest of the time he wallows in a vat of gloom.

Fellow inmates slip in and out of sight and imagination: Lola scuttling, or Goob hanging like fungus off the side of a post. He never sees Esther or Adeline. No one mentions their names and he wonders if he imagined them. Self-doubt balloons. He is so alone.

Next time he passes Goob, Andy flickers a smile and says, 'G'day.'

Goob briefly meets his eyes, then hawks and spits a yellow-green blob that hangs off the lower leg of Andy's jeans.

'Get lost, ya loony loser.'

Goob chuckles and Andy stumbles, not for the usual reasons, but because stinging tears blind his eyes.

Chapter Thirteen

There is darkness, then daylight, then darkness again. Andy hasn't eaten or drunk since he lay down after Goob spat on him. He's wet himself but doesn't care. If he's a lower form of life than Goob there's no point in getting up ever again. He hasn't seen Esther or Adeline in the days since Leo brought him home from hospital. Home? It's an absurd notion. He had dreamed of rescuing them, even hoped they might rescue each other. Perhaps Esther never existed, perhaps she's a fantasy and that would explain why she hasn't appeared since he returned from hospital.

One thought persists: *end it, end it now, end the pain.* When he feels the urge to get up and cut his wrists, Standing Andy, the narky bastard, says, *You have to discontinue from uni first,* and *You need to tell your mum which friends to give your CDs to,* or *What about a note to Esther?* and *What about River?*

Crap! Why bother with any of those things? Andy suspects it's a warning system from the part of his mind that wants to stay alive, so it prompts him to give out signs and drop hints so someone will save him. Pathetic! If he wants to do it he should just do it, but he has no energy to either kill himself or put out signals, so he lies and waits for an answer.

DAYLIGHT COMES AGAIN and a different urge strikes—he's hungry as hell but there's nothing to eat. That's a good sign for survival because he could have starved to death. Standing Andy must have got to him while he was asleep.

Andy figures Leo won't care if he dies because he's no big cog in Leo's schemes, but Andy doesn't want to be thought a loose cannon or it will be off to the funny farm. Leo said he could go to the shops and Andy will let him know where he's off to, just to be sure there's no retaliation.

He spruces himself up enough not to attract attention, and finds Leo wedged in the timber throne, swigging from a long neck and studying the auto parts section of a newspaper. A swarm of flies is the best of his aura.

'G'day, Leo. How's things?' Andy asks briskly.

Leo eyes Andy for few seconds without moving his head and grunts, 'Whadaya want?'

'I need to go to the bank and to the shops for food. Can't live on air and petrol fumes.'

Leo scowls, 'Yeah, all right. There and back. No friggin' round. Remember what I said.' Andy has turned to go when Leo adds, 'That stray mutt is still hangin' round. Don't give it any reason to stay.'

Andy doesn't realise how weak he's become and his strength almost expires before he shambles out the side of the park through a hole in the fence. It's the shortcut but it may not be short enough. Posts hold him up while he gets his breath back, and front garden fences steer him down the street like a cave diver's rope in the dark.

If he looks down for firm footing, he can't see ahead, and if he looks up, he gets vertigo. Up, down, up, down—he gets dizzy and wobbles like a drunk. This must be how old people feel when they see their goal at the end of the street and can barely get there, let alone return.

Outside a familiar cottage garden, he sees Bert on the veranda: there's doggedness in the man's long jowls and weathered face, but alert concern also shines. Andy thinks he's looking at Gandalf from *Lord of The Rings* and feels stronger just with eye contact.

'Oi, Andy. What's up, mate? You look like crap... even worse than last time.'

He helps Andy up the steps and into a cane armchair. That galls. He must be far gone but the peace of an unsought haven reassures. Andy sits like jelly setting in a mould while Bert gets a cup of tea and biscuits, and when Andy wolfs them down, Bert gets a meat sandwich, then another, then the whole cold roast and tomatoes and more bread.

'So, who's had you locked in solitary confinement on a starvation diet? You can't stay there, Andy.'

Andy explains that he's been in hospital and it was Leo who got him out. He can't go anywhere yet because he doesn't have anywhere to go or any way to get there. Besides, if he tries to leave, Leo might make him go somewhere he doesn't want to go.

'Ah, bullshit! Leo can't do nothing to you. He's been a bully all his life. Mind you, he's in thick with bad types but all you people up there would have more on him than he's got on you, and don't forget it. Come on, get out from under and tell him to shove his standover tactics up his fat arse. He can't run a mini Fascist state. This is Australia in the twenty-first century, not 1930s Nazi Germany. Now, get some more food into you.'

Bert is fully riled and let's fly again while Andy munches. 'You start making plans to leave that dump, Andy. Take this bag of food and when you need more, come here. Homecare takes me shopping so it's no trouble to get some for you. And remember, you can always make my place your first stop.

'Tell you what, Andy. Come back here the day after tomorrow at lunch time. I bet I can come up with something useful for you. Promise me now. I don't want to do a lot of hard thinking for nothing.'

He hands Andy a piece of paper with *Bert's place. Wednesday (two sleeps) lunchtime* scribbled on it and pokes the note in Andy's pocket. What Andy can see of Bert's aura is shifting yellows and greens: he emanates wisdom and compassion.

Fortified with encouragement and a full stomach, the walk back is easier. There's also a glow of excitement that he remembered to ask Bert to get dog food, and he's comforted by the bulge in his pocket of a wrapped bone and meat scraps. Andy can't shoo away the only living creature that wants to be with him. Casper will have to spend more time in the van.

Mulling over Bert's words about the twenty-first century, Andy has a flashback and remembers this is the same advice he gave Adeline. What Bert says is true: he has to take positive steps on his own behalf. Now the world has changed again for him in half an hour—a bit more time than the split second he needed, but didn't have, to avoid the cars on Parramatta Road.

•————————•

On Wednesday Andy locks Casper in, walks past Leo to say he's off to the shops and goes to Bert's. Bert has a lady friend there named Clara. She's a big, bustling, business-like grandmother type, but there's no fuss. Andy feels that however hard he leaned on her, she'd never fall over.

Clara is the boss of local Homecare. She tells Andy how she used to be a social worker with youth groups in western Sydney, then Redfern, and around the kids' courts, till it all got too much for her and she retired to the Hunter. Working for Homecare is no breeze but it's not the battleground of youth work. They're both under-funded, she says, but there's more policy disputes in youth work, and too many do-gooders and not enough good-doers. Clara doesn't ask questions about where he's living, which is good, because Andy is too scared to say anything about Leo in case it gets back to him.

Bert must have told her about Andy's uni course and she asks how far he got. She's impressed and asks what he'll do if he doesn't finish. Bert must have told her that, too. She asks if he's considered being a psychologist, or a counsellor, or a youth worker. She could help, she says, find volunteer or part-time work to see if he likes it, then see what courses he'd need to do.

What she says cheers up Andy heaps. Maybe he

104

could have a proper job and earn money: Esther might see him as a real man, and Dad, too. Maybe not Dad. In the meantime, Clara offers to take him to a local GP for the medication he needs. Bert must have also told Clara about the awful spasms he'd seen Andy have, and how people think he's having a fit.

Bert makes Andy promise to return on Friday and gives him another piece of paper. Clara will make enquiries in the meantime. Andy almost floats home, even with the bags of food Bert loaded him up with. Thinking of the van as *home* again makes Andy laugh for the first time in weeks. Now it is funny because he does have an alternative.

He's still on a high when he sees the same scraggy mother and two kids who taunted him once before. The kids are trailing behind her with their lips, hands and T-shirts red from melting ice-blocks. They shape up to deride him again but he's ready this time. He lets them get close before he hunches his back, screws his face into a Quasimodo look-alike, and croaks, 'I'm the boogie man and I'm coming to your house tonight!' The little buggers run screaming to their mother who glares back at him—and the ice blocks on the ground. Some days are diamonds...

Andy dreams of Mum and Dad for the next two nights. He tells them about an interesting day at work in his new job and shows them his first pay slip. Mum hugs him and Dad tries to hide his tears. Andy is not sufficiently tuned in to his new abilities to see that the dreams have meaning.

ANDY SLIPS OUT the through the side fence on Friday without consulting Leo: he walks taller and less awkwardly, with an air of independence. Outside Bert's is a pale blue Mercedes that Andy hasn't seen before. It reminds him of the flash cars he saw daily in Sydney: he pauses in admiration and peers through a window at the leather upholstery. One of Bert's neighbours must have visitors.

As Bert walks him down the hall to the kitchen, he can hear Clara talking but he doesn't know who's with her. Andy falls against the doorway when he sees two glowing lights seated at Bert's kitchen table. Inside the lights are Mum and Dad. Mum's familiar Maroussia perfume and Dad's aftershave entangle and, like ammonia, sear a path into his brain. They are just as he saw them in his dream: Mum with immaculate, spray-laminated hair, wearing a tailored skirt and stylish blouse with gold chains around her neck and bold earrings. Dad has on a soft, open-necked shirt and cravat with up-market beige trousers.

Frozen faces fill the room like a sculpture gallery: lips begin to move but there's no sound; tears well but don't flow. Mum gets up and meets Andy in a hug. Dad joins in and the three lock together and rock, maybe for a minute, maybe for ten minutes. Mum asks how he is, what does he eat, where does he wash his clothes? Dad asks what does he do with his time, has he made friends here?

Mum and Dad run out of questions at the same time. The three sets of arms disentangle and Bert guides them to the dining room where there are enough chairs for everyone. Bert talks while Clara makes the tea.

'Sorry if this gave you a shock, Andy. Me and Clara wanted to get you and your mum and dad together to sort things out, and for you to be able to get home if that's what you want. I found their number and gave them a call. Told them you'd been doing it tough, which you have.'

Mum and Dad stare at Andy whose eyes flick between Bert and Mum.

Dad's turn. 'I had a long think after your terrible results. I understand now what happened: you got back into study too soon without enough help. I have discontinued your uni enrolment so you can take another year off. It was not easy to persuade them to do that. I hope you appreciate it. Now you have more time to get strong again and revise the old work. It will be all right. We will all go home today, and your mother and I will take care of everything. You need only to get well and study.'

Home! There is no more welcome word. Escape from this hell in little boxes and Leo's threat to put him in the loony bin. 'Yes,' says Andy. 'Yes, I'll do that. I'll collect some things from the van and we can go.'

Bert catches Andy's eyes as the biscuits pass between them, and the old man's scrutiny breaks the spell. Options flash through Andy's mind. His parents' willingness to come to Greta means he has a safety net, so even if he doesn't leave with them today, they'll surely welcome him home another time—maybe they'll even come again to pick him up.

But he can't go now. To leave Esther, or the others bogged in the netherworld at Leo's, would be to abandon someone he loves and others who need him. The small part of himself he has grown to respect can do good here, perhaps better than the good a doctor might. And he's positive Dad won't let Casper onto the Merc's leather seats.

He must get out of this mess himself, not be uplifted like a sailor rescued by helicopter from a sinking ship. At home, he'd be Mum's sick puppy and Dad's pet project: he'd be their broken toy.

Dad's jumpy to be off and Mum's run out of conversation with Bert and Clara. They want to pick up what they've come for and get going. They're on the front veranda and Dad's telling Andy how much he's forgiven him and how hard it's been for him to make this trip. He's had to revise his standards, lower his expectations, and commit to helping Andy so much more. This is a big chance for Andy, Dad says, so hurry up and get in the car. Say goodbye to these kind people, and we'll be off.

Andy looks him in the eye and says, 'Sorry, Dad, Mum, but I can't come home yet. I appreciate that you've come all this way for me and I love seeing you, but there's stuff happening here that I can't walk away from.'

Time stands still like the instant that elapses before the body of a beheaded soldier drops. For that moment Andy thinks Dad understands, but then Dad erupts.

'Stuff? Stuff! Like what? More friends like the ones you had in Sydney, for sure! Wasting your time with girls and parties and drinking beer. I knew it was a mistake to let you go away. I knew something bad would come of it.'

Mum puts a calming hand on Dad's arm, but also for support. She's sickly white beneath her olive skin. Dad tries a different tack. 'Andy, be sensible. You need our help. We are there to help you, in your home. We cannot be up here for you. Your mother's heart will break if you don't come. She cried and cried for me to come and get you, but I will only do it once. A father will not beg a son to do his duty. The consequences are on your head. Get in the car, now.'

Andy looks down and shakes his head. He looks up to tell Dad one last important thing, but Dad is already walking away. He's leading Mum down the path and through the gate. Hers is a twisted walk, a little like Andy's, because she's turning back to look at her son as Dad steers her to the car. She looks twenty years older than half an hour ago, and the dark colours of despair hang over her.

Andy calls out, 'Dad, I'm not staying for me, I'm staying for other people,' but he doesn't know if Dad hears.

Dad slams Mum's door, then his own, and revs the engine. Andy has never seen Dad slam a door before, let alone roar off the way he does, spraying roadside gravel as he fishtails, then burning rubber on the bitumen before disappearing around a corner, elbows and hands flailing across the top of the steering wheel.

Go, Dad! Andy urges in admiration of the unexpected hoon machismo.

Andy is not upset by Dad storming off: alone on the veranda, he feels solitary but strong. He would never have made this decision before the accident, so maybe it's another change for the better—although he has disabilities in his body and brain there's more good in his character. It's an odd thought, but comforting.

Bert limps out and puts a hand on Andy's shoulder. 'Well done, young fella. I like your mum and dad. You're from good stock. That was a tough call and it took guts and the right upbringing to make it. Come and have another cuppa and we'll see what Clara's lined up for you.'

Clara appears at the screen door and hustles out when she sees Andy is still there. She hugs him gently. 'I was coming out to console Bert and tell him he's done the best he could. I'm so pleased you've stayed. It's the right decision.'

Chapter Fourteen

Bert, Clara and Andy have a long chat after Mum and Dad leave. Clara apologises again for any shock she and Bert caused Andy by having his parents appear in Bert's kitchen, but they believed Andy needed a chance to go home.

Clara says, 'We're so proud you stayed, Andy. It was hard to see your mum upset. Perhaps she suspected you wouldn't go because she slipped Bert an envelope for you. What did she say, Bert?'

Bert plops the envelope on the table. 'She said it was for any debts you might have here, or for expenses in case you stay. Maybe she knows you better than you think.'

Andy looks inside the envelope. It's full of cash. Andy says, 'That's a help, but I wish Dad hadn't stormed off. He always makes such a big deal of everything. He'll probably never talk to me again.'

'He'll settle down,' offers Bert, and follows up with an uncharacteristically touchy-feely comment. 'Even though you've lost them for a while, you're finding yourself.'

Andy draws comfort from that. He says, 'And you know what else? I'm taking Dad's advice. He used to say stuff like *A metal never tested is never proved*. I reckon it's easy to live a good life and be a nice person when there's no crap hitting the fan, but when bad things come your way, that's a chance to grow and find new strength. Another thing he said was that people should be judged not on how well they make a plan and stick to it, but on how they react when things go wrong. I guess that's what I'm working on now.'

Bert and Clara both smile.

'Hey! On the topic of things going wrong, what's happening about Leo's place and the casino?' Andy asks. 'The last I heard was about three weeks ago, before I was in hospital. If I remember right, Leo said he was waiting for Spider to pay him money. Sounded like he needed it.'

'I haven't seen or heard anything definite,' Bert says. 'It takes a bit to get one of those forced sales together. Council has to issue final notices and the like. Don't worry, I'm onto it, and you'll be the first to know.'

———•———

CLARA HAS LINED up places for Andy to go as a volunteer, like *Youth off the Street* and the *Safe Sleeping Centre* for homeless people. She also wants him to visit the Maitland Disability Advisory Committee. Clara says it's a group of lovely people, only some of whom have a disability, and they all live in the area. He'll fit right in. There's no pressure to join and it's just to see what goes on. The committee is organised by council to advise on the needs of people with disability—and he must remember to call them that, not *disabled people*—like how they can be better integrated, and where access needs to be improved so they can get around.

It sounds interesting and worthwhile, but something jolts because if Andy signs up, it's like joining a club for second-best people. Part of him still doesn't want to admit he's disabled. He doesn't want the baggage that comes with the label. The realisation surfaces again that he does have a new, different real life... but it's hard to let go of the old one.

Clara reads his mind and says, 'You don't need a disability to join. The committee is for anyone with an interest in disability issues.'

He tells her he'll give it a go. Bert removes the tea cups to make space for filling out the heap of forms Clara produces. They're like tickets to a new life; Centrelink registration for a Disability Pension, application for a new bank account, tax file number application, and a list of employment agencies. They fill out a request to redirect mail to Bert's, and a TAFE enrolment application because he might do a counselling course. There's even a form for the Disability Advisory Committee which they complete just in case he decides to join. Self-perception is hard to change and in Andy's dreams he's still whole and healthy. When he becomes wonky in his dreams, he'll know he's adjusted.

Clara offers insight into the life of some people with disability. She says Homecare is badly underfunded and she's heard of clients spending three days in bed and totally unattended because, basically, there isn't enough money to get someone there to get them up and showered. No one expects the government to support people in luxury. Modest comfort and safety would be enough. Carers have a hard time securing resources to transport people with disabilities to medical appointments for which they've waited months. Most people with mobility problems want to keep living in their own homes, which is cheaper for the community, but that means they'll need help in daily life: shopping, appointments, socialising.

Bert beams as Clara's enthusiasm escalates. She makes a strong case for helping the disenfranchised. They're the ones, she says, who have paid taxes, or their parents or relatives did and do, but who are now so marginalised that their life is entirely taken up with the struggle to survive. All day, every day, is a struggle. Will someone come to get them up, wash them, feed them, do the washing, hang the washing out, take them shopping or to a crucial appointment? Forget about recreation, hobbies or friends—anything that makes life worth living—getting through the day to face tomorrow is the goal.

Clara says, 'Andy, if you want to make a mark and be remembered for having made a difference, you need go no further than the disability circus. In some local government areas, and this is one of them, twenty-five per cent of the population has a disability and the main one is mobility related. Just think of all those people stuck at home with inadequate services, or unable to get where they want to go. And that can be places like a post office or a bank or a doctor's surgery. We're talking essential services here, not entertainment or whimsy. Lots of people care but no one has the answers.

'A new political party has just formed up with social equity as its platform. Most of that twenty-five per cent also have friends and family who pitch in to look after them. Some are paid a Carer's Pension that in no way replaces the wage they give up to look after a loved one, and a lot of care is provided gratis by friends and family. That's a big electorate waiting to be tapped.'

'Wow,' says Andy, impressed and thoughtful. 'It's not the same as being a doctor, but it could be a way to do good and earn a living. I wonder what Dad would think?'

———•———

THE NEXT MONTHLY meeting of the Disability Advisory Committee is the following Monday. At nine o'clock Clara picks Andy up at Bert's. She chats as they travel into Maitland: she knows all the members of the committee. There are men and women, young and old, many of whom have had bad luck: some were born with conditions that have dominated their lives; some have ended up in wheelchairs after accidents; and others have just got sick and can't look after themselves.

'Got to admire them for pitching in to a community group, but disability runs their life and their families' lives. They manage to get to meetings and come up with ideas but for most of them, that's it. All their time is spent organising what others take for granted: just getting up, getting dressed and fed can take them till lunch time.'

Before they go into the meeting Clara tells Andy she's submitted his forms a couple of days ago so he'd feel more at home with the group. But that still doesn't mean he has to join.

They enter the old part of the council chambers: it's colonial vintage, built from sandstone with high ceilings and thick walls while the sturdy, panelled doors and massive window frames were made from cedar cut in the Hunter Valley. A musty smell, a bit like Casper when he's wet, hits Andy at the door. The meeting room is grand but shabby, with thick, dark carpet bunched in tidal rows that obstruct wheelchairs. However, the huge, antique table suits people who get around that way, because once they reach the table, it's high enough to get their legs under. The multi-toned decorative frieze is flaking and the windows are too high to see out.

A middle-aged woman with faded reddish, fluffy hair takes the chair. She introduces herself to Andy as Nicola Throsby and tells him, in case he's curious, that she uses a wheelchair because of spina bifida. After general chit-chat and introductions, the meeting gets underway. Andy is invited to join in the discussion whenever he likes.

Nicola works through the agenda and there's nothing Andy connects with until under New Business an item piques his interest. *Proposed Casino for Lower Hunter.* He reads that Leo's Hunter Holiday Park is one suggested site. They talk about the casino and feel sure council wants it in Greta. Apparently, it's common knowledge that Leo's place is about to be resumed because the rates haven't been paid. Andy is surprised Leo would be so stupid as to get into that position.

Suspicions are quietly voiced that some councillors are linked to developers who hope to get the land cheap then have it rezoned. Council would get the rates, and developers and their associates would get a bonanza. If it's built up the valley, the same guys might still have a stake, but it's a different council area, and the land would cost more. Nicola has found out there's only one casino licence available for the whole area—from Newcastle on the coast to Mudgee in the west—and different backers are after it. If the Greta-Maitland cabal can't get the Greta site, they'll want to nab the vineyards option quick smart.

Committee members have differing attitudes: some (the ones who live in Maitland) would like the casino in Greta: it would be progress; there would be new jobs; the RSL club is shabby and the casino would be a classy replacement. Most committee members think it would change the town too much: houses would be pulled down; the RSL club, which actively supports locals, would go under; the whole place would be too busy. People, especially the members from Greta, like the town the way it is. Even the 'No Casino in Greta' camp didn't mind the idea of a casino further up the valley in the vineyards or at a golf resort because there would still be jobs but less impact on local area.

Nicola asks Andy if he has an opinion on the matter.

'Well, yes,' he says. 'I haven't been in Greta very long and I do like the town, well, most of it anyway. I wouldn't like to see it get too busy. It's nice like it is. I do have a general problem with casinos, though.

'I had an older sister... Lydia. She was great, and so smart. She looked out for me and I could talk to her about anything. She was a Med. student and doing well but she mixed with guys who gambled every weekend and she went with them to illegal games... not to gamble herself, but because the blokes did. One thing led to another and she was in the wrong place at the wrong time. There was a knife fight between the gamblers and she died trying to help someone who was stabbed.

'There's always an outside chance of hold-ups at a casino, and those thieves mean business—they carry guns and knives. Thugs know people bring cash or jewellery to dress up and look flash so all sorts of crims are sucked into the area, some just to steal, others to entice gamblers to private games to launder money, or for the chance of an easy win.'

Andy adds Dad's rant about gamblers. 'They're wicked and greedy,' and his own new thought, 'There are so many other ways to enjoy life.' He tells the committee that the further away from Greta the casino is, the less chance there will be of criminals in town.

The committee takes a vote after Andy's response. They are united in their opposition to the casino anywhere near Greta or Maitland. They agree to go to the next public council meeting to raise objections. Nicola promises to speak for them but she wants Andy to speak, too, because what he describes is so convincing. It's a real-life experience from the heart, she says.

Andy promises to think about it. He tells Nicola just talking to this group is a big step for him. The idea of making a speech to a room full of people, especially when many of them won't like what he says, is terrifying. There's a chance he'd turn to jelly and melt away between the floorboards.

Some of the committee doubt the process is worth the effort. Sure, it's democracy in action, but one cynical bloke who's been battling for years to get council to fix the footpath outside his house so he can get down the street is already muttering, *For what it's worth! It'll take more than that to swing it.* They don't doubt Nicola's dedication and ability for straight talking but believe the council, especially some councillors, have made up their minds and are there to line their pockets. Open meetings are a formality.

During the discussion Andy dreams up a crazy idea, but doesn't let on because it's so bizarre and he has to talk to Bert about it first. He doesn't know if it would work, so best if he says nothing. Andy registers a boost when he recognises logical thought processes taking place.

Clara has sat through the meeting but when it's over she goes off to pick up a few groceries while Andy has a cup of tea and a chat with his new acquaintances. They're still talking about plans for a survey of access into shops in the business district, and how they hope to convince owners with stepped entrances to take up a council offer for assistance putting in ramps, when a young woman in stretchy clothes clinging to a generous figure enters the room and climbs over the carpet in six-inch heels as if she's wading through snow. She approaches Andy with a generous smile and says, 'Mr Contos, if you're free, the mayor would like to meet with you in his office.'

The committee members look at Andy as if he's won the lucky door prize but there's a fair chance it's booby trapped. Maybe all new members are honoured this way, but he doubts it. Andy concentrates hard not to stumble as he follows the secretary.

'Ah, Mr Contos, we met recently at Greta,' the mayor says as he extends a hand.

What a bastard, Andy thinks. If he remembers me, then he remembers I can't shake hands. Andy just nods, and nods again as the mayor introduces his colleagues, Councillors Freestone and Croft. They're all out of the same mould: choking on conceit and wearing expensive suits overdue for a clean. There's a clubby air of good prospects around them as if they know where the Easter eggs are hidden. They're certainly not inviting Andy to join their club, but he must have something they want, and the answer is likely to be no.

'Andy, may I call you that?' Mayor Twigold goes on. 'Congratulations on joining the Disability Advisory Committee. New blood refreshes these groups and I'm sure you'll make a valuable contribution. This part of the Lower Hunter Valley is racing ahead and we want to do it right for everyone in the community. We can't afford to leave anyone behind or have them put up with second best. Maitland is fortunate to have Councillors Freestone and Croft as local residents. They're major players in this growth and have generously invested in the future of the town. Business takes all the risks, you know, not the public sector, and council does what it can to support them.'

Can a fox look apologetic before it raids the hen house? They try. The mayor hits his oratorical straps and it's not bad entertainment, as long as Andy can resist gagging. The colours moving around the mayor flit and vary. He must actually believe some of his own propaganda. He strolls to and fro behind his desk—it's as big as a full-sized pool table—and the huge executive chair almost obscures him as he passes it.

'Their company, Grabbengraft Constructions, is behind the fabulous expansion planned for Greta. Just yesterday I saw on your application form for the committee that you're living at Leo's Hunter Holiday Park. Imagine that! Right on the planned site of a great new development.'

The mayor pauses as if hoping for a show of enthusiasm but Andy is thinking what a patronising ass he is.

'Andy, there's an opportunity for you to be involved in something big here. Not many young men, and newcomers at that, have such a chance. The venture can't start till the site is available, obviously. Mr Schwartz hasn't yet offered his land for sale. The matter might soon be out of his hands. That is to say, it may be a forced sale. That's not up to me.'

The mayor chooses his words carefully. 'Alternatively, there's a provision under the law that if a person is convicted of a criminal offence then his assets might be confiscated as the proceeds of crime. Now I'm not saying that will happen here, but if it were to, we'd like to do the right thing by you, Andy, and by the other tenants, and give adequate notice so you could find somewhere else to live.

'The police and council are gathering evidence to see if there's a case. That's where you come in. Because you're a resident you might see things of interest to the police. They could look like normal day to day activities but they might also be part of something criminal. What we're asking is for you to keep an eye on the comings and goings there—you know, number plates, people, times, conversations, things that get taken in and out. You'll be compensated for your efforts.'

Andy tells them he'll keep an eye out. Of course, he'll keep an eye out but he has no intention of snooping for the council. No way will he help bring a casino to Greta. Besides, if Leo finds out Andy is spying on him things could turn ugly so fast, he wouldn't be able to escape to Bert's, let alone get Esther and Adeline out and warn the others. Nonetheless, he's tickled that the mayor thinks he could be a sleuth.

The mayor tries to stitch up a deal. 'We owe these courageous developers our support and the community will be in their debt once the project is up and running. You could be part of that successful team. The alternative doesn't bear thinking about. If evidence builds up against Mr Schwartz it would be a tragedy to see you tarred with the same brush when you have the chance to distance yourself from him now.'

Andy understands what he's getting at. Flashbacks

to truckloads of car parts, Leo and the bikies smoking dope, and the small matter of arson at Spider's, make Andy break out in a paranoid sweat. He manages to keep a plastic smile on his face. What if it's not paranoia and they want to twist things round? Might he go to gaol? Would that be better or worse than the psych ward? Dad would probably move back to Greece if that happened. It's a stab of insecurity and self-doubt when the day was going well.

Councillors Freestone and Croft are nodding like demented cockies on a perch, studying Andy's face to see if he's been sucked in. Mayor Twigold offers to show Andy back to the meeting room but Andy opts to find his own way. Andy thanks the mayor for the meeting and is relieved to make a dignified withdrawal. They could probably smell his panic.

Clara is waiting in the hallway. She tells Andy he must be run down because he looks knocked up. He just wants to get going. For a hefty woman Clara sets a cracking pace. Her car is parked down the road, which is okay because it's a chance to see a bit of the town. Andy was too nervous on the way in to pay attention. Out on High Street, away from the mayor and his cronies, Andy relaxes and is pleasantly surprised by the streetscape. There are impressive buildings from the 1800s when, Clara narrates, Maitland had more banks than Sydney and was the hub of a thriving rural industry: everything from timber to tobacco, fruit and livestock. Nearby Morpeth was a busy river port even before Newcastle got underway.

They pass three-storey sandstone premises: one formerly a bank and now a restaurant and function centre; another, gloriously decorated in stone as the technical institute, is now an art gallery. Commercialism in the form of a pawn shop, a tattoo parlour and a hydroponic equipment outlet, has encroached on the grandeur of another old building, but the place has soul. Clara shows Andy where there used to be a magnificent theatre with two semi-circular marble staircases in the atrium. It was pulled down in the seventies by developers to build the tackiest of supermarkets. Andy wonders if those developers were also councillors.

He ponders the little town of Greta. It certainly needs tarting up, and Leo's is a blight on the landscape, but people like Bert who have lived in Greta all their lives don't want a casino or a supermarket or a MacDonald's in town. They want a say in how their town looks and what it's like to live in. They want the power to control their environment.

In the car he tells Clara about the meeting with the mayor and the councillors: not everything, of course, because she might be less willing to help if he's committed anything illegal. She's outraged at their gall. She riles at the skulduggery of the mayor's request and works herself into a hooting, gleeful anticipation of a full-on confrontation. The loose skin underneath her upper arms wobbles non-stop as she takes one arm then the other in turn off the wheel to punctuate her exhilaration.

'If they're so desperate to build a casino,' she says, 'they'll do something stupid to get their way. Bert knows how to get under their skin. He'll roll up his sleeves for the next meeting and ask the right questions. He might be old, but there's a lot of fight in him, especially for a good cause. He's reviewed development applications before, so he knows where they'll come unstuck, and he's not afraid of a stoush.'

Clara drops Andy at Bert's and keeps going. Bert's keen to hear how it all went as soon as Andy walks in the door. He nods as Andy tells him about the casino item on the agenda and his meeting with the mayor. Bert has been alerted to the casino plan and has made some phone calls to see where it's up to.

Andy runs his mad idea past Bert who nearly falls off his chair laughing. He wants to know how Andy came up with such a scheme and Andy wonders himself. He did Legal Studies for the HSC and was on the Students Representative Council at uni, so something must have stuck. What he suggests is this: could they pay Leo's outstanding rates with a cheque that bounces? By the time the error is picked up, council will have met and been told Leo's land is not available for resumption, and they would have had to make the decision to go up the valley or nowhere. Bert tosses in that his daughter just happens to work in the accounts department at council so she'll know what the time frames are.

They entertain themselves with other less legal ways to thwart the developers. Bert promises to check the feasibility of Andy's idea and they celebrate with a strong cup of tea, after which Andy saunters, or so it feels, back to the park.

Casper is waiting in the van. The dog now wags his tail when Andy returns instead of merely slinking in close when called. Andy gives him a pat—he still won't be cuddled—feeds him and lets him out for a walk as soon as it's dark. He's back in a few minutes.

For the first time since Andy returned from hospital he's not depressed. In fact, he's happier than he's been for ages. He did something positive and feels capable of more of the same. Leo might not want him to go to the shops alone, or to see Bert (he probably knows about Bert), or join the Disability Advisory Committee and attend a council meeting, but he can do it. He knows he can. Leo is a bully but Andy can either persuade him, or tell him to eff off, and just do it. He can.

Leo gives the impression that he has something over every tenant but it's bullshit. For sure, most of them are on the shady side... not bad, just dubious, but Leo twists reality so they aren't sure what to believe, and he manipulates them into doing things they know are wrong so he can blackmail them into doing worse stuff. It snowballs. Light-fingering hubcaps leads to car rebirthing and before they know it, they're in so deep it doesn't matter.

Andy wonders why he's in awe of Leo but can't think of anything personal. He's stuck there because he can't find his way home. Some guys fall in line behind Leo as easily as putting on an old T-shirt. It's what they want: someone to tell them how to get by on the fringe. Others are victims of the bullying and can't get out from under.

That night Andy enjoys the best sleep he's had for

weeks, but he wakes up troubled because he's dreamt of him and Esther in some kind of nirvana, when in truth, he doesn't even know if she's still alive.

Chapter Fifteen

Andy wakes up confused. He's had wonderful dreams and yesterday's meeting made him feel like a genuine person: he discovered there are people like him who achieve worthwhile things and they pressed him to believe he could do the same. That, and scheming with Bert to thwart the council's plan, put him on top of the world. But now he lies, thinking about the decision not to go home with Mum and Dad. What an idiot he was! But that's not what's wrong! It's Esther! She's what he needs.

He hasn't laid eyes on her since before he went to hospital. It's been a little over three weeks but seems like an eternity. He tries not to think of Leo pressuring Esther to go to work for him, and what if he, Andy, made Adeline sicker by confronting her? Esther might never forgive him. He'll still try to persuade Esther and Adeline to leave, but there are so many others who can't be left behind.

There's Goob's sad little friend, Fiddle, and what about River? Andy has asked Clara to find out if the boy is making progress. Last night Andy thought he could move mountains, but today problems are insurmountable. Shifting his legs to the edge of the bed and sitting up is too much.

Andy senses malevolence outside, and Casper must have too, because he disappears into the bottom of the hanging space. With no warning knock the door swings open and light spears in. The van tips dramatically to one side as Leo heaves himself onto the step and squeezes inside, rocking the cabin. Leo perches on the end of a low bench.

'Social visit...' he gasps at Andy who's wedged in a far corner of the bed with a blanket dragged around him. 'Feelin' better?'

Andy nods grimly. He's naked in every sense of the word and freezes like a rabbit cornered before a dog pack. Leo's huge hands are planted on his bulwark knees with rounded fingers spread like grappling hooks. He sniffs coarsely, scans Andy's paltry possessions, and says, 'Since I been so good to you, thought you might like to return the favour.'

Andy trembles. What now?

'I got a dicky tooth that needs pullin'. Been givin' me 'ell for weeks and I figure pullin' it will hurt less than keepin' it but I'm not going to any of them shysters in town.'

Andy splutters with relief. 'I'm not a dentist. No way!'

'Aw, sonny, I've tried to get string round it and yank, but no luck. Worked when we was kids. That's how my pa did it. Never went to a dentist then, and ain't going now. I got heaps of pliers, so what else do you need?'

Andy can't see a way out, but he can buy time. 'Okay,' he says. 'But you need to get some things first; mouth wash, Dettol, gauze, cotton wool...' He makes the list as long as he can.

Leo thinks it's all sissy stuff, but Andy insists. They sort out the how, where and when of the extraction but Leo lingers. Andy thinks he's waiting for a confession of sorts, such as an update of what Andy's been doing, and weighs up how effective Leo's spies could be. Andy was supposed to stay in the park except for shopping and he's been to Bert's and the committee meeting.

'Say, Leo,' Andy begins tentatively, 'I went to a meeting yesterday of the Disability Advisory Committee... didn't think you'd mind... seemed like a natural for someone like me. Um, your name came up. Well, not your name, but this place was mentioned because it seems, and you probably know, that council wants to take it off your hands and put a casino here. Apparently, you haven't paid rates for years. That's what they're saying, anyway.'

Leo stares at Andy as if he'd like to pin him to the wall.

'There's a lot around town don't want it within cooee, especially the disability people. They want me to attend the next council meeting, and put the case to take it further up the valley. If that works, it would suit you, too, so we'd all be winners.'

Leo growls through tightened lips, wondering how much is being put over him and is the payoff worth it? Andy wraps the blanket around him like a shawl and feels he's finally got the upper hand.

'Yeah, all right,' Leo agrees, 'but I'm watchin' you.'

Andy draws the blanket up to his eyes to conceal his satisfaction. He's finally scored a point and the low mood lifts. As soon as the big man is gone Casper emerges.

The dog's coat has grown longer and more glossy with better food from Andy than he used to forage and he behaves with the confidence of a handsome dog. Casper's quivering lips show distaste for the departed visitor but that settles into a canine smile.

———•———

WHEN ANDY SEES Leo leave to purchase dental supplies, he slips to Esther's van. Leo has probably taken Goob as a gopher, and could have left another overseer, but Andy is unconcerned. Leo will still want his tooth pulled and will still want Andy to steer the council away from his land.

He knocks and waits, and waits, and knocks again. Esther opens the door a crack and Andy reels at her aura. Her love festoons them both like an exploding dandelion, but anguish and fear flood out the door as well.

'Oh, Andy, dearest Andy! Why have you not come for so long? Mother is very ill! More harsh words from Mr Leo may be too much for her and he will be cross if he finds out that we talk.'

'Let me in, then. He's gone to Maitland. He won't know.' Andy squeezes past a barely compliant Esther. The last time he was in this van he confronted Adeline for putting her head in the sand, and Esther threw him out. But now they stand close, each holding the other's two hands. They melt and fuse for a fleeting, eternal second.

'I'm sorry,' (he wants to call her *darling*). 'I've been in hospital, Esther,' he says. 'When I came out Leo told me to stay away or he'd make things worse for you and I didn't want to do that. I've been dying to see you. Are you all right?'

'Yes, I am all right. Why were you in hospital, Andy? What was the matter? Are you well now?'

Andy reassures Esther he's okay. She squeezes his hands and leans forward to softly kiss his lips. Andy's knees go weak and he wants to sink with her to the floor.

Adeline is resting, propped up on pillows. She is drawn, greyish, and her eyes dart anxiously between Andy and Esther. She settles when Esther tells her that Mr Leo is away and won't know Andy is here.

'You see, Andy, how ill she is.' Esther drops onto a chair at the tiny table, and Andy sits opposite. Their foreheads almost connect as they talk in whispers. 'She cannot walk to the shops anymore and gets breathless going even so far as the shower block. I am not permitted to leave the van park in her place and Mr Leo brings us only the bare necessities. I want to take her to the hospital but she will not go. She thinks we will be separated: that I will be deported, and herself also, whether she recovers or not. Andy, if she does not receive help soon, she may die. What can we do for her?'

Andy agrees with Esther's prognosis. He proposes they call an ambulance, and the officers would just take her, but Esther vetoes the idea.

'She would be terrified. She would resist, and that would be the end of her.'

Andy has a rising sense of frustration. 'Yes, Esther, but it will also be the end of her to do nothing. She can stay here and get worse or take a risk and see a doctor. I know a lady called Clara who knows all the right people to talk to. I'll ask her to speak to the social worker at the hospital to get things moving for you. Just tell your mother you've decided it's the only way for both of you. Don't give her a choice. Tell her you don't want to lose her and this is not where she should end her life. Tell her I will fight tooth and nail to keep you both in Australia.'

Andy drops his gritty tone, takes her hand and says softly, 'Ask if she wants to see you living a free life with someone who loves you. Ask if she wants to see grandchildren. If she wants those things, she must move.'

Tears roll down Esther's face as she whispers, 'I will try, Andy.'

He tells her about the committee and the council meeting he hopes to attend, partly to impress upon Esther and Adeline that there is a social support network in Australia, but mainly to show Esther how manly he is.

Much as he would love to spend all Leo's absence with Esther, he must use the opportunity to best effect. 'I have to go,' he says. 'I've got something else to do. Tell your mother everything will be all right, but get her ready to move. Take care. I love you,' he adds as he slips out the door, and is immediately irritated with himself for having half-said the wonderful words and not knowing if Esther heard them.

Chapter Sixteen

Andy makes straight for the hole in the fence, contorts through it and heads to Bert's. He heaves his right side, hobbling and wobbling along the street: feels like he's flying but knows he looks like a robotic spider. Doesn't care.

'Lucky I don't live at the other end of town,' Bert says as Andy drags himself up the front stairs, 'or we'd be placing bets on whether you'd make it. So, what's the latest?'

Andy pants a smile and Bert reckons it's the first time he's seen Andy looking positive like a young fellow should. He lets Andy get his breath back while he brings him up to speed on how Leo's outstanding rates will temporarily appear to have been paid: at least for long enough to make his land appear unavailable to the casino developers, so forcing them to commit to a site further up the valley while they have the chance.

Bert himself has written a cheque and his daughter— the one who works in the accounts department at council, is processing it through the system so the rates will show as paid. By the time the cheque bounces, the developers should have gone elsewhere.

'Howzat?' Bert quizzes with a fielder's enthusiasm and an old man's stiffness, 'Couldn't be simpler, eh? The fee for a dishonoured cheque is a small price to pay for getting rid of carpetbaggers and scumbags. Can't see what else they can do to me. Ain't worried, neither.'

Andy is delighted by the simplicity of the plan and nods approval. He adds, 'Don't want you in trouble, Bert... any sort, like court or bills or lose your home.'

Bert dismisses the notion. 'Nah, that won't happen. Besides, I like a good stoush. Can't swing the fists anymore, but can still launch a broadside and enjoy it. On the other hand, I'm happy with a little calculated skulduggery, just the size of a signature, that whips the rug from under their feet. So, how's things at your end?'

'There's progress. Leo's not going to stop me going to the council meeting because I've convinced him it's in his interest. Maybe I don't need to go if the cheque thing works, but I told the disability group I'd go, so I will, and we want to make sure the whole town knows the downside of casinos. There's that, and a big thing: I've nearly persuaded Esther to take her mother to hospital. Adeline looks really sick, like, aweful, so we've got to keep her calm while we do it. No arguments, no choice, just get in the ambulance and go.'

'Well done! When's all this going to happen?'

'It's got to be soon. Can you ask Clara to line things up at the hospital? She knows who to speak to. Otherwise, it will be as if Adeline's dropped in from another planet. There'll be no record of her or Esther anywhere. It would be good if Esther could stay with her mother, or very close, like Mum did with me in intensive care, because that'll stop Adeline stressing out. It's no good having them get to hospital and be carted off somewhere as illegal arrivals. Guess who'd never speak to me again! Do you think Clara could do that?'

'I'm sure she would. She's a force of nature, that woman. Does everything by the book, but like she's driving a steamroller, whereas me, I'll use any tactics but only for the right reasons. Reckon she and I have a lot in common... just prepared to use different methods.

'By the way, she rang last night 'bout River, the young chap you took to hospital. Seems they saved his leg but it'll always be weak. Community Services has stepped in and he'll most likely go to a foster home. Clara's spoken to a youth worker who says River is behaving badly, even in hospital. He wants to go back to his mum and dad and blames you for where he is. River's parents can't understand what the problem is and blame Leo for taking their boy. They blame Leo because they found out you took River to hospital and they reckon you're one of Leo's gang.'

Andy cracks up at the notion of being anyone's enforcer but dulls at the implications. 'Oh, shit! That's not good, is it? The bikies will be mad in a big way and they'll make it known. If Leo works out it's my fault, he'll want to settle the score.'

'Probably,' Bert concedes, 'but shit happens, as you know. You just got to duck when it's coming your way. And pick it up and throw it back.'

They're both thinking, *Yeah, duck or run faster.* Nonetheless, it's fair advice, and vaguely reminiscent of philosophy debates with other students in first year at university. It's far more practical, however.

They enjoy a cup of tea and a snack on the veranda, chatting generalities. Bert tells stories about work in the underground mines. Andy marvels at other ways of life, and how things change. Even yesterday, or first thing this morning, the thought of bikies after him would have blown his mind, but talking to Bert, who underscores success and who points out whimsy and humour where potential disaster lurks, gives Andy a sense of control. If he can keep this perspective, he can stay on top. That's the plan, anyway. He's desperate not to spiral down to that numbness that leaves him bruised and drained, lacking spark or confidence.

He's on a high when he leaves Bert and has just turned into the dirt laneway that leads to the hole in the fence when motorbikes descend on him. He backs up to the cyclone wire that's lined against prying eyes with rusty tin and battered colour bond. He steadies himself, mind and body, by grasping the wire. He feels like a sacrificial goat staked on a rocky outcrop.

Four riders form a line then close to a semicircle. They edge in till the front wheels almost touch him and each other, and rev like hell. Andy turns his head away, closes his eyes, and waits to be pummelled. Will the same bones be broken? Are lights still as bright in hospital? Do those places smell the same? It seems like forever, but is probably only a few seconds before the bikes roll back and roar off down the lane: a mini tornado of dust and fumes in their wake. Andy blinks the dirt from his eyes, finds himself twitching and gasping, but still standing. It's an effort to disentangle his fingers, and he pants as he plods, more heavily on one side, back to his van. It's strange to find a sanctuary inside Leo's, but it will have to do. Casper is there and allows Andy to fondle his ears. The warmth of the dog's body and his friendly eyes calm Andy like a mother's lullaby.

The dust and buzz of engines still fill his head but he tells Casper, 'It's all right, boy, we got through that one.'

●————————●

GOOB ARRIVES THE next morning. 'Leo's got all that stuff you said, so git over there and do it.'

Andy prevaricates and says his hand is shaky today. He's hoping the tooth is agony in the meantime, but Goob won't buy excuses. He tells Goob to go and boil water, to clear a space inside Leo's van, and he'll be there soon.

Goob protests and quips, 'He ain't droppin' a kid... it's just a tooth.' Andy threatens to repeat Goob's mimicry of the big man's wimpy moan so the spineless lowlife scrabbles away.

An hour later Andy rocks up to Leo's van. Noxious-smelling liquids leak from garbage bags outside, and inside the air is worse. Nothing has improved since Andy used the phone a few weeks ago; fat-filled electric frypan, grease coated hotplate, dishes multi-coloured with adhered food, filthy clothes draped and dropped anywhere, and cockroach droppings sprinkled like hundreds and thousands. It's a big van, but Leo more than fills it. Goob pops out from behind a curtain that conceals the bed, but Leo tells him to eff off. Goob vanishes back the way he came, and Andy sees him through the window, walking away.

So, there's a concealed door.

A corner of the table is cleared, and various items connected with tooth-pulling are laid out. Leo sits beside the table with his unshaven, multiple chins quivering every few seconds and one paw firmly gripping a bottle of bourbon. Andy's mouth is dry as he washes his hands at the sink but there's no sign of soap. He inspects the tools, selects the most likely, pours hot water over them, and adds Dettol to the mix in the sink.

Leo hasn't spoken since Andy came in, but his eyes follow the preparations. He shudders and clenches his mouth as Andy approaches.

'So, which one is it?' Andy asks.

Leo's mouth jerks open. He sticks a finger in and grunts, 'At un at er 'ack, I ink.'

Andy peers in and is reminded of a long-drop bush toilet: the colours and shapes of rot and decay are all there.

Andy sits on the adjacent chair. 'Looks like a cesspit in there, Leo,' he says. 'There's more than one rotten tooth and sometimes pain can be referred from another tooth. I can pull out the worst, but it might not be the one that's hurting. You should go to a dentist.'

Leo looks as if he's about to cry. By way of support Andy adds, 'They'll give you a needle so you don't feel any pain.'

Leo groans at the word *needle* and swigs urgently. 'Just pick the one you reckon is the worst, and hurry up,' he spits.

Andy sits back and looks thoughtful. The word *needle* has an interesting effect on Leo. Andy takes time to run through the process of how it would be done by a dentist, how more than one *needle* can be administered to achieve total numbness, how all the teeth could be attended to over many visits, with several *needles* each time... for pain free treatment.

Leo's head judders from side to side in denial. 'Just do it!' he barks.

Andy fingers the tools and feels Leo's fear mount. 'Here we go, then.'

Leo snaps his mouth open, clenches his eyes closed and stops breathing. Andy inserts the pliers coated with gauze for grip, fiddles a minute and withdraws.

'Is that it?' a relieved Leo asks. 'The piss did the trick. Didn't feel nuthin'!'

'I didn't get it, Leo. Couldn't get a good grip. You know... my weak arm. You'll have to sit different. Try this.' Andy sets Leo's sweating head at a better angle, comes at him from the side, grips and yanks. Andy drops back in triumph. 'Got it!' He waves the pliers and the tooth like a regimental banner.

Leo howls as if he's been whipped with a cat-o'-nine-tails then swigs at his bottle.

'Bite on this to stop the bleeding,' Andy instructs, handing him a wad of cotton wool, 'and change it often till the bleeding stops.'

The bloody, extracted tooth—chunky, discoloured, rotten, lies on the table still clasped in the pliers' jaws. A whimpering Leo tries to avert his eyes but curiosity gets the better of him and he studies it disdainfully. 'Ain't meant to look like that, are they, Doc?'

'No, they ain't!' Andy replies in language he hopes will register with Leo. 'But most of yours *do,* and you could also have *abscesses*: rotting infections that go from the tooth to the jawbone. You need a dentist and antibiotics to deal with them. They get *really* painful. They can make you very sick, in fact, poison your whole system and maybe kill you, but before that they are excruciating... worse than...' Andy describes a ghastly wartime torture that, once read, he's never been able to forget.

Leo winces and shrinks. For the weak or phobic, association is quick in the face of fear. Andy hopes the notion resonates with Leo any time he has dental pain and drives him to have his decaying teeth attended to. Andy is happy about the job he's done but wonders if he got the right tooth. Either way, Leo's got more pain ahead of him—it might be a distraction from what Andy is up to but it might also predispose Leo to erratic decisions.

Chapter Seventeen

Andy allows a couple of days for Esther to talk Adeline around and for Clara to line things up at the hospital. He loiters near his van feigning indolence, all the while quivering inside. He's almost asleep on the second night when there's faint knocking. He ignores it because it could be Goob getting him out on another job. Then a woman's whisper has him out the door in a flash and around the side. A wiry hand grips his arm and keeps him against the side of the van. It's Lola.

She burbles, 'It's happening, Andy boy. It's happening.'

'What?' he asks fearfully.

'Lardarse is putting the hard word on me.'

'On you?' he asks in disbelief.

'No, no, no, not for that. For me money, you dope.' Her weak but emphatic blow on Andy's chest almost sends him rolling. 'He says he's got a cash cow problem and I'm his flow cash... or something like that. Anyhow, he's taking me to Maitland tomorrow to get all me money from the bank, or else!'

'Or else what?' Andy asks.

There's a pause before Lola answers, 'Well, I dunno. I suppose he could kick me out and where would I go? He could tell the police 'bout that fire years ago when me husband died. He could tell Goob to beat me up, but

I'd show that faggy little sparrow what for.' She gives a barely visible but surprisingly agile display of shadow boxing.

'Come inside, Lola, and we'll work something out.'

Andy hangs clothes over the window before lighting a candle. They talk for a while and he writes two notes on separate pieces of paper and hands them to Lola, instructing her to slip the one that says *I am making this transaction under duress* to the teller. The rest of the outcome will be up to her and Andy has no doubt that Lola, the ex-showgirl, can pull it off.

Before she ducks out, she hugs Andy and says, 'You're a white knight on a shining charger!'

<hr />

THROUGH HIS WINDOW the next morning Andy sees Goob escort Lola to the people mover van—that's what it takes to move Leo's bulk. Lola looks smart in a fifties style dress and hat but the canvas bag lets the outfit down. Goob tries to steer her by the arm. She shakes him off with a withering look and hobbles ahead in leather shoes whose uppers are stiff as boards. Despite the crook shoes and a rough path Lola puts her nose in the air with a combative demeanour that augurs well. Goob slithers along behind.

Andy gives them ten minutes to get clear and hotfoots it to Bert's to give him a message and is back at his van within the hour. There's no sign of Leo so he ducks over to see Esther. Her hug fortifies him enough to take on ten Leos. Adeline is perturbed when they cuddle but grows distraught when he tells them Lola's problem and the plan.

'This will upset the balance,' she moans. 'Mr Leo will become desperate and do something bad to get what he wants. We will all suffer.'

Esther agrees. She and Andy understand it might take a showdown to get Adeline to hospital, and that's fine as long as no one is hurt in the process. Leo is due back so adrenaline-charged Andy struts back across the corral.

●────────●

PRIDE COMETH BEFORE a fall. There's a similar saying in Greek but neither version occurs to Andy early enough to warn him. He's in his van contemplating the next smart move when Leo's vehicle roars in and skids to a stop with a bang as it hits a row of forty-four-gallon drums. Leo is haranguing Goob before they get out. Andy can't hear the words—just the rant of an enraged bull elephant. It sounds as if he's lost it this time. An apoplectic fit for the big man would be useful right now.

There's quiet for a few minutes and Andy is optimistic the crisis has passed till a pitiful female scream rips the air—it's blue electricity barbed with grief. Andy rushes out to see Leo lumbering toward his precinct, marching Esther ahead of him with a hand thrust up through her hair at the back.

Adeline rushes to Andy, wringing her hands and sobbing with no pretence of dignity. 'He has taken Esther,' she wails as if her soul is being dragged out of her on the end of a fish hook. 'He says it is your fault and you will know why. She must stay with Mr Leo till he gets what he wants. You were right about him.' She grips

Andy's arm with unexpected strength. He has as much chance of getting away as a rabbit struck by an eagle. 'Please, you must help her. Save her!'

Andy is shocked by Leo's savagery and can't get words out. He turns towards Leo's but Adeline holds him back and they retreat into Andy's van. He attaches the dicky security chain, for what it's worth.

'We must have a plan,' Adeline says. 'Mr Leo has a gun and men to help him. He might kill us all.'

In a moment of clarity, Andy says, 'We should call the police. He can't kidnap her. This is worse than locking you both in your van because he's keeping her prisoner and...'

They both jump at a thump on the door and Adeline flattens herself against the wall. Casper growls but hides at a wave from Andy. The door starts to open but is stopped by the chain. It's a cocky Goob who says, 'Oi, Andy. Get yer arse out here and see Leo. And he says tell Adaleen to get home and stay there. Make it snappy 'cos he don't want to have to come and get ya.'

Adeline slides down the wall in a faint. Andy snaps the door shut, hoping it will crush Goob's snotty beak. He's not afraid of the acolyte any more, just the master. He would break the little creep in half if he was strong enough but that wouldn't stop the bigger threat. Andy tells Goob to eff off and he'll be there in a minute. He needs to think and to overcome his trembling.

Adeline has almost slipped to the floor so he hoists her up and settles her with a drink of water. He urges her to go down the road and call the police. 'Go to any house. Just ask them to call the police. For Esther.'

LEO IS WEDGED into the thunder throne. He occupies the chair like a huge timber-encased slug. Gigantic forearms, thick with dull, red hair, resemble lichen-covered buttress roots. Andy tries to look casual, even pleased to see him. Leo is calm but his colour is up and his breathing is laboured. Andy's greeting doesn't break the ice and Leo's steely expression doesn't flicker. He signals with his eyes for Andy to sit on a low box in front of him and Andy's bravado evaporates. Goob stands behind Leo at the van steps as if guarding the door. Andy's blood rises at the thought of that slime bag coming between him and Esther.

Leo stares at Andy, silent and unblinking. If the menacing hush is intended to unnerve Andy, it works.

'Suppose you reckon you're smart, Mr Professor,' Leo growls, 'but you've crossed the wrong person. Lola couldn't have thought up that trick on her own. You're the only one round 'ere could have put her up to it. I'm surprised she had enough brains or pluck to carry it off, but she did, and that leaves me, and you, sonny, in a pretty mess. Guess you know who my house guest is.' He signals to Goob, who waves a piece of clothing in the air. 'Just in case you aren't up to date.'

It's Esther's skirt and Andy doesn't hear Leo's next words because of the blood thundering in his head. He rises.

'Siddown, sonny. The little bitch is all right, and she'll stay there till I get what I want. You put me in a fix, so you'll have to get me out of it.

'Those bastards at the council want the rates. They

been sendin' me letters for years. I give 'em dribs 'n drabs, but it's crunch time and they want the lot. Sent me a Letter of Demand with a deadline that runs out in a couple of days.' He waves a letter at Andy. 'I need a spot of cash real bad, about twenty-three thousand dollars or they'll sell me up. You know that already. And I know what they're up to... a friggin' casino is what they want to put here. A man's land ain't his own no more.

'Lola was going to solve my liquidity problem but you put the kybosh on that so now it's up to you. Your dad's a doctor so he's got to be loaded and 'ave somethin' put aside for a rainy day. Well, there's a bloody deluge about to arrive and until I get the money little Esther stays where she is. You can come up with it, or you can talk Lola round.'

Andy protests. 'I haven't got any money and Dad has disowned me. You seem to know everything that goes on so you'd know Mum and Dad came up and we had a fight and now Dad won't talk to me. No way would he give me that much money... any money.'

'Then you'd better catch up with Lola,' Leo says, and catching Andy's glance at the van he adds, 'and you can't see Esther. Now get going and get back here this time tomorrow with the cash. Don't fuck me round on this one, sonny, 'cos there's a lot at stake.'

Andy has had to pull himself back from blurting out that the rates have been paid: he has no proof for Leo, and they've been paid with a cheque that will bounce. That's all been a ruse to keep a casino out of Greta, and it's not enough to get Esther freed.

Andy feels as if he's been punched in the head and pummelled in the stomach. He can barely stand and when he does, he's rocking. Goob's grinning as if he's watching the horror sections of a *Mad Max* movie. Leo blinks slowly.

Andy keeps his mouth shut and hopes Adeline didn't call the police because Leo would take horrible revenge on all of them, and on Esther first. That slow blink and dead, cold stare are chilling. Each nasty or illegal thing Andy has witnessed Leo do is another tick of the clock in a time bomb. Even handing over money may not ensure a safe outcome, but anything less will certainly provoke mayhem.

Andy heads straight to Adeline to assure her Esther is all right for now. She hasn't called the police, and she begs him not to provoke Leo further. Andy agrees.

———•———

ANDY STRIKES OUT for Bert's, wishing he could run like he did when he was a kid playing soccer. He falls in the door, breathless.

'Whoa there, Andy. Steady on mate, and get your breath back. I'll make a cuppa.'

Andy tells Bert how Leo has kidnapped Esther and that he needs Lola to get her money out of the bank or Esther might be harmed. Bert wants to call the police but he accepts Andy's assessment of Leo—that he is unpredictably violent and provocation is dangerous.

'You're a bit stuck then, Andy, because Lola ain't here. That was a clever plan to get her away from Leo at the bank and it worked a treat. She passed the note you wrote her to the teller, and the teller kept a straight face. Then, when Lola said she was having a turn and had to lie down, they whisked her away to a back room—Leo couldn't go through for security reasons—and once the manager confirmed she was there under duress like the note said, they called her a taxi and she escaped out the back to come here. You should hear her version. That woman has a funny turn of phrase. You warned me she was a character and that's not the half of it!'

Bert slaps his thigh, enjoying the humour of it all, but Andy interrupts, 'Where is she? I have to find her.'

'Clara took her to a refuge in Maitland. Some suggestion she's going back to Sydney to make a life for herself in the old haunts.'

Andy is so deflated he feels half his normal size. Esther's lovely face appears to him. He straightens up and looks at Bert. 'I don't know what to do but I'll think of something. I have to get Esther out of there. Maybe I should have put in Lola's note a message to the bank manager to call the police. I thought it would be too dangerous for Esther. But maybe I should have.'

'Hey,' Bert says, 'now I've got an idea. You know I wrote the cheque and my daughter, the one who works at the council, can give me a receipt. That should do the trick. Call by in tomorrow morning, Andy, and I might have something to help you out.'

Chapter Eighteen

Bert, chortling and waving a piece of paper, greets Andy at the door mid-morning next day.

'Here's a receipt for what Leo is supposed to pay. Francine looked it up for me and that's what I wrote the cheque for and this is a receipt for that amount. And see, it's made out with a reference to Leo's property. Easy-peasy! The finance committee of council meets tonight and she's making sure information of the payment gets to the general manager and whoever does the financial reports.

'When my cheque bounces in a few days Francine will reverse it. She's a chip off the old block is that girl of mine—a touch unscrupulous but no harm done and no brown stuff will stick to her. In the meantime, give this receipt to Leo and tell him to let Esther go.

'It should do the trick getting Esther out *and* shutting down the casino guys. When the mayor and his dodgy mates hear Leo's rates have been paid and his place is lost to them, they should zoom up the valley to the other site. That will leave Greta for us residents.

'After the cheque bounces Leo will still have to pay up or lose his place, but by then Esther and the casino will be out of the equation.'

LIKE A LOYAL serf Andy appears at the appointed time. Leo oozes part-way through the door like sludge on an outgoing tide. He studies the receipt.

'Don't believe it,' he says, shaking the piece of paper in Andy's face. 'I wanna see the money. What if this ain't for real?'

'I couldn't get cash,' says Andy. He has to stick to the idea of the money coming from his parents: that's what Leo expects. Andy explains, 'I had to persuade Mum to transfer the money from Dad's account. That's the only way I could get it and that's how they move money around these days. You know that. Ring up the council number on the receipt and ask if your rates have been paid. Come on, Leo.'

'Don't *Come on* me, sonny. This flippin' bit of paper ain't going to get you off, or get Esther out. I wanna see hard cash, not this crap.' He waves the receipt in Andy's face.

'Well Lola's gone and that's all I can do, Leo. You're off the hook, so let Esther go. I've filled my part of the bargain.'

Leo almost concedes but grumbles a new objection and contracts back through the door, saying he'll think about it. Andy retreats to his van, at a loss for what to do next: he and Bert have done what they can. Andy hopes nothing bad happens to Francine at work. Bert says she always sticks up for the underdog.

There's no one else to turn to: Andy can't ring his parents, Adeline is in shock, and he doesn't trust the police to storm in and rescue Esther. Spider might welcome an invitation to sneak up on Leo and get one in, but Esther's safety wouldn't be his first concern. Options are running out.

Hours pass and despair looms. Andy recognises the first signs of strangling lethargy licking at his feet and he jitters to stop them taking hold. If he falls apart there will be no one to help Esther. He works himself into a rage in his tiny private space, hoping for a thump on the door that will be Esther, or Goob to say she's free, but none come. The afternoon passes in a frenzy of frustration at his own ineffectualness. Esther may never think well of him again, let alone love him, if he can't help her now.

There's a faint tapping on the outside wall. It's not what Goob would do, unless to spook him, so Andy ignores it. Tap, tap, tap echoes again so he peers out and sees nothing in the gathering gloom.

'Psst! Psssst! Andy, you deaf or what?' Lola peers around the end of his van. She darts to the door and slips in.

Andy grabs her shoulders in amazed relief. An ally! 'What are you doing here? I'm so glad to see you! We thought you'd gone to Sydney.'

'Do you think I'd leave me mates?' she queries. 'I knew you'd have more problems with Lardarse and I couldn't rest easy till they was revolved. I was only in Maitland at the women's refuge, and oh, it's a lovely place after this dump. Some other dames I seen round 'ere was there, too. They been keeping tabs on how Leo's getting too big for 'is boots. Brighter than I give 'em credit for. Just slipped out a couple of days ago while Leo was in Maitland with me, and hitched a ride. Don't think 'is Royal Fatness knows they're gone yet. It weren't them Curry women. They're dumb as.

'What a place it is in there! You should see people walking round the streets like they was free, or something. Must be great to live like that instead of being stuck 'ere with that bully. Come and go as you please... no one playing the lord like they was your husband and gaoler.

'I caught a cab back out here. I know how to get in and out without being seen. There's holes in fences only me and a rabbit fit through. I been 'ere so long I reckon I know the place better than the rats. I been down every tunnel, under every van, and behind every piece of junk. F'rinstance, bet you didn't know Fat Boy's got a back door to his van. Always prepared, he is... must have a guilty conscience. On the outside there's that ripply tin stuff standing up against the wall, just tight enough not to blow away. On the inside the door is behind some clothes hangin' off a hook.'

Andy confirms he thought there was a door there and tells her she was brave to have gone in Leo's van.

'Yeah, one time when he and Goob was gone for the day I treated meself to a squiz. Disgusting, but interesting. Was just about to drink his grog but remembered in time he might have backwashed into it. Braah! Changed me mind quick smart! So, what nasty tricks has he come up with since I nicked out the back door of the bank? God, I wish I could have seen his face.'

Andy tells her the bad news. 'When he couldn't get your money, he took Esther and locked her in his van. He won't let her go till I've given him money to pay the rates he owes. I've given him a fake receipt so it looks as if they've been paid, but he's not satisfied and he won't let her go. I don't know how to get her out. What else can I do?'

'Oh, Lordy,' Lola says, and goes quiet with a faraway look for a minute. Slowly she says, 'I reckon this will work. We've gotta just have it out with him—all of us. He has to stop thinking he owns us.'

Andy waits, but that's all there is to her plan. He asks for more.

'He's losing the plot, love,' Lola says. 'Going to Maitland he was yelling at Goob that he has to get rid of his free-loading nancy friend, and Goob's the only one Leo can trust to stick by him, but not if Fiddle has to go. And he said to me, he said, "I reckon that Andy is on his way to the funny farm 'cos he's so fucked in the head he'll never be any use." You gotta put it to him for all of us. You know the right words. You can help these poor sods get out from under. I've made a break but there's heaps of others like that truck driver, Bobby, and the rest. Even Silo that Leo says is a Hannibal is all right. Got some funny habits, but he's all right. It suited me to stay a few years but I'm sure most of them others would like to move on.'

She drags on Andy's arm, entreating him. 'Say you'll do it, 'cos you're the only one can steer us straight. I'll round everyone up. They'll be there, you'll see. And we gotta do it tonight before he spirits Esther away to some place you'll never find her. If you wanna see your lovely lady again you have to fight for her. Think of Prince Valiant.' She manages half a pirouette.

The possibility of Leo moving Esther had not occurred to Andy, and now it strikes fear into his heart. As for Prince Valiant, that comic strip was before his time, but he understands. He visualises himself as one of King Arthur's knights—that sort of thing used to work when he played soccer—but he never learnt to ride a horse, and the next image is of himself crashing to the ground in a heap of metal armour, looking like one of Leo's wrecks.

'Okay, Lola, we'll do it.'

She claps her hands in glee. 'I know me way round here in the dark, so I'll sneak off now and speak to everyone. I'm persuasive when it matters, don't you worry none. We'll meet at Leo's ten o'clock sharp and make him come out. We'll all tell him at once that he don't own us no more and he's gotta let Esther out. What can he do if we stand together? He can't take us all on. We have to stand firm. There's a heap of bad things we know he's done. Tell him that, and if he don't cooperate, we'll dog on him. Simple as that.'

'All right, I'll be there,' Andy says, 'but you've all got to be there too. If he can pick us off one at a time, he will. One thing though, I'll get Adeline. She's different to the others.'

'Tonight's the night, then!' Lola hoots, scrunching her

shoulders in excitement as if they're about to premiere a new dance show. 'You're a trouper, love,' she adds. 'And bring matches, Andy. We'll have a bonfire in the drum out front for celebration. You'd be surprised how a fire gets people excited. Might be just the thing to brazen them up, like.'

●────────●

THE LONGEST TWO hours of Andy's life drag by: he waits dressed and ready, pockets stuffed with matches, rehearsing what to say. If Lola's strategy doesn't work it will be a disaster—Esther will still be locked up and he doesn't know how to run away to Maitland. The latter doesn't concern him because he'd be staying near Esther but if Leo's got wind of their plan, he could have a gang of heavies waiting to do the upstarts over—he would laugh in their faces and send them cringing back to their holes. And any time Leo chose he could catch Andy here or at Bert's and drag him off to hospital or worse.

Andy sits on the edge of his bed, hoping ten o'clock will come before he chickens out.

Chapter Nineteen

Just before nine o'clock the power goes off, as it does every night, but there's enough moonlight to discern shadows. Andy peers out the door and sees shapes flitting between vans. He urges Casper inside, but the dog slinks off: he knows something is afoot. The night air prickles Andy's nose as he sneaks to Esther's van. Leo has re-padlocked it since Adeline went back in.

He knocks gently. Adeline shoots back, 'Who is that?' The poor woman must be very afraid. He responds and she says, 'What is happening? I can tell something is happening.'

Andy tells her there's a meeting out the front of Leo's to demand Esther's release. Andy has come to take her there. Adeline hesitates and Andy can almost hear her hands wringing as she says, 'I have been praying. That is all I can do.'

In case she's thinking of telling Andy to go away, he rolls a drum under the window, clambers up, shoos her back, and breaks the window with a rock. He crushes the edges, lays his jacket over the broken glass and topples in.

Adeline writhes with fear. 'Oh, Andy! What will Mr Leo do? You have broken his window and you are out at night. He will hurt Esther!'

Andy calms her and explains what's going on. 'Think of history. Dictators come and go. They go when the people they persecute rise up and throw them out. That's what we're about to do. We need everyone there, especially you. Leo has intimidated you for years. If he sees you there, he'll know the game's up. You have to come, Adeline. You're our strongest weapon. Seeing you front up will knock his socks off.'

'What is this *knock his socks off*? We cannot have violence. That will lead to more of the same.'

There's a brittle underscore of panic to her otherwise regal voice. Andy explains the terminology but she's not convinced about why she has to join in. He tells her it's the safest way to get Esther back, and tries to make it sound totally logical and watertight. Bullies aren't brave, he assures her, especially when the numbers are against them.

A few minutes before ten o'clock Andy helps Adeline out the window onto the drum. She leans on Andy's back to slither to the ground. She's already struggling for breath. Fluttering figures converge on Leo's van; slaves and bondsmen, stooges and enforcers. They gather in the deepest shadows and link arms for mutual support. Adeline steadies Andy and he supports her. He boosts her spirits and she praises his bravery. They move to the open space outside Leo's van where the darkness pulses with a chorus of booming hearts. Shuffling and muttering burble with each arrival. Even Silo turns up, shyly accepting the hands extended to him. The last to arrive are Mrs and Miss Curry, who move as conjoined twins and are absorbed into the fold like a droplet of mercury.

Streetlight faintly illuminates the patch of ground between the insurgents and their quarry. They hang back in the shadows like a weakling wolf pack—circling yet too timid to nip at the prey. A buzz of audacity catches and they surge forward, but lose momentum when no one will lead. The mob energy begins to melt and the pack starts to fray. Andy knows he must act or the group will disintegrate. It's now or never to rescue Esther.

Andy steps forward into the light and it feels like the biggest step he's ever taken. He turns and tells the mob to listen up: he'll knock on Leo's door to get him out, and they must all come forward and stand behind him. No one is allowed to drift away. They have to keep calm, stay together and tough it out, and they must not let Leo rattle them, because that's what he'll try. This is an all or nothing chance and it won't come again. They mumble assent and move forward in unison.

The first faint rap on Leo's door sounds like a thunderclap but nothing happens. Andy knocks, then thumps. Leo could be dead drunk. A light comes on inside and then another outdoors. Leo has his own power supply.

Andy retreats to the group.

The fire drum outside Leo's van works as an outdoor heater and mustering point for shindigs with the bikies. It's fuelled up and ready to go. Lola pads forward and uses a lighter to ignite dead leaves on a branch which she plunges into the drum. Fire flares and flames shine in twenty pairs of eyes.

Lola hollers, 'Oi, Leo, come out and hear what we got to say, ya big gas bag.' She scampers back into the shadows.

Burly Bobby, the truck driver, steps up with hands cupped to his mouth and lets forth. 'You been lying to me, Leo. I got someone to check at the police station and they ain't looking for me. Me missus never lodged that complaint. I've been living in this pig sty and doing your dirty work for no good reason, you great lump of dung. Reckon you owe me big time.'

And Toby yells, 'You promised to send my family money if I took the rap for them car parts but you never did. And when I came back 'ere you said there was another warrant out for me, but I bet there ain't. I'm still shifting them lousy car parts for you and you still ain't paying me. You're a scumbag, Leo!'

Others shout about how Leo has done them wrong. Andy is happy for them to spearhead the attack. The test will be when the big man appears. Suddenly the door opens and he's there, wearing a towel the size of a bed sheet around his waist, with saggy man tits hanging over his belly. There's instant silence and some of the band scuttle from sight.

Leo squelches half out the door. 'What the 'ell's goin' on? Who lit that fire? You there, Goob?'

They hold their breath as one beyond the ring of light.

Leo bellows, 'If it's you, Spider, or your flunkies,

better step up. I got the message youse was coming to collect and if the best you can do is light up the drum, then good luck and get off my place. If you're tenants then get back to yer rat holes.'

A mass impulse carries the collaborators forward.

Leo scowls, shading his eyes against the firelight to see them. 'And what do you lot think you're doing? You ain't allowed out now. Go on, get out of here. What's the matter... you all got the trots and this is the queue?'

Leo is sussing them out—still bossing but not provoking.

Lola jabs Andy in the back. 'Now, Andy, tell him.'

'Tell him what?'

She shoves him forward. His insides are quivering and his body contorts in spasm.

Leo sneers. 'So, the smart guy's going to tell me what's up. Watch that arm don't knock you out, Andy.'

Those behind Andy wilt at the taunts. It's the same old story: they're circus animals and Leo, the trainer, has whipped them into the corner of the cage. If the poor buggers go whimpering away, they'll never stand up to him.

Leo is wide awake now and on his game. 'You're back, Lola. Pleased to see you've recovered from the fainting fit at the bank. We'll have to get down there Monday 'cos you owe me. Toby, you can try to find someone else to drive for but it will be hard without a licence. Andy, son, boy, looks like you're hanging out to go to the funny farm.'

Leo grips his towel and drags the rest of his body out through the doorway. With a minor convulsion, he pops back into his globular shape, plods down the steps and advances like a bulldozer. Andy is so scared that he can't make words and munches his tongue trying to talk. The pain and the taste of blood cut through the frustration and help him focus. He hates this man so much. Leo picks up a baseball bat and rumbles closer.

'That's far enough!'

Leo stops at the tone and the others freeze.

'This has to end. Let Esther out right now. You can't treat people like this. We're not your slaves and you're nothing more than the owner of this disgusting dump and even thinking you're the owner is stretching the facts. You might have something on every one of us but we've got the acid on you ten times over. We know about the car parts and the drugs and the dole cheques and the stealing, and we're happy to tell the police about the whole lot, so you'd better do as we say.'

As Leo roars and advances, a voice yells, 'Make a circle!'

Some of the men pick up weapons and one hurls something small, probably a spark plug. He throws it like a cricket ball from the outfield but it's only going a few metres. It hits Leo on the head and he's momentarily stunned, but storms on and stops beside the drum. The circle forms up and rotates around Leo so he can't fix on a target. It's a macabre ring-a-ring-o-roses dance: the halt, the lame, the idiot, the aged and the dispossessed.

Andy gets clear of the prancing figures and lurches to Adeline's side. She's leaning on a post and moving her head as if she's gliding with the dancers. Lola moves in loping leaps and others cavort in crazy gaits. Around and around they go, chanting, 'Down with Leo! Down with Leo!' They brandish pick handles and sticks as if a weapon is the key to release from Leo's thrall.

Leo swings his bat to clear a path through the circle. The revellers laugh as they twist and dart aside. Leo heads for the van, yelling, 'I'll fix youse all! I'll fix youse all!'

When he turns to look back, he trips and crashes against the throne. His head thumps onto solid wood. He struggles up, collapses again, and rises in slow stages, one hand holding his head. Blood trickles between his fingers. The towel slips off and there are howls of derision at his enormous, wobbling, hairy arse struggling up the steps and wriggling through the doorway.

'So that's where the two little pigs live!' and 'More like the whole litter! Woo-hoo! Go piggies!' They hoot and yell like pagans around a fire celebrating a kill. Andy sees Leo in the van topple forward clasping his injured head. He doesn't get up. Andy watches for Esther to step over Leo and run out, but she doesn't come.

Anything that will burn is thrust into the drum: cinders fly up into the dark sky like souls escaping purgatory. The heat and the danger and the dancing drug the frolickers who pull brands from the fire as they pass, and wield them, waving sparks to eternity. They career around Leo's forbidden space; his throne, under his tarpaulin, around his van. They poke and spit at car engines, boxes of tools, greasy pallets of contraband—at any extension of Leo.

A dancer gambols under the awning. It's Lola. She

punches her torch high, right onto the tarp. It catches, ignites, explodes and collapses, spreading flames to all the combustibles Leo has stashed around his van, and to the oil and grease those things have dropped. Rags and paper on the ground catch fire. There's plenty more will burn if the fire spreads.

Bobby drawls, 'S'pose we better look like we tried to do the right thing. I'll go ring the fire brigade. It'll take a while, but. Ain't my fault the phone on the corner's trashed and the next one's up at the servo.' He salutes a wave and wanders off.

Cardboard boxes burst alight and the onlookers exhale, *aaah*. The pile of oily junk underneath the van erupts into a fireball that sends sheets of flame leaping over the doorway.

'Esther!' Adeline screams.

Andy has never heard a sound like it. He's already heading for the concealed rear entrance. At the back of the van he sees two hulking shapes—they can only be bikies—being harassed by a large white dog. It's Casper. Andy yells at him to stop because the men could help, but they run off. The smell of petrol is strong.

Reefing the sheets of corrugated iron from their shaky ties, Andy finds the concealed door. The internal panel collapses when he thumps it. Andy pushes his head through a curtain of foul-smelling clothes into a soup of fumes and smoke and calls, 'Esther, this way. You can get out this way.'

He hears her splutter, 'Andy, I am tied. Help me!'

He pushes the clothes aside and follows the voice till

he bumps into her. They're both trying not to breathe. Andy runs his hands down her arms to the ropes around her wrists that secure her to the wall. The rope's wet where she's been fretting at it with her teeth, but tugging has only made the knot tighter. He jiggles it and wrenches at the rope where it's attached to the wall, but it doesn't come away.

Esther croaks, 'Knife. There.' She nods her head towards the bench.

With one hand before him Andy takes a step and knocks into a cupboard. A strange moan, somewhere between a grunted threat and a pitiful cry, rises from the floor beside him. It's Leo and his hand is searching the floor for salvation. He finds Andy's ankle and latches on, still strong as a gorilla.

There's more air down low and Andy hears Leo growl, 'Get me out or we'll burn together.'

Flame glows through the smoke at the far end of the van as sections of the wall and ceiling melt into noxious vapours that transform into licks of flame. The stench of burning vinyl doubles the effect of the smoke and the poisonous vapours shoot through Andy's head and chest like darts.

His fumbling hand finds a bread knife. Esther pulls the rope taut so it will cut more easily and it gives. Her hands are still tied but as he turns to huddle her out, he's anchored by Leo's grip. Esther can hear her tormentor's moans and understands what's happened. She feels with her foot for his head and kicks as hard as she can. Andy's foot slips free and they stumble to the false door and roll out onto the ground gasping and coughing, and crawl back from the heat. Goob is there, too, on all fours, spluttering and wheezing.

Adeline has made her way to the back of the van. She moans with relief to see Esther emerge. Mother and daughter cuddle on the ground and Adeline works on the knots. She extends an arm to Andy, brushing his face with the back of her hand and stroking Esther's cheek at the same time. It's a blessing on the two of them.

Goob is vertical again, gibbering and leaping from one foot to the other. He's whimpering, 'Where's Leo? Is he in there? Where's Leo? Get him out.'

Andy struggles up and steps toward the entrance. The fire races along the van and has almost reached the opening.

Esther sits up and says hoarsely, 'Andy, no. It is too late. You cannot do it. He is too heavy.'

Andy looks at her, then at Adeline. Their eyes lock on him and they're both moving their lips, so he doesn't know who says it, but he hears, *Let him burn. He must burn.*

Goob looses a demonic, wailing *Shiiit*! and flashes into the smoke. There's silence apart from crackling and some airy, whooshing sounds, then a single, baboon-like shriek as fire races along the rest of the van. The three pull back as a wave of popping flame consumes the rest of Leo's lair. Nobody emerges.

The group at the front is still romping like kids on cracker night. They greet Andy, Esther and Adeline with wild whoops as if they're gladiators who've survived a bout with beasts in the Colosseum, but come to a puffing standstill as sirens blare in the distance. They stand in silence, transfixed by the dwindling inferno, the black spires of burnt oil and the heat.

The result of confronting Leo is sinking in. They are free and he must be dead. Even so, they're half-expecting, even hoping for a climactic, night-rending death scream, or for a volcanic human torch to erupt from the flames, but there's nothing except for Lola's cackle. 'Have you seen how long fat burns? That van'll go all night.' And she chants, 'Now there's a sight to warm the cockles of your heart. Now there's a sight to warm the cockles of your heart.'

Ambulances and fire engines and police arrive. Andy tells the paramedics about Adeline's chest pain and she's loaded into an ambulance. Oxygen is administered to her and Esther, who's climbed in beside her mother, and to Andy. Other van park residents still on the scene— and many have already slipped away—are checked out and some are bandaged.

When Andy clambers in to say goodbye, Adeline draws him down and says, 'That Goob person... he went in behind you and came quickly back out, before you and Esther, with a box, the metal type for the safe-keeping of valuables. He took it a short way off and he dropped it into a drum before returning to where you saw him. It will still be there.'

The police arrive and set up a crime scene when they hear someone has died. Onlookers are lined up to give their details and told to report to the police station next morning. Most will disappear in the night, and because they're known only by colourful nicknames, they will, for all intents and purposes, vanish off the face of the earth. They may well turn up in another place like Leo's.

Chapter Twenty

Andy is drawn to the fire site the next morning before he goes to the police station. There's more to smell than to see in the pink, hazy light; a nauseating concoction of burnt rubber, fuel vapours, noxious fumes, and the stench of burnt meat. The throne stands like a monument before the charred remains. He spots the drum Adeline mentioned. It looks secure for now.

The police and fire brigade have been there all night, both to guard the scene and to stop the fire from flaring up and spreading. Four men shuffle near their vehicles, hands clasped around mugs of coffee, close to a thermos and McDonalds bags on the ground. A figure dressed in jeans and sports coat strides along the driveway from the road. He imposes himself on the men, asks questions and surveys the scene while they answer. He takes in Andy's presence, points at debris, queries, and nods at responses. The group moves closer to the barrier tape, and to Andy, who ambles off.

———•———

Andy calls in at Bert's.

'Been expecting you, Andy. You all right? Heard some of what happened. What did you see?'

Andy gives him a rough outline and says he's due at

the old police station to give a statement.

'Reckon you're in shock, mate. Sure you're okay? Yeah? Well, come back here after you see the police and we'll go from there.'

'I want to know if Esther's all right... and Adeline. Will you ring the hospital and see how they are?'

'Course I'll do that,' says Bert.

'Hey, Bert,' says Andy as he's leaving. 'Casper didn't come back to the van last night. He's followed me here a couple of times, so he knows your place is safe. Keep an eye out for him, will you?'

Andy makes his way past the former Greta Court House: it's a Victorian era brick building with sandstone quoining; painted cream at some time—probably several times judging from the depth of the paint chips. Both the court house and the similarly constructed police station next door were closed and locked up in the sixties in favour of Maitland and Cessnock. The court building now houses the local history museum, and the station is opened only to coordinate emergency services or to suit police activities, such as interviewing witnesses. The building is shabby: paint peels from wooden window frames, and timber on the veranda looks as if steel teeth have combed away the wood fibres. The panelled double doors, two metres tall and with a cement quality brown paint, stand open. Despite its dilapidated state the building oozes tradition, stability, assurance—all of which Andy needs.

He lingers in the doorway while his eyes adjust to the interior.

An officer sitting at a bare desk behind the dusty counter rises. 'Good morning, sir. And you would be...?'

Andy appears not to hear. He takes in the empty steel shelving, the noticeboards and walls covered with faded, drooping posters and dated announcements.

The officer repeats, 'Good morning, sir. And you would be...?'

'I'm Andy Contos, Contopoulos, actually. You asked me to come here today to talk about what happened last night. The fire.'

'Good. I'm Sergeant Tipps. Thanks for coming. We appreciate your help. We need to establish what happened last night. Detective Crossley from Newcastle viewed the scene this morning. Him and me'll be present in the room while you tell us what you saw. We'll both make notes. Do you agree to the conversation being electronically recorded?'

Andy agrees.

Sergeant Tipps leads Andy to an interview room. The same man Andy saw at the caravan park is on the far side of a laminex table. The only other furniture in the room is a desk and chair suitable for a schoolroom, and a spare chair. It's been months since the building was open, and this room reeks: sweat, urine, stale cigarettes. Perhaps it's a squat, or local youth use it as a de facto clubhouse for whatever they can't do at home. It stinks.

Andy is left seated while the two officers fuss and chat. He knows he doesn't rate highly in their eyes but he's offended at their casual behaviour when he's come to talk about dead people. The officers exchange snippets about the Newcastle Knights' big win last week, but the sergeant has a different game on his mind now.

Sergeant Tipps changes his tone and says in a measured voice to make sure his fellow officer hears, 'It's the Pumpkin Pickers playing today... against Singleton. I'm down to be a linesman but they've got a replacement if I don't make it. Love to get there, though. Should be a doozey: it's always a grudge match between these two. There's more fighting that try scoring. Big crowds, brawls and all... and I can stand back and enjoy.' He waits for the information to sink in.

The sergeant turns to Andy. 'Can I call you Andy? Fine. This is Detective Crossley.' And to Detective Crossley he says, 'Mr Contos, Andy, has come of his own volition to tell us what he saw last night. He has been informed that we will take notes and he has agreed to the conversation being electronically recorded.'

The sergeant speaks with great deliberation and winks at the detective to convey his concern about Andy's capacity for intelligent communication.

Andy rests his arms on the table, trying not to catch the sleeves of his jumper on the splintered edge. Acceptance of what has happened and the fact that he must now talk about it overwhelm him—his body subsides and his head sinks onto his arms.

Detective Crossley eases his coat and settles into the chair. The policemen study the slouched Greek then exchange a perplexed look. Andy's dark, thick Mediterranean hair stirs envy in the detective, who strokes his own thinning dome.

Sergeant Tipps fidgets. It's still early on Saturday morning, and if the detective is not pedantic and if Andy's story flows...

Tipps articulates as if speaking to a deaf foreigner. 'Andy, can you hear me. We need to get started.'

Andy raises his head but he's having trouble focusing.

Detective Crossley leans forward to make eye contact. 'There was a fire last night at Leo's Hunter Holiday Park in Greta and fatalities occurred. Were you there?'

Andy keeps gazing through the wall. He doesn't know where to start. He hears the detective hiss, 'Should this guy be in hospital? We're not going to get much out of him at this rate. Even idiots have the effing sense to make something up, or say they can't remember.'

The word 'hospital' slices through Andy's fog and makes him pay attention.

Tipps scowls. 'The ambos checked him out last night and said he was okay.'

The detective, out of the corner of his mouth, says, 'Looks like he's Captain Rats to me. If he won't talk, we won't get a statement out of him, but our Legal Services guys need somewhere to start and it would be good to have something for the Coroner's report. He's here so let's get what we can. We'll keep trying.'

Detective Crossley turns to Andy and repeats, 'There was a fire last night at Leo's Hunter Holiday Park in Greta and fatalities occurred. Were you there? Do you understand what I'm saying? We want you to tell us what you saw. It's possible the fire was deliberately lit, in which case a crime may have been committed.

Your statement could help us find the person or people responsible. Two other residents of the park came here this morning and made brief statements. We haven't got much to go on. Tell us what happened, Andy. You could have a solicitor with you, but we're only asking for a witness statement.'

Andy nods. Detective Crossley has his pen poised but it's Tipps who's panting with readiness to take notes. Crossley signals Tipps to start the tape recorder. Tipps states, 'Interview commenced at eight minutes after ten in the morning. Andy Contopoulos, were you present last night when the fire started at Leo's Hunter Holiday Park?'

Silence. The officers glare at Andy but he's glazed over again, looking right through them as the odours of the room soak into him: mouldy walls and cheap disinfectant that doesn't mask the beery sweat and cigarette smoke wafting from last night's clothes. The detective's sickly, musk aftershave is an aggravation. Then there's the fear. His own fear. Throbbing expectation in the air cripples him as severely as dazzling lights. Andy gasps, wraps his arms around his head and folds forward. The recorder clicks off.

Andy can hear what they're saying, but he can't respond. Sounds of exasperation from the sergeant suggest rising blood pressure, and as Andy raises his head, he sees the sergeant's finger poised to push the button at Crossley's nod.

Andy tries to rally. 'I want to say what happened but I can only remember things in order. I had an accident a while back and it affected my head. It means that I have to tell you from the beginning. If I get out of sequence, things get mixed up or don't come at all.'

Detective Crossley had planned to join his mates on a fishing weekend. The boat leaves at eleven a.m. from its berth an hour's drive away. He's got no show. It's always on the cards that work will upset weekend recreation and he doesn't hold it against Andy, but the lad is more exasperating than most. The detective deals with all types; deros, ferals, druggies, roid junkies, drunks, psychopaths, sociopaths, dealers, robbers, paedophiles, and wife beaters. They can be straight, gay, bent, bi, queer or tranny, mean and cunning, or violent and abusive: anywhere from cretin to Lex Luther... or any combination of the above. Some make him want to puke, some he could almost share a drink with at the pub: others put the cold, sweaty fear of god into him. But the ones he finds most tedious and draining are guys like this Andy Contos: he is part smart, part dumb, and wants to give the history of the world in his statement—all or nothing.

The detective's voice is heavy with resignation as he says, 'Whatever works for you, Andy. Let it out.'

Andy takes a breath and perks up. Maybe he can do this.

Before Detective Crossley nods at Tipps to start the recorder, he interjects. 'Listen, Andy, if you've got to tell us events in order, keep it rolling as fast as you can. Just tell us what's relevant.' He rotates his forearms around each other for visual reinforcement.

'I can try,' says Andy, 'but everything matters.'

Sergeant Tipps withers like a deflating balloon.

Andy focuses and launches into his account. 'A few weeks ago, I was at the Great Southern Pub with mates from Sydney...'

As best he can, he describes his arrival in Greta, how he came to Leo's, and how things unfolded. After half an hour he asks for a break. Detective Crossley steps outside for a cigarette while Tipps brings in a plastic jug of water and paper cups. Andy savours slow mouthfuls. Tipps's eyes narrow with impatience. Andy uses the quiet time to review events involving Esther. He doesn't want to talk to these men about her and he wants silent time to revel in the best memories. Maybe he should tell everything he knows about Esther and her mother in case something happens to him. The police might step in and help. He will tell, he decides, but in his own time. Andy sinks into agreeable reminiscence: the exaltation of his early meetings with Esther and their first kiss. She's what kept him going and besides, all else is pushed aside every time she enters his mind.

Andy is unaffected by the purpling sergeant's aura. The changing colours are curious but not intimidating.

When the three men are again seated the sergeant blurts, 'Andy, can you tell us where you were when the fire started?'

'I can't tell you that yet,' Andy protests. 'I have to work around to it or I'll miss something important. Okay?'

They nod because they have no choice.

'Did I tell you, Sergeant, pretty soon after the last

176

thing I told you, I went to a meeting at the Maitland Council Chambers? It was the Disability Committee—or whatever its proper name is—and it opened my eyes. Clara took me there, and she told me all about it... like, what they do and why people join. I need to tell you what happened because it affects Leo's place.'

The officers sigh and Detective Crossley waves dispiritedly for Andy to continue.

'Clara picked me up at Bert's on the day of the meeting.'

'And who are those people?' the detective interjects.

Andy explains who Clara and Bert are. 'She knows all the members. There's different ones go; men and women, young and old. Some of them have had totally crook luck: maybe born with something that's wrecked their life; or they're in a wheelchair after an accident; others are too sick to look after themselves. You know, disability runs their life, and their families' lives, but they still try to help. They go to meetings and come up with ideas to help other people like them, but that's it. Just getting up and dressed and fed can take them till lunch time.

'Anyway, turns out they're opposed to a casino in Greta whereas the council wants it here in Greta, on Leo's land. The story is... was... that his place might get sold from under him because he hadn't paid the rates. That's why Leo kidnapped Esther: he knew I liked her so he locked her up to make me get the money he needed. He thought that because my dad's a doctor I could get it.'

'Whoa there! What did you say? Leo kidnapped Esther? Kidnapped? So, who's Esther?' Detective Crossley is animated. He might be on to something.

'Esther lives... lived, at Leo's, with her mother. We used to talk... when we could, and Leo knew I liked her. She's lovely and so clever.

'Anyway, Bert and I kind of did get the money— we played a trick to make Leo think the rates were paid—but Leo still wouldn't let her go. That's why we all gathered out the front. It was to stop Leo from being such a bastard and to make him let Esther go. He took advantage of everyone and liked to have them at his beck and call. In fact, I reckon some of the guys were happier having Leo think for them while others were just down on their luck and had nowhere else to go.'

The detective and the sergeant exchange looks. The latter makes notes. Detective Crossley offers an official caution, reminding Andy that anything he says can be used against him. Crossley asks Andy to talk about the fire but Andy insists on talking about Leo. Andy doesn't realise he's given a motive for revenge.

He says, 'This is what I saw soon after I got there. Leo used to give his tenants the impression that he was protecting them. It was all bullshit, although most of them are on the shady side... not bad, just dubious. He twisted reality so they weren't sure what to believe, and he manipulated people into doing things they knew were wrong so he could blackmail them into doing more suss stuff. You know what I mean? It snowballs. Light fingering hubcaps led to car rebirthing before they knew it, and they were in so deep so fast it didn't matter anymore.'

'Why were you there, Andy?' asks Detective Crossley. 'What did Leo have over you?'

The question stops Andy dead. He blusters before answering, 'I was there to start with because I couldn't find my way home. Then I got to know a few people and I liked some of them. I thought I could help them, maybe. Leo let me stay if I helped with first aid.

'It took me a while to work Leo out. He was friendly and helpful to start with. He gave me something I needed—a place to stay, but he asked for a lot more back.'

'But the fire, Andy. What about the fire?' asks Detective Crossley.

'I have to tell you about the bikies before I talk about the fire. Some of them were there when it happened, when the fire started. I reckon they were up to something.'

'We'd better hear about them then,' sighs the detective.

'They came mainly at night. They'd roar in at all hours, drink beer with Leo... smoke pot. Sometimes they just partied, at other times it got down to arguments and fights. Leo made me go with Spider to fix his dog. Leo and Spider pretended to be friends but they were wary of each other and Leo kept a gun handy, like, buried in the pillows around his chair when Spider was there. And when Spider's kid was injured, I made sure he got to hospital.'

Detective Crossley intervenes. 'Who's Spider?'

The officers keep Andy on a roll and he tells as much

as he knows, and without thinking, he mentions the psych ward. There are more questions about why and for how long, and had he had psychiatric treatment before he came to Greta? The memory trips his mind into a black hole—he closes his eyes and subsides: he knows where his body is, but the rest of him is reliving what happened in Maitland Hospital after Goob roared off.

Andy mumbles, 'There were three of me for a while. I could hear voices. Do you get those voices, Sarge?'

The sergeant shakes his head and makes another note.

'Mmm,' says Andy. 'I thought about doing myself in.'

The sergeant writes again.

Andy falls silent and stares sideways out the window. His mind is in another place. The sergeant stops the tape.

'Andy, are you with us?' asks Detective Crossley. 'We've talked about the psych ward and the bikies. You wanted to tell us about the bikies because you believe they were there when the fire started. Can you tell us how the fire started?'

Tipps presses the button, states where and when this interview is taking place, and waits. And waits. Andy raises a zombie face, and drops his head again. The sergeant spits obscenities after he turns the machine off. The clock's ticking. If a fight breaks out at the game and he misses a punch-up, they might as well cancel Christmas.

'All right, Andy. Let's just go to the fire. What else can you tell us about last night?'

Andy pulls himself out of his trance. He says, 'We were out the front of Leo's as a show of force. We thought he'd buckle if we all confronted him at once. He came out of his van when we called, he wouldn't let Esther go, he went back in, someone lit the fire in the drum—Leo often had a fire there—and it caught on to the shelter and spread. I'm not sure who started the fire in the drum. It wasn't me, though.'

The detective needs more information. 'Try to remember who lit the fire in the drum.'

'It could have been Lola. She likes fires.'

'How did the fire get from the drum to the tarpaulin?'

'Lots of people had burning torches: things like a rag on the end of a stick. They were all running round, dancing and calling out. I think the flames jumped from a torch to the tarpaulin when someone ran underneath. I couldn't see who it was. It was chaos. I was over on one side with Adeline. She can't dance. Neither can I.

'The fire was worse around the back along from Leo's secret door. That's where it took off, in all that stuff. The petrol smell was really strong. And I'm sure it was Spider and one of his mates running off when I went around the back to see if I could reach Esther that way.'

'What secret door?' the sergeant probes. 'How did you know about it?'

Andy tells them how he discovered the door, and about rescuing Esther.

The sergeant makes notes, but not as eagerly as before.

Detective Crossley leans forward. 'That was a brave

thing to do, Andy, but why didn't you get Mr Schwartz out as well.'

Andy looks at him, dumbfounded. 'The fire... the fire just took over,' he says. 'I think Goob tried to. Anyway, he ran back in and never came out.' That's the first mention of Goob so Andy fills them in.

Sergeant Tipps says, 'I think that's all we need from you, Andy, for the time being. You've given Bert Foster's address for contact. Is that correct?'

Andy nods.

'Please answer in words for the recording,' the sergeant asks.

'Yep,' Andy replies.

———•———

SERGEANT TIPPS BOUNCES around the room disconnecting equipment. 'Two o'clock. I might make it to the game,' he mutters half to himself and half to Detective Crossley.

'You can go, Andy,' Detective Crossley says. 'We'll be in touch if we need you again, and let me tell you that if you're cleared of any connection with the fire you could be nominated for a bravery award? It takes a lot of guts to dive into a fire, a lot of guts.'

Andy nods. Dad would be impressed with an award... for a few minutes. The detective said he could go, but Andy is stiff from sitting and moves slowly through the door behind the officers.

Detective Crossley lights a smoke and turns to the sergeant who's almost skipping toward his car.

'Thanks for your help today, Tipps. Looks as if it's all

the info we need. This statement might save us chasing the other witnesses who've taken off. Those two this morning: that weirdo Silo, and Bobby what's-his-name-truck-driver, gave us nothing. It's a big ask to believe what they claim: that the sirens woke them up and they got to the fire at the same time as the brigade. Their consciences can't be so clear they sleep that well.

'Oh, Tipps, one more thing: get this tape straight into Newcastle so it can go to Sydney on Monday for transcription. I'd take it myself, but I've just remembered the mates on the fishing weekend are calling in at Forster tonight so I can catch up with them there. Might still have a good time. Thanks, mate.'

Sergeant Tipps's face had been florid for most of the interview: it had faded and his eyes had brightened when he stepped outside, with a mere pink glow enlivening his cheeks. Now, after the detective's request, his face resembles a convulsive, plum-coloured cabbage.

'Aw, gees, sir. Can't it wait till Monday? I could still get to the game today. Tomorrow's no holiday 'cos I've got to mow the mother-in-law's lawn.'

'Sorry, Tipps. Better get it there today. Cheers.' He saunters off.

'Aw, what a bummer of a weekend!' the sergeant mutters.

Andy senses the sergeant's glare as he heads to Bert's to find out what's happened to Esther and Adeline.

Chapter Twenty-one

B ert's face lights up when he opens the door to Andy. 'Come on in and take the weight off. You look tuckered. How did you go with the coppers? Must have been tough,' he says, hobbling ahead down the hall. 'I was thinking maybe you should have had a solicitor there.'

'But I didn't do anything wrong. They just wanted me to say what I saw and what happened,' says Andy, trailing one hand along the wall for support as he catches his breath.

'Yeah, but I've heard say they got a way of making the facts fit the story they want to come out, and loading up whoever they can get their hands on if it's too hard to get the actual culprit.'

'But I didn't do anything wrong.' Andy is adamant.

'I know that,' Bert emphasises. 'But like I said, even things a person had no part in, or that happen by accident, can be sheeted home to them if there was negligence or 'reckless disregard' or some such. We'll have to wait and see. Hey, there's good news though. Look out the back.'

Andy leans over the sink and through the window sees Casper sleeping on a mat on the back porch. He goes out and kneels beside the dog which wriggles against him, thumps his tail on the wooden floor and submits to an ear caress. Andy sighs: at least one thing he loves is safe.

Watching from the doorway, Bert says, 'He turned up after you called by this morning. God knows where he spent the night. I can't guess why he didn't go back to your van, but maybe he knew he was best out of there. Paws were a bit roughed up and sore... looked burnt. I've put salve on them.

'Come and get spruced up. I'm glad you got here when you did. There's a photographer from the local paper due at three o'clock to snap yer ugly mug. Good publicity don't hurt none. I'm not sure how he cottoned on to the fact that you'd be coming here but he's heard you were a regular hero last night, saved lives and all. I'll sit in, if that's okay, just to make sure he gets the story straight.'

Andy, still on the mat with Casper, stirs suddenly. 'Can I ring the hospital about Esther and Adeline?'

'All done, Andy. Esther doesn't have injuries but she'll stay with Adeline to keep her calm, and Adeline's in the best place for care and will see a heart doctor on Monday. Clara's up there right now talking to the social worker. There's all sorts of officials will want to see them: Community Services, Immigration, bloody ASIO for all I know. Adeline doesn't have the right paperwork for a migrant, but Esther was born here. I can't believe they'd be deported... it would be criminal to send them away after all these years. Clara's suggested we see the local member pronto to push for a quick decision from Immigration. You and me will go to the hospital tomorrow, when they're more settled. How about that?

'Get scrubbed and you'll feel a whole lot better.'

———•———

LATE IN THE afternoon, Jason Lemesurier, a reporter from *The Maitland Comet,* arrives. He's wearing jeans, an open-necked shirt and a sleeveless vest. He's about thirty and very much on the ball. There's a guarded intensity in how he stands, alert to threats and eyes scoping as if he's expecting to be picked up by his collar and britches and evicted through a wall. Perhaps that's a career hazard. He doesn't look as if he can fight, but he could be fast on his feet. His interview technique is reassuring and he's willing to share insights into police procedure, perhaps to relax Andy and Bert in the hope they'll give him a gem for his story.

Bert declines permission to tape the interview but adds, 'You can take some notes. And this is just for half an hour. The young fella's buggered.'

Bert closes his eyes and lowers his head. He listens intently as Jason probes Andy's memory. Andy says he's told the police all this and it took hours because he had to do it in chronological order and he's not up to going through it again now. Bert smiles to himself and tells Jason a few pertinent, colourful facts that flatter Andy. Bert suggests that with the interviews Jason already has and a photo of Andy, there's enough for a story.

The reporter doesn't want to leave yet, and at Bert's prompting, is happy to speculate how the investigation might run. His bailiwick is local courts and crime, and because Maitland and the whole Lower Hunter are active, so to speak, there's no shortage of material.

'It's understood,' Jason says, 'that Leo Schwartz had criminal connections. I don't know how big time he was, but everyone knows he was into car rebirthing, and drugs at some level. Nobody's sorry he's gone, but his offsider went too. They have to work out if there's been a murder, a murder-suicide, or whatever. There's lots of options. And because there was a fire, the firies get involved. They'll give an opinion about its cause and if there's any stiffs, they do a report on the circumstances: the police call in their scientific unit: a doctor does a post-mortem and verifies the cause of death and provides a death certificate and proof of identity.

'Then, because there's been deaths other than in the most predictable and normal of circumstances, all that information goes to the Coroner. Putting it simply, he or she decides if any one or more persons can be identified as responsible for the deaths. The matter would then be referred on to the Office of the Director of Public Prosecutions for their consideration as to whether charges should be laid. It goes on and on. I wouldn't be caught up in it for quids. And the coppers are always looking for an easy explanation—you know, someone who's not likely to stick up for themselves, or who can't afford a good lawyer.

'Here's a tip. If you need a lawyer, don't get your local bloke who does everything from drafting wills to shoplifting charges, even if he does say he can get Legal Aid for you. Go to Legal Aid central in Newcastle. They do nothing but criminal stuff and they're the best at it! Seen them in action plenty.'

Andy trembles uncomfortably at the mention of criminal law. Bert raises his head and stares at the journalist through slits.

Jason rethinks and says, 'Why do you think investigative journalists have come into their own? We get a bee in our bonnets and follow a lead for months or years about a story, and unearth stuff the coppers never have the time or inclination to follow up.'

Bert has shut his eyes again and Andy's expression is still fixed. 'But I didn't do anything wrong!' he stresses.

'I believe you, mate,' Jason sympathises, 'but it's a tough way to spend a few months... waiting for the Coroner or the cops to decide if they'll lay charges. Best thing to do is get on with your life as if everything is hunky-dory, and it most likely is. Don't let the bastards get you down. The delay isn't all their fault, it's just that so many labs and people have to put in their two bobs worth. That's the law... ass or otherwise. Just don't let your guard down, or get your hopes up, or say anything stupid.'

Jason snaps pictures of Andy, and one of Bert for good measure. Andy asks him as a favour to take one of him and Bert and Casper all together and send it to him. He agrees, of course. Bert is happy Andy thinks to ask.

●———————●

IN THE LAST of the clear evening light Bert and Andy relax on the front veranda with mugs of tea. They're tranquilised by the glowing green vista of lucerne fields across the flood plain. Casper snoozes on the doormat. Andy fills Bert in on a few details of last night that recur to him, unbidden and out of sequence, but including Adeline's account of Goob and the box.

Andy asks Bert, 'Those mates of Spider's, the bikie guys, who were around the back of Leo's van during the fire, do you reckon they were after the box? They might have thought Leo had money stashed.'

'True,' muses Bert. 'Could be ill-gotten gains, or maybe Leo had something they wanted real bad... something he had over them. Could be that's why they kept doing deals with him. He could've told them whatever the thing was, it was in a bank vault or hidden elsewhere. They might have got desperate for it and decided to raid the van, or if they couldn't do that, then just burn it.

'On the other hand, what about this? Suppose Spider was pretty sure Leo had the item in question in his van, so he and an offsider went to have it out. They could have been planning to force Leo to hand it over, then bump him on the head and set fire to the van. They had the petrol already poured around the back, ready to ignite when they came out, but they never went in. Esther would know if they went in. Could be some petrol ran under the van and was ignited by the fire out front. Whoosh! Up she went. Spider and co quite sensibly decided not to charge into the flames and they bolted. It's a coincidence they were there on the same night you lot took Leo on, but bad blood was building with Spider and his gang, and all Leo's bad luck, or justice, came at once.

'You did tell the coppers about the bikies?'

'Sure did,' says Andy.

The two men sink into their own thoughts. Casper sighs. It's been a huge day but they know there's more to come.

Chapter Twenty-two

In the laneway behind Leo's—they still think of it that way—Bert and Andy chuckle at their absurd unsuitability for a stealthy jaunt: an old man hobbling with a stick, a young fellow half-dragging a leg, and a skulking white dog. Around midnight they climb through the back fence into the shadows, and for Andy, back into fearful breathlessness.

While Andy snoozed in the early evening Bert took a reconnaissance stroll and spotted the police car parked in the driveway of Leo's to guard the crime scene. The officer is probably asleep by now, and Andy knows the place well enough not to need a torch.

The men try to close off their nostrils to the stomach-churning air that has settled around the site but they must go where the smell is strongest—right behind the burnt-out van. In the faint moonlight they push under police barrier-tape to reach the drum, and then tip it over gently to minimise noise. Water gushes out and a safe deposit box topples forward and clunks on the side of the drum. The sound is cushioned by silt that flows with the water. Andy imagines floodlights exploding into life, guards and whistles and troops of armed men rushing toward them. There's absolute silence except for their breathing, and Andy's is thunderous in his head.

Bert slides the box out onto the ground and they stand the drum up. The box is heavy so they take turns to carry it back to the laneway where they look around, and carry it between them, one handle each. They try to look more like strollers than burglars, and with their ungainly walks, could easily be returning from a late session at the pub. Back at Bert's, the box sits like a stolen idol on a towel on the kitchen table. It's locked, of course, and leaking water.

'Hope there was no documents in there,' says Bert. 'Tell you what we gotta do. Tempting as it may be to use any cash that *might* be inside to right a few wrongs and help the needy, us included, first thing Monday morning we take it to the police. But,' he stresses, 'we insist on being there when it's opened. There may or may not be valuables, or valuable information inside, but as the finders of this box we're entitled to know what's in it before it disappears into the black hole of bureaucracy. Proceeds of crime can be confiscated and stolen goods should be returned to an owner or the insurance company, but where no owner can be located etcetera, the finders may have a claim... after a period of time. Who knows, you might come up trumps.

'And the reason we need to be there is because sometimes, rumour has it, not all the stuff that comes into a police station finds its way into the said bureaucracy. Some of it falls on the floor and goes into the pockets of whichever officers happen to be there on the day. Yep! Me and that journo, Jason, would make a good team. Maybe we should ask him to come with us. That would really keep the bastards honest, knowing that the papers could get hold of it.'

Bert pulls back a mat on the kitchen floor and lifts a section of floorboards to reveal a cavity under the floor. He wedges the box inside.

They turn in around two-thirty. Each in their own room, Bert and Andy lie awake in the dark. They hear motorbikes cruise down the road and return a few minutes later. The bikes pause at the front fence, rev once or twice, and head off.

Bert confirms his weapon is under the pillow on the other side of the bed. As he sinks into sleep, he chuckles to himself about how these bikies need to get around in groups. Down the hall, Andy checks his window is locked and lies awake for another hour before drifting off. It's been a bit more than twenty-four hours since he rescued Esther and he's relived his entire life in that time, and then some. He dreams he's riding a motorbike alone at breakneck speed. The action alternates between him chasing the bikies and being their prey.

•————•

BEFORE ANDY WAKES up next morning, Bert gets a Sunday paper from the servo. On his return, as he's opening the front door, Jason Lemesurier pulls up and bounds onto the front veranda. He hands Bert a large envelope and says, 'Preview enclosed. Tell Andy he'll get front page in tomorrow's *Comet*. There's a snippet in that Sunday rag in your hand, too.' And he's off.

Bert finds the snippet in the paper—and that's all it is—about ten lines in one column mentioning a fatal caravan fire in the Hunter Valley. It's not rare news and insignificant in the scheme of things.

On the other hand, Jason's article ticks all the boxes: Andy is a hero; Greta is saved from a casino; and there's juicy detail about how council works.

Bert hollers as he hears Andy stir, 'Come and get an eyeful of this. Jason's dropped off a copy of what will be a great spread on the front page of the *Comet* tomorrow. Bit of bad news, though.' Bert's voice drops as Andy meanders down the hallway. 'The young fella Goob had with him... seems he necked himself. Poor little critter, living at Leo's with Goob and then he dies. That's not much of a life.'

Andy wanders into the room and grimaces. There's more to healing someone than bandaging their wounds. He turns his attention to the preview pages.

Local Hero Saves Girl from Horrific Caravan Fire. Three Men Die

Andy Contos, a resident at Leo's Hunter Holiday Park, sprang into action last Friday night to rescue Esther Schönburg who was trapped in a caravan that burst into flame at Leo's Hunter Holiday Park in Longine Street. Ms Esther Schönburg and her mother, Adeline Schönburg, are currently recovering in Maitland Hospital. Tragically, Mr Contos's efforts to save Leo Schwartz from the same fire failed and Mr Schwartz perished. Another resident of the caravan park, known locally as 'Goob' also perished in the fire. He was last seen attempting to rescue Mr Schwartz. Both Mr Contos and 'Goob' may be nominated for bravery awards when investigations are complete.

Another male was found deceased in the caravan previously occupied by 'Goob' but at this stage there are no suspicious circumstances regarding that death. Police have been unable to identify that deceased male.

A small number of residents are assisting police with their enquiries but investigations are being hampered by a scarcity of witnesses. Some residents of the caravan park claim to have slept through the night and have no recollection of the fire, while others cannot be located. Police are appealing for further witnesses or people with relevant information to come forward.

Tragic as these events are, they impact on a contentious matter currently before Maitland Council. It has previously been reported that the council and local developers favour the site of Mr Schwartz's property for a casino. There has been strong opposition to this proposal from the Greta community who are prepared to fight 'tooth and nail' to keep the development at bay.

It was rumoured that unpaid rates would make Mr Schwartz's property the subject of forced acquisition, but sources have revealed the developers signed a contract last Thursday for a site in the Vineyards. This followed an announcement

195

at Wednesday night's council meeting that Mr
Schwartz had paid the outstanding rates that day.
The developers' hand was forced to quick action as
failure to secure a suitable site immediately could
have meant the Hunter Valley licence could be
taken up by another party.

Mr Schwartz's death would have provided a
second opportunity to secure the Greta site, but
residents of the town are celebrating because they
are now safe from the imposition of a casino in
their midst. The future of Leo's Hunter Holiday
Park is uncertain.

Andy reads and digests the article. Bert reads it for
the umpteenth time and chuckles again.

'Jason got that together snappily. He was only here
yesterday arvo. Do you realise, Andy, we beat them?'
Bert asks. 'We beat the bastards at their own game. No
casino! Greta will still be Greta, but even better because
Leo's gone. Whaddaya reckon, mate? What a great win!
It's almost enough to make a man turn religious and say a
prayer of thanks. Not quite, but almost. As they say, *God
helps those who help themselves* and that's what we did.

'Here, write your mum and dad's address on this
envelope. I'll get an extra copy of the paper tomorrow
and send it to them. They oughta know what their son's
been up to. Now, get that breakfast into you then we'll
go see the ladies.'

Casper trots to the front door with Andy and Bert as
if he's part of the team. He's learned how to sneak inside

the house by opening the back screen-door with his nose and letting it slide along his body to close silently behind him. Bert isn't keen on having a dog inside but usually, by the time Bert sees him, Casper is asleep at Andy's feet, or pretending to be. The pricked ears are a giveaway.

'You stay here today, Casper. Guard the fort.'

Andy puts him in the backyard. The side gate is closed. Casper would be over it in a flash if he wanted to take off but at least stray dogs can't wander in.

IT'S BEFORE VISITING hours at Maitland Hospital but Andy and Bert are allowed to see Esther and Adeline in their private room. Adeline, propped up and dozing, has a good colour. Esther rises from the bedside chair, steps straight to Andy and takes his hands. They exchange stares, neither knowing what to say or who should speak first.

At last Esther says, 'You are well? You are not injured?'

Andy can't find words so he wraps his arms around her and breathes in. There are scents of hospital shampoo and charity issue clothing, but her own musky floral aroma is still there and goes straight to his brain. He wants to cry with relief and happiness, but holds Esther close while he regains his composure. He leads her into the hallway and Bert comes too. Esther replies she's fine when Andy asks.

Bert chips in to ask for an intro. 'And I'm pleased to meet you, my dear. You and your mother have had a shocking time in that hellhole at Leo's. I'm sure everything will be fine from here on.'

Andy and Bert both ask about Adeline at the same time.

'A doctor has come to see her. A Registrar, I think he said he was called, for the heart. He was very kind. She will have more tests and is likely to need an operation or a procedure of some sort. Andy, what would that be? Is it safe? I don't want her to have a dangerous operation. And we cannot pay for it. Would we go to gaol for debt? What will happen if we cannot pay?'

'Esther? Esther?' A fretful call comes from the room.

'I am here, Mama,' says Esther pushing the door ajar. 'Do not worry. I am close by.' It's as if she's now the carer. Esther turns back to say, 'She worries if I am out of sight. I am permitted to sleep in the room with her or she becomes anxious. The chairs are comfortable when pulled together and the bathroom, ah, it is luxurious.'

They all go in and Adeline smiles when she sees the men. Andy introduces Bert as a great friend and makes the link with Clara. It's Clara who's been in and out talking to Esther and Adeline to get the paperwork moving.

Andy steps to the bed and says reassuringly, 'Esther says you'll have more tests. You mustn't worry, Adeline. None of it will hurt and there are many simple things that can be done for heart problems. There have been great advances in medicine, and it will cost you nothing.' Even if it does, he tells himself, they'll cover it.

Andy hasn't planned anything in advance but he continues, 'Bert and I are going to take Esther outside for a walk in the fresh air and maybe get a cup of coffee. We won't be long. Just rest and you'll be fine. If you need anything press this button and a nurse will come.'

Esther masks her surprise at Andy's composure. 'It's all right, Mama. I would like to be outside for a short time. I will return.'

Adeline is concerned but agrees. She lies back, eyes darting from one person to the other in search of a hidden agenda but finds nothing to worry her.

Andy and Esther fall easily into holding hands as they stroll. Bert sends them off to do a lap of the block while he rests in the sun. Clara catches up with them all back in the café.

'Oh, my,' she says. 'Life is altogether too complicated when a person, or two people, drop out of the sky. Far be it from Big Brother to allow a body just to be. But I suppose if we want pensions and allowances and Medicare cards someone has to keep lists somewhere, not to mention being obsessed with knowing who's living in the country and might be planning to smuggle in criminals. Anyway, so far, so good. Esther, the hospital has agreed to let you live-in as long as your mother is a patient because they understand her state of mind and after that you'll be eligible for emergency housing. That might be a motel room to start with, but you're on the list for something better.

'Now, I haven't heard back yet from the local member's office—he's a politician who's a member of parliament.'

Esther tenses at the mention of politicians.

Clara reassures her. 'He might be our best ally. His own parents arrived from Europe after the war.' Clara pauses and slows. 'And I'll let you know as soon as the Department of Immigration gets back to me. Look, you and your mother are a pair of lovely, intelligent women who've been here for years. You are no threat to the country, and your own father was probably an Australian citizen. You've committed no crimes, as far as I know, so there's no reason to deport you. Besides which, Bert and I are happy to go guarantor in any way required.

'And, my dear, there's always the press. There would be a lot of public pressure for you and your mother to be granted permanent residency visas. In due course, you might even be eligible to apply for citizenship.'

They return to Adeline and find her picking at dinner. If she was stressed by Esther's absence, she wouldn't be eating at all, so nibbling is a good sign. She smiles a relieved welcome, pats her mouth with a serviette and extends a hand to her daughter.

———•———

ANDY AND BERT spend all day around the hospital and Clara is there on and off. She and Bert sit with Adeline for a while to give Esther and Andy more time together. During the middle of the day Adeline is left alone to rest and the others drink too much machine-made coffee. While they're sitting in the café a nurse wheels a child past in a wheelchair. He looks familiar but very different to the desperately ill boy Andy brought in.

'River!' Andy calls out. 'How are you?'

The nurse stops and turns the chair to face Andy's group. River is suspicious and sullen.

Andy explains to the nurse. 'I'm Andy Contos. I sort of brought him in. How's the leg?'

'He'll keep it,' says the nurse, 'but only just. He's in the dumps because he won't be able to play football. We tell him there's other sports he could try.'

River chips in. 'Nah. Only want to play league. Nothin' else is any good. All wussy stuff.'

'I'm sorry,' says Andy. 'It's hard handling a big change like that. It might not be much consolation now, but at least you'll have two legs to stand on and walk with, and ride a motor bike for that matter. It's all easier with two legs.'

Andy thought the last suggestion would appeal to River, but instead, he bristles.

'How's things at home?' Andy wants to know about Sweetie Pie.

'Mum came yesterday. First time. Said Dad's gone to Queensland. On business.'

'What about Sweetie Pie?'

'Never came back. Mum heard she bit the guys trying to catch her and they shot her. Don't matter none. She weren't no use any more for fighting and she was a bitch to look after.'

'Well, we'd best keep going,' the nurse said. 'I was just giving young River a change of scene and a bit of sun.'

She pushes the chair a couple of steps, applies the brake and turns back to Andy. She says quietly, 'I think he understands you saved his leg, and probably his life. We've told him how lucky he is that someone brought him in. You did a great thing but don't expect gratitude.

I don't think he's got it in him. Maybe when he's older he'll get all this in perspective. Right now, he's confused about who his friends are.'

When River and the nurse are gone, three questioning faces confront Andy.

'I guess that was River,' says Bert.

'You guessed it.' They want more so Andy picks up the thread at the first time he saw Sweetie Pie, and tells them the story over another cup of coffee.

———•———

IT's DARK WHEN Bert and Andy reach home. They call Casper from the back door but he doesn't come. They search the yard, find the side gate open, and call him up and down the street. He still doesn't come.

Chapter Twenty-three

B ert leans over the sink peering out into the darkness while Andy paces between the kitchen and the dining room. Where is he? They're about to set out searching for Casper in the direction of the van park when a knock sends them scrambling to the front door. It's Dotty, a neighbour.

'Hello, Bert. Just saw your lights on. That dog you got 'ere. Well, some blokes come round the side while you was out and 'e just let rip. I heard their bikes pull up then there was a ruckus out back. I couldn't do nothin'. I was in me yard peerin' through the fence. I could see they were no-good types: you know the sort, bare arms and tatts. Anyway, that dog drove 'em off at first but they laid about 'im wiv sticks and beat the bejeezus outa 'im. After they left, I rang the vet and they sent the pet ambo, so that's where 'e'll be.'

Bert and Andy surround Dotty to hug her. It's the most male arms she's felt for decades.

She giggles and trills, 'It weren't nothin'. I woulda done the same for me old man.'

Bert rings the vet and asks that everything possible be done for Casper. No matter that it's Sunday and after-hours rates apply. The next call is for a taxi. Bert checks under the floor after Dotty leaves. The security box is still there.

Poor Casper! He's flat out in a cage with one front leg in plaster. The vet opens the door so they can pat him.

'Softly,' says the vet. 'He's got contusions all over. Just let him know you're here.'

Casper's eyes open to slits and his tongue hangs out. He considers Bert and Andy groggily, lifts his tail once off the floor and manages a flicker of the lips. Andy understands. Bert goes out to speak to the vet and Andy kneels to comfort the dog with gentle strokes.

He praises Casper's bravery and whispers, 'I love you, boy. You gotta get better. We all love you. You're a great dog. Never had a dog before you. You gotta get better. I'll look after you.' Andy wipes tears away before going out to Bert and the vet.

The vet says, 'He's had a pounding, for sure. Must have kept going back for more. A dog that size could run faster than his attackers and get away so he must have been standing his ground. There was plenty of blood on him but he doesn't have any broken skin, so it looks like he got some bites in. People who'd do this to an animal could retaliate so keep him indoors unless you're outside with him. Watch out for baits thrown over the fence.

'Come and see him whenever you want. I'll get the surgery van to drop him home when he's ready to go. By the way, I'll have to report this to the RSPCA in the morning so you and the neighbour who rang might get a visit.'

Bert grunts, 'That's all right. Has to be done.' He turns to Andy and adds with humorous resignation,

'Looks like we got ourselves an inside dog.'

Back at home Bert rings Jason Lemesurier. 'Yeah, yeah. I know what time it is. Sorry 'bout that. Didn't think you'd mind if it's something you can print, and it'd be good to get it in the rag asap. We need a favour. We need your help to protect our dog. Yeah. You heard right—dog. That picture you took the other day of me, Andy and the dog, Casper... well, some arseholes beat the crap out of Casper in the yard here. I think they were trying to break in looking for something in particular, or more likely, something they don't want the cops to know about. Get the picture? Casper drove 'em off. Could you do a follow-up to the piece about the fire—use the picture if you want, but it's important to get this across: *items possibly associated with criminal activity found at the scene of the fire have been surrendered to police.* Something like that. If the bastards can read, they might understand what they're after ain't here. Could you do that for us? Great! Thanks, mate. Wouldn't hurt to add that the RSPCA is also after whoever did it. Arseholes! See ya.'

ON MONDAY MORNING Bert packs the locked box into a battered Gladstone bag, and he and Andy catch a bus into Maitland. They go to the police station where Bert explains what they've brought in.

'It came from where the fire was at Greta last Friday night... at Leo's Hunter Holiday Park. We ain't opened it and we'll leave whatever is in it with you, but we want to be present when it's opened and to have a list of what's in there.'

They're shown to an interview room where two officers force the box and examine the contents, then they wait while a list is typed. Bert slips a copy into his coat pocket.

'Insurance,' he says to Andy, tapping his chest as they leave the station.

⎯⎯⎯⎯⎯⎯⎯

ON TUESDAY MORNING Andy and Bert are back in Maitland. Andy visits Esther and Adeline while Bert goes to Maitland Police Station again. He's been ruminating about what came out of the box and he wants to speak to someone senior but it's not so easy. He goes to a public phone and rings Newcastle Detectives and asks for Detective Crossley, the name Andy gave him. Bert dangles a juicy bait.

'Morning,' he says. 'Name's Bert Foster. I live at Greta. You the bloke that came out after the fire at the caravan park? Right. I understand you're looking for more information. Yeah, 'bout that and another matter that you've recently offered a big reward for, a 'cold case' matter in the Sunday papers a few weeks back— something about the ambush and murder of a police officer twelve years ago in Kurri Kurri. No. You'll have to come to me. I don't drive. This is the address...'

It's close on an hour from Newcastle to Greta and two detectives are at the door in not much more. Wearing jeans and shirts and driving an unmarked car, they want to travel below the radar. Bert knows he's piqued their interest. Andy was nervous when Bert told him on the bus home that detectives were on their way.

Bert reassured him. 'It's all good, young fella. It's all good. This talk should shift any suspicion away from you, and generally have a good outcome, maybe a lucky one. You never know.'

Bert had been studying the signed inventory of contents of the box. The most startling item is a handgun: a .357. *Nice piece*, the officer at the station called it. There's also a men's gold signet ring with a date engraved on the inside, seventeen items of ladies' jewellery (all gold and some with stunning large gems that look the real deal), eighty Krugerrands, and a set of keys. Also on the list is a plastic bag containing sodden newspaper cuttings, which, if handled correctly, may be decipherable.

The visitors sit at the dining room table when invited to do so. Bert asks if they've heard yet from Maitland police about what he and Andy handed in yesterday. They haven't.

'Good. I'm telling you now. There was a handgun in a box retrieved near Leo Schwartz's van after the fire. Also jewellery, a men's gold ring, keys and other stuff.

'A few weeks back there was a review in the Sunday papers about cold cases. I generally browse through them. You might remember a big jewellery heist in Sydney about thirteen years ago: some Bellevue Hill old money family who didn't bother with safes and they got cleaned out. Huge reward offered by the insurance company but nothing turned up. The robbery made the news then because a housekeeper was killed when she came in on the thieves.

'Then twelve years ago a copper, some Detective McMaster, was shot at a house in Kurri Kurri. Different stories said he was lured there and ambushed, others that he went there on the take. Anyway, got himself killed. No arrest. I can understand you blokes getting upset when one of your own dies on the job, so that murder also was described again in all its detail. Because it was a cop, the reward for helping to solve it is right up there.

'I recommend you take a look at what was in that box: the gun, the jewellery and the other stuff. Reckon it all fits together. I can only imagine the jewellery was too hot to offload, 'specially if it became associated with the murder of a police officer. I couldn't say if Leo Schwartz or the local chapter was connected to the robbery. Either one of them could have been involved in the murder and it was probably the bikies if Leo had a gun they wanted back.

'And the men's signet ring: check the date engraved on the inside. It's the kind of ring young blokes were being given back then for their twenty-first birthday. How old was the detective who died? About thirty-four? So, the date on the inside of the ring is about right for when he would have turned twenty-one. Anyway, go figure. You just remember where the leads came from, and put up young Andy here's name for the reward. He's the one who found the box at Leo's and gave it to the Maitland cops.'

The detectives query how Bert and Andy came into possession of the box. Bert tells them everything they want to know.

Chapter Twenty-four

A ndy collects his remaining items from Leo's and settles in at Bert's. It's a definite upgrade from the caravan. Casper comes home in a few days and is allowed inside. Bert sighs at the sight of a dog in the lounge room and says his poor departed missus would turn in her grave if she knew. They have to help Casper to and from the yard, and keep watch while he's there, but it's a labour of love. Bert and Andy compete to look after him.

Going home to Sydney is not on Andy's radar, but nor is he comfortable imposing on Bert.

'It's no problem, mate,' Bert says. 'You're not putting me out but if it makes you feel better, you can cover your costs like you said, or pull your weight however you like. I enjoy your company. Look at it this way: you're doing a community service, helping an old bloke stay happy in his own home.

'Anyway, you'll want to be round here for Esther and her mother. You're free to come and go, and you can stay as long as it takes to get things back on track. And speaking of 'on track,' let's take Jason's advice and see those solicitors he mentioned—the Legal Aid mob in Newcastle. We can catch the train from Maitland and make a day of it. Interviews aren't fun but if we do something good with the rest of the day, we'll come out ahead.'

Bert makes an appointment for the following week, and he and Andy have a long chat with a bloke called Thomaso Scarpetta who specialises in criminal law. As far as Andy is concerned, Mr Scarpetta asks too many questions that are hard to answer. Bert helps out with time frames, scenarios and players. Bert adds the qualification that it is *to the best of his recollection of what Andy has told him.*

Mr Scarpetta winds up the meeting with, 'I'm glad you came in. This way, if anything comes to pass, I've got all the background. If anyone is going to be charged, it can be sooner or later, depending on how long it takes the police to get everything together. And don't let your guard down as far as the bikers are concerned because they never forget.'

Andy has mentioned that he's heard bikes in their street at night—just a low burble to and fro past the house, and that he can't get back to sleep. Bert hadn't heard them except for the night they brought the security box home.

They leave the Legal Aid office planning to have lunch in a nearby corner café. It's adjacent to the court precinct so it's filled with legal types and clerical staff: men in business suits and black shoes, the women in tight skirts with sheer black stockings and heels. There's a young Nordic-looking couple in T-shirts, but not a tradesman or blue-singletted labourer in sight. The menu is all wraps and melts on focaccia. Bert is not even sure what they are, and neither he nor Andy wants to sit amongst the boisterous crowd. Bert buys two ready-to-go plain meat and salad sandwiches and two bottles of orange juice, all of which he can carry in a bag, and they amble toward Newcastle Beach. It takes only a few minutes to stroll around a corner and down the hill to the esplanade.

It's not a great day for the beach but it is holiday season. A few ardent surfers are taking a lunch-time dip and some wetsuit-wearing boys bob on boards out the back, waiting for a wave. Bert and Andy find a bench on the concourse to sit and eat. The salty heaviness and fresh tang of the sea air stir Andy's beach memories. He hasn't been in the sea or close to it for a long time but his physicality recalls the surf: chilly at first and tugging at his legs; sand shifting under his feet with the flow of water returning from the shore; the shock of cold spray lashing his trunk; and the moment of total immersion diving under a wave. Then, further out, the lifting swells, the slap of curling crests on his face... He wants to do it all again.

'I want to go for a swim, Bert,' Andy says.

Bert responds, 'Looks okay, don't it? We can't today—no swimmers—so let's aim to get here another day before it cools off. I doubt we'll get Clara into the water but you never know.'

Andy looks at his legs and then at his right arm. 'It wouldn't matter in the water, would it... that they're no good?'

Bert nudges Andy's shoulder. 'They'll be just dandy in the water.'

There's plenty to watch: a posse of bikini clad girls on the water's edge giggle and kick splashes of water onto each other in view of four youths playing tip; a lone, burqa-clad woman plays in the sand with two youngsters—perhaps a single man on another seat is her husband; a lean old man in budgie smugglers and joggers, with sagging, dark brown, leathery skin like an ill-fitting glove, shuffles along the concourse. It calms Andy to see the rest of the world having a good time.

He and Bert stroll around the flat foreshore past the ocean baths to Nobby's Beach. They continue to The Breakwater and walk along the broad concrete path till they're level with Nobby's, the mound of a headland that is the southern land edge of Newcastle Port. They've walked a long way but they're not in a hurry and can rest when they please. Andy is intrigued by the colossal pieces of rock that make up the breakwater wall. It stretches further out for hundreds of metres but they don't go all the way.

Bert says, 'Nobby's was much higher and an island when the colonials first got here in the early 1800s. They thought it was a good place to send the difficult convicts from Sydney—the extra hardship of tougher conditions, and all that. The army got the convicts to cut the top off Nobby's and used the rock as fill to make a causeway to the shore. Then they could get out here easily and use the high point for a lighthouse and lookout.

'They found coal hereabouts early on, and look what that's led to: the whole bloody Hunter Valley being dug up and carted away. Underground is one thing—it's more dangerous for the miners, and more expensive, but open cut rips the guts out of everything. Mining companies reckon they *remediate* the land. Bollocks! A hundred years later it still won't be any use for farming! It's all very well to be earning export income for Australia, but we've still got to live here. What's more important than being able to feed ourselves?'

Small boats have been dallying around the harbour mouth and two tugs powered past half an hour ago to a vessel not far out. A helicopter went overhead with the port pilot, and now the massive coal carrier is approaching the narrow harbour entrance.

'They must have known we were coming. What a whopper!' Bert is agog at the size of the ship.

They have to look up steeply to see the superstructure and grin as the bow wave rushes to the breakwater and slaps up between the rocks. Fishermen wind in their lines and snatch up their gear till the ship passes. Walking back toward the train station they pass a small beach on the harbour side of the spit of land and breakwater.

'Look at that!' Andy points in delight at the sight of dogs frolicking on the beach, feinting and teasing, chasing each other or sticks thrown into the water and along the sand.

Bert looks at a sign above the beach and reads, '*Horseshoe Beach. Dogs permitted off-lead.* Well, I'll be... That's good to see. Dogs aren't allowed to run around in most public parks and beaches.'

'Casper would love it, wouldn't he?' Andy adds, grinning.

Andy is quiet on the trip to Maitland. Recollections have been stirred and he's been alerted to pleasures that are still available to him, even in his new life. The interview with Mr Scarpetta recedes and he's happy to let the bad memories of the fire and Leo fade: he may never have to trawl through them again.

Chapter Twenty-five

Three weeks later, just when life is beginning to feel normal, there's a telephone call from Newcastle Police.

'Mr Contopolous, will you attend Newcastle Police Station tomorrow morning at ten o'clock to assist with our enquiries into the death of Leo Schwartz? You may bring a legal adviser with you.'

When Andy's face freezes and the phone falls to his lap, Bert seizes it and continues the conversation.

Clara drives them in the next morning and Mr Scarpetta meets them outside the station. Andy is shaking so much that Clara has to help him through the door. She hugs him when they're inside.

'Don't you worry none, Andy. There's good people looking out for you,' she says. Clara fidgets and Bert glowers in the waiting area as Andy and Mr Scarpetta are led to an interview room. Exchanges take place between the solicitor and the officers, there's a brief interview, and Andy is told he will be charged. He's led to the custody area adjacent to the cells where the charge is read by the sergeant on duty: *You, Andreas Contopoulos, on the fourteenth day of January two thousand and one at Greta in the state of New South Wales did murder Leo Schwartz...*

Mr Scarpetta explains to Andy, 'You are now under arrest. That means you're in custody and must go to a cell downstairs. I'm applying immediately for bail for you and we should get it. If we do, you can go home with Bert today. If I can't get before a magistrate today, you'll have to stay in custody, in the cell overnight, and we'll go before a magistrate tomorrow.'

What Mr Scarpetta says barely registers with Andy. He's numbed by the charge: that he, *Andreas Contopoulos... did murder Leo Schwartz.* The few words of Mr Scarpetta that Andy hears are gobbledegook.

A custody officer helps him up and escorts him along unfamiliar hallways and down stairs. He's admitted to the cell and the door clangs shut. Andy feels like a puppet inserted into a movie set. He sits on the bed and wonders how he got there; he merges with the steely coldness of metal bars and bed frames, and is in the same position two hours later when he's checked on.

Mr Scarpetta manages to get the application for bail heard mid-afternoon. Andy is taken to the court where Mr Scarpetta appears for him. Despite the Prosecution's opposition, the solicitor convinces the magistrate that although the charge is serious, Andy is not a flight risk and is not likely to commit further offences, and he will comply with any bail conditions. Bail is granted and Andy is remanded to his next appearance. He goes home with Bert.

THE DAY AFTER his arrest Bert mobilises Andy to see Esther.

'You can't drop your bundle now, Andy. Get up and get going. Come to Maitland with me on the bus. There's one of them new ones running today with the drop-down entrance platform. It'll be like a ride at the Easter Show. And by the way, it was the Access Committee started calls for that bus.'

During the ride Bert repeats to Andy the conversation he had with Clara that morning.

'Adeline's heart problem has been fixed with stents, whatever they are. They should do the trick and she'll be fine for the rest of her days with medication. The doctors want her to stay in a bit longer for observation. And get this: Adeline told Clara she thinks you're a fine young man and she's very pleased for you and Esther to be keeping company.'

'Really?' Andy swells and smiles, but then deflates. 'She may not think the same when she hears I've been charged with murder. It gives me the heebies just to say it.'

Bert doesn't want to think about it, either. He says, 'The big news for the ladies is that they've been granted refugee status: they can live in the community and they can apply for permanent residency straight away.

'Clara reckons that's most of the battle won. They'll get emergency housing in Maitland as soon as they leave hospital. She's been badgering the local politician on their behalf to get some sort of minimum benefits for them. The reward for the pollie is that Clara has told the *Maitland Comet* all about it, so it should make the paper and there'll be heart-warming karma all round.'

At the hospital Bert visits Adeline while Andy and Esther go into the garden. They hold hands as they walk but he won't talk.

'What is wrong, Andy? You are unwell?' Esther asks.

When they sit he turns to face her. 'Something awful happened yesterday. The police think I killed Leo and they arrested me for his murder. I'm allowed out, though, on bail.'

Esther draws back as if Andy is contaminated. She moves further away along the bench and gasps, with two hands holding her face. Fear of police with trumped-up charges, and dread of association with criminals could be in her genes. Does Andy know she kicked Mr Leo in the head so they could escape the fire?

Neither can speak. They stare at each other as the sparkle in their eyes dies.

———————•———————

ANDY AND BERT meet with Mr Scarpetta, or Tommo, as he says to call him, who explains the legal process: the Brief of Evidence will be served and must be replied to; a Committal Hearing date will be set. Andy must appear in court on each occasion and he will be remanded to the next appearance. Mr Scarpetta will apply for bail to be continued each time.

Mr Scarpetta says, 'I'll be your solicitor, Andy, and you'll need to make a Legal Aid contribution toward costs.'

Bert undertakes to cover it.

'Now, a Committal Hearing is where a magistrate decides if there's enough evidence for a trial. The

Prosecution has to put all their evidence together and give us a copy—that's the Brief of Evidence. It includes the evidence they will rely on, witness statements, forensic information and medical reports. Charges are almost never thrown out at the committal stage, so because a trial is likely, the Defence, that's us, establishes as much as we can to our advantage at the Committal stage.

'We will have a Public Defender to represent you at a trial, Andy. Public Defenders are barristers employed by the state to appear for people on serious charges when they can't afford to get their own. They're all top notch. I'm trying to get a Mr Davis: he's the best of the lot in my book.'

The subtleties are lost on Andy, who offers, 'I did nothing wrong, and even if there's a trial, I'm innocent and people will say so.'

Tommo adds, 'Just so you know, the Coroner ruled that Goob Spitall's death was accidental, and there are no suspicious circumstances surrounding the death of the young fellow who shared his van, but there are questions hanging over how Mr Schwartz died. The police think you know how the fire started and that you had a hand in it. In their eyes, if that's true, then you are responsible for Mr Schwartz's death.'

———•———

WHEN THEY NEXT see Tommo he tells them, 'The Prosecution brief has been served on us. Their witnesses include Lola Montgomery, Adeline Schönburg and Esther Schönburg.'

'How can they do that? They're my friends. They all

know me. Will they say bad things about me? That's not fair. Why are they witnesses for the other side?' Andy is perplexed.

Tommo says, 'That's how it works. We'll get to ask them questions, too.'

Tommo quizzes Andy on the fire again. 'You said in your statement you saw the fire start when someone danced under the tarp with a firebrand. You also said there was a strong smell of petrol at the back. Even though you risked your life to rescue Esther, people have been known to start a fire just so they can be a hero by putting it out, or by rescuing someone. You didn't know Esther was tied up inside, so you could have thought she'd just run out. The Prosecution will try to make a case that you did start it, and that you knew what you were doing.'

They've talked about Lola, but Andy hasn't told anyone how sure he is that it was Lola's flaming torch that set the tarp alight. Mr Scarpetta has been to see her at a women's refuge in Newcastle and he's still wondering at her unusual slant on the world. *Not quite in touch with reality and a weird way of seeing things* was how he summed her up.

Adeline has reluctantly given a statement. It's short and she tries not to take a position:... *Mr Leo looked after me and Esther but he was not kind in other ways. I could see he was not a good man when he took Esther away...* She covers how Andy rescued Esther, how Goob went into the fire and came out with a metal box which he dropped into a drum, and how he plunged back into the flames.

Adeline's doctors have issued a statement to the effect that her health precludes attendance at court.

Strangely, Esther shows little interest in the preparations for Andy's defence. She has recovered from the shock of his news and treats him tenderly when they're together: they see each other often; he takes her to the movies and for walks and shopping and out for lunch; he's even been looking in jeweller shop windows at diamond rings. He saved her life and would have died trying. Now she appears uninterested in what's happening to him and won't talk about the committal.

Clara has been to see Tommo and has taken a shine to him. From her time as a youth worker, she knows most of the hard work for the Defence in a trial takes place after the committal, but she's seen Tommo throw himself into the preparations for Andy's matter already. He's been casting the net widely to gather information and background statements from Sydney doctors about Andy's injuries.

Clara has offered to do whatever she can to help. 'I've known Andy almost as long as anyone up here and before that I worked with young people for yonks. I know a good one when they come along.'

Clara also advises Andy to put his best foot forward. 'If it comes to a trial everything helps, including character. Folk in the jury box will always run their eye over you, and some might fancy they can read a lot into your appearance. All the kind and positive things you do will show in your face. That's what I believe. Look at Bert's rough head: that shows he's been up to no good most of his life… just kidding, Andy. I think he got off to a difficult start as an ugly baby. I'm still kidding,' she adds in response to Andy's perplexed look.

Andy enrols in a small business management course at TAFE—not that he wants to go into business, but it will show what he's capable of doing. And if character becomes relevant, it will be an indication to the court that he's prepared to work hard and be constructive.

Clara persists in trying to persuade Esther to do some HSC subjects at TAFE. She's clearly intelligent and Adeline has given her a good grounding, but Esther demurs.

Thanks to Bert regularly feeding titbits to Jason Lemesurier, there's been a steady trickle of items in the paper about Greta's fortunate evasion of a casino, and about the fate of residents from Leo's. Andy is mentioned several times, often on the same page as articles about where Maitland is heading and the upcoming local government elections. Clara is checking if Andy is eligible to be a candidate. If he wants to stay in the area, and if he did want to stand, good publicity is an advantage.

Chapter Twenty-six

Andy's mum rings on the morning of the committal. She's frantic.

Andy says, 'Don't worry, Mum. It's a committal hearing. I've told them I didn't start the fire. It will be all right.'

He's forgotten Tommo's warning that charges are unlikely to be dropped at the committal stage.

'And thanks for sending up my suit and the new shirt, and the money. Don't make Dad angry, though.'

Mum has told Andy that she takes the money out of the housekeeping. She doesn't care that his dad asks where is the lobster or exotic fruit-out-of-season they used often to eat. She doesn't tell her husband where the money is going, just that she hasn't been to the markets. Nor does she admit she'd rather eat bread and water, if she must, in order to help Andy.

She rings when Andy's dad is out. She started doing that after they received the newspaper article about Andy's heroism in the fire. 'He read it and put it away,' she tells Andy. 'But I see him get it out and read it when he thinks I'm busy. He loves you, I know.'

•———————•

CLARA ADJUSTS THE knot in Andy's tie before they leave the house at Greta. Andy isn't embarrassed by the attention because his mother always trimmed his appearance before he went out. Clara usually has something upbeat to say at difficult times but today she is quiet, concentrating on driving during peak hour. Bert gazes out the window, lost in thoughts punctuated by growls deep in his throat.

They park close to the courthouse and Clara helps Andy twist into his coat when he gets out of the car. Mr Scarpetta meets them on the footpath.

The upcoming process has been explained to Andy many times. During the proceedings he must be calm and appear interested: the accused can't take a favourable outcome for granted even though he knows he's innocent of the charge. He's told again that matters are rarely dismissed at this stage.

Bert and Clara make their way into the public gallery. Andy and Mr Scarpetta take their seats in the body of the court and the process begins. Neither side is calling witnesses at this point. The magistrate listens intently to submissions from a senior solicitor from the DPP, that's from the Office of the Director of Public Prosecutions, and from Mr Scarpetta, who draws attention to the fire officers' report that found evidence of accelerants on the ground behind Leo's van.

He tells them to come back next week, by which time he'll have made up his mind whether Andy will be committed to stand trial. The court is adjourned.

A WEEK LATER Andy's heart is pounding as he again sits beside Mr Scarpetta at a table near the front of the court. He's dizzy with apprehension. Just a few minutes ago he was sitting in the public gallery with Bert and Clara, and saw a man vanish from the dock, down stairs into a cell in the bowels of the building. It was the matter listed before Andy's—another committal.

The magistrate's words ring in his head, '...strength of the Crown case... sufficient evidence to commit to trial... bail refused... remove the prisoner from the court...'

Prisoner! And the man was gone! Whisked out of sight as if disappearing from the face of the earth. Would he himself also be going down those same stairs before the day was out?

Andy screws around to look into the body of the court and sees Bert giving him the thumbs up. Clara is there and he wishes Esther was there, too. There's also a sheriff's officer at the door and a uniformed policeman standing to one side. The room is unbearably hot: sweat trickles down his legs behind his knees and down the middle of his back. He's struggling for air.

Andy's matter is called on. The magistrate eyeballs Andy and starts to read. He hears the same words as were read out for the previous matter: '...strength of the Crown case... the nature of witness statements... there is a reasonable prospect that a jury would convict the defendant. I therefore commit the defendant to trial.'

Andy is dreading what comes next. To his great relief the magistrate announces, 'Bail continued.'

•————•

THE TERRIFYING TRUTH sinks in over a few days. He's going to be tried for murder. At least he was not spirited away down the stairs to a holding cell, then to a prison van and off to Cessnock Gaol. 'Bail continued'! It's not as if he's free, even if he is allowed to walk around. Part of Andy wants to run back to the psych ward at Maitland Hospital and beg them to shunt him into a drug induced haze, to a pretend peace, a peace of any sort.

'Hrrrh!' growls Bert at the kitchen table to Clara and Andy. 'Told you that Scarpers was suss.'

'Well, I think he did all he could,' says Clara. 'He might appeal against the outcome of the committal, Bert, but he says it rarely changes the fact that there'll be a trial. Let's hope some new evidence comes to light.'

'Hrrrh!' is all Bert can offer.

The phone rings. Clara picks it up and passes the receiver to Bert. It's an old-style unit and the handpiece only just reaches him on the end of the fully-extended coil cord. 'Yeah,' says Bert. 'Yeah,' again after an interval. 'Well, well, well, that's great news, Jason. Thanks for letting us know.'

Bert hands the phone back to Clara who hangs up the receiver. He chortles and rubs his chin.

'Well, Bert, what is it?' Clara demands.

'All in good time, woman. I'm savouring the moment.' But he can't hold back. 'All right then... that was Jason. A professional contact up north has told him that one Spider Dragovic was taken into custody in Queensland a couple of days ago. I reckon our chat with the Newcastle Detectives did the trick.

'There was a warrant out for Spider's arrest in relation to the box me and Andy handed in. The one in the drum at the back of Leo's, with the gun in it. And the bloke he was with, someone called Hippo Jack, from round here, no less, was arrested for good measure at the same time. Apparently one Hippo had a bit to say about a recent fire down this way. Could be good news for you, Andy.'

Bert pauses and adds, 'Poor bugger. Cooperating with the police in Queensland might get him out of gaol up there but he won't last long anywhere if his bikie brothers reckon he's broken the code. Poor bugger.

'We'll get on to Scarpers first thing tomorrow. It's certainly worth following up. But don't get your hopes up because Spider could come up with an alibi for that night, 'specially if he's got someone sharper than Scarpers,' Bert concludes.

Clara ignores the barb and says thoughtfully, 'Lola said in her statement she was one of the people dancing with firebrands. And Andy, you've said that you weren't dancing and that you're sure the fire started when someone went under the tarp? I might go and see Lola. If I explain how important that part is, her memory might improve.'

Andy confirms that's when it started. 'At the front of the van, anyway. And Lola was one of the dancers, but I wouldn't want to say for sure who actually caused it. Don't frighten Lola, though.'

'You know me better than that, Andy.' Clara pauses. 'Tell you what. For Lola's sake, we'll find a solicitor to advise her of her rights. We don't want her to incriminate herself. Surely she'd qualify for Legal Aid.'

Chapter Twenty-seven

'Oh, dearie me,' says Lola. 'That's a shockin' proposal. For him to be charged like that, with murder, I mean. Andy never hurt nobody. He helped us all. Course I'll make another statement. If they end up charging me with something... well, that will be the time to confuse 'em with what goes on inside me head. I'm not stupid, y'know.

'Poor Andy. I'll tell 'em 'ow it 'appened. Leastways, I'll tell 'em what it takes to get Andy in the clear.'

'No,' says Ms Wright, Lola's solicitor. 'Tell them exactly how it happened. It must be a truthful statement that stands up to cross-examination.'

'Yeah, that's right,' says Lola. 'It all 'appened on the sperm of the moment. I'll be very pacific. There was a fire in the drum, we was all dancin', I stuck a branch in the drum, it caught fire and I kept on dancing. Away from the drum it was pretty dark and I couldn't see I was dancing under the tarp. Suddenly it caught on. Whoof! Up she went. What a beautiful sight! Pretty soon after the front fire started she went up at the back, too. Took off like a tornado. Don't you love a good fire? What a beauty that was!

''cept that it killed people,' Lola adds, controlling her zeal. 'I'll tell 'em again, simple like, so they understand.'

Clara wants Andy to be cleared, but not by dumping Lola in deep trouble. Chances are Lola will be believed as to how the fire started and her age and diminished understanding of what she was doing could reduce the likelihood of prosecution. Clara suspects Lola knew full-well what she was doing.

Lola agrees to make a fresh statement at Newcastle Police Station in the company of Ms Wright.

⸺•⸺

ANDY FEELS AS if he's in suspended animation: hung on a high hook and watching the earth spin beneath him. On bail he has freedom of movement and thought but he can't think of anything other than the imminent trial. Mr Scarpetta didn't manage to get him off at the committal, so will the trial go the same way? At least a Public Defender will represent him next time. Those PDs are top notch criminal barristers. Jason Lemesurier told him that.

Andy sits through hours of meetings with Mr Scarpetta. Sometimes Mr Davis, the PD, is there. The ground they cover is staggering: Andy's whole life; his family; the accident; his psychiatric and medical background; why he was at Leo's; everything he knew about Leo and other people in the van park; the bikers and whatever he knew about them. Esther is a frequent topic. After all, her presence in Leo's van triggered the rebellious gathering that led to the fire.

Andy's lawyers have to be sure of his motives for being present when the fire started. Was it possible that Esther spurned Andy and had chosen to team up with Leo? If Andy believed that was possible, would he have lit the fire to have revenge on them both?

Andy is flabbergasted by the question and manages only a ragged response: there's a thousand reasons why Esther would never voluntarily go to Leo, and even if she did, there was one reason—one reason that was bigger than his life, why he would never hurt her.

Mr Davis gets Andy's drift. He says, 'Andy, the Prosecution will ask you questions like that. They'll try to establish motives that discredit you. We need to know how you'll answer.

'So far, the police have got you lighting the fire at the front. We want to show that the fire at the front was accidentally caused by another party, and that the fire that actually set the caravan alight was started at the rear by persons unknown. There were other events at the back: you saw two figures running off, and Adeline saw something while you were getting Esther out.

'On that score, though, we have the information about Spider Dragovic and his off-sider, Hippo Jack, being arrested in Queensland. Spider is facing other charges but Hippo panicked and spouted off about a fire at a caravan park at Greta and how he didn't know that's what Spider was up to. And, what's more, he was 'shocked and horrified' to see petrol poured under a van which may have belonged to a man called Leo Schwartz. At the same time there was some kind of riot going on out front, he recalled.

'He's back in New South Wales, but not in custody, and Mr Scarpetta has been out to see him. We're going to call him. We couldn't ask for anything better than his statement. As long as he stays alive or isn't got-at to shut up, he's our best witness. Mr Scarpetta warned him to keep a low profile because his former associates might be after him. Unfortunately, we can't offer him any protection.'

Mr Davis pauses and adds, 'I don't like his chances long term. Let's hope he stays safe long enough to get to court.

'Moving on now. We've had an independent scientific investigator go over all the forensic evidence for the fire: you know, where the seat of it was, and whether accelerants were used. What he says supports what you say, Andy. He believes petrol was poured out at the back and that it's likely some of it ran under the van and was ignited by a spark from the fire at the front.'

In his interview as a witness at Greta, Andy described his stay in the psychiatric ward of Maitland Hospital, but Mr Davis won't introduce the episode in evidence.

'It's not in our interest to do so,' he says. 'If we run a mental illness defence and you're found not guilty but on the grounds of mental illness, there's no sentence, just ongoing detention with periodic assessment to see if you're fit to be released. You could be held for the rest of your life.

'Nor are we claiming Diminished Responsibility— it's called *Substantial Impairment* now. If we raise it, it could work in the Prosecution's favour as it suggests a greater likelihood of your doing something silly and would give the jury an easy way out to find you not guilty of murder, but guilty of manslaughter. So, you would still get a sentence, possibly mitigated because of impairment. That's an option we don't want to give them. Andy, I'm after a straight *Not guilty* for you.

'But we will use medical reports about your accident in Sydney because that runs to your physical strength. Our position is simply that you didn't light the fire, not that you did it and there were mitigating circumstances.

'We've had all reference to your admission to the psychiatric ward removed from the transcript. I've had a meeting with the Crown and they won't insist on introducing the Maitland Hospital stay, either. We'll confirm the Crown's position in court before any evidence is given. I'll talk to the judge prior to the trial.'

Andy struggles to follow the legal arguments. With the mention of mental health, he asserts, 'But I have changed. I'm better than I used to be before the accident. I mean, I think I'm nicer to other people. I understand why they do things and what they're thinking, and even what sort of person they are.'

'Mmm,' says Mr Davis. 'We'll think about that. By the way, how's things with Esther? You're still seeing her, yes?'

'We're good,' Andy says weakly. 'Her mum is out of hospital and they've been living in hostels and motels till something better comes up. Bert invited them to his place but Adeline wouldn't do it.'

Tommo says, 'Just as well, Andy, because your bail conditions have changed. Because Esther is a Crown witness, they don't want you seeing her or her mother before the trial. You can't visit them again till it's finished.'

Andy would like to be with Esther all day every day—she's the font of his hope for the future. Her love is a cloak against adversity, and her auras reassure him, but since the committal she's been slow to take his offered hand and less responsive when they kiss. It's as if she doesn't want to disappoint him. Bert and Clara keep him grounded and focused on what needs to be done, but being near Esther and winning her heart has been the motivation for every act of self-improvement. This new restriction takes him back to when Esther was imprisoned in her van. At least he knows she's safe now. Andy doesn't know how much separation he can take and retreats into his room at Bert's.

The trial is a week away.

———•———

Mr Scarpetta receives a communication from the Office of the Director of Public Prosecutions. If Andy agrees to a plea of guilty, they'll reduce the charge to *Manslaughter*. There would still be a conviction on his record and a lesser sentence than if he were found guilty of murder. The lesser sentence could be eight or nine years. Tommo has to put the offer to Andy but he and Mr Davis are not in favour.

Bert is ropeable at the very suggestion. 'You didn't do it, Andy. Get in there and fight the bastards. The offer just means they're worried their case is weak.'

'That's right,' says Andy. 'I did nothing wrong. They'll see that.'

———•———

ON THE DAY before the trial Tommo rings with bad news: Hippo Jack has been shot and he died in hospital. They've got the record of interview from his arrest in Queensland but a live witness would be better. The police rushed to get a further statement but Tommo doesn't know what's in it, or even if they got one. Such statements can be powerful evidence in court.

Tommo reminds Bert, 'Spider's in custody in Queensland in relation to the gun in the box. The ballistics must have added up and the charge is likely to be murder of the detective at Kurri Kurri. It can only be a suspicion at the moment—could have been Leo fired the gun. But I guess if it was in Leo's possession and Spider was trying to get it back, it points at Spider again. He'll be extradited to New South Wales.

'The police would have been keen to get Hippo's statement because he was a long-term associate of Spider's and could have witnessed the detective's murder. We know Hippo had a loose tongue, so Spider couldn't risk him 'assisting the police' further. Spider could have got word out to silence Hippo. That's an assumption, of course, just a possible scenario.

'Perhaps all Hippo had time to tell the police was who shot him. He might have thought there was no risk with Spider in custody, or that he was too good for anyone who came after him. I'd say the last thing on his mind would have been the fire at Leo's but we've got to hope he said something about it.'

Bert tells Andy only the parts that will boost his confidence.

Chapter Twenty-eight

The trial is underway. Andy is sure his jacket is moving in rhythm with his drumming heart.

As instructed, Andy was at court early to run through a few points. He was composed mounting the steps of Newcastle Court—that challenge distracted him from the day's business, and the chat in the Defence conference room was similar to many over recent weeks. The courtroom itself, on the other hand, has focal points of attention: the judge, the jury, the accused made prominent by isolation in the dock, and the table near the front where the Defence and the Prosecution sit—Defence to the left and Prosecution to the right, closer to the jury box. The Prosecution comprises a Public Prosecutor who is a barrister from the DPP, and a solicitor instructing her. Andy has managed to remember some new information.

He tries not to look at the Prosecutor, whose name is Ms Kemble, and she could change his life. There's a slight rock in her walk yet she reminds Andy of an old-style steamroller: she's not that big, of course, but she's tall and solid and relentless in manner. She's gruff with her instructing solicitor, a tense young man, whereas by comparison, Mr Davis is paternal with Tommo.

Andy wonders why someone would work hard to have

him convicted and gaoled rather than to cooperatively discover the truth. What an odd job she has. Such is the adversarial system Mr Davis described. The Prosecution will attempt to prove beyond reasonable doubt that the charge is valid by presenting evidence and witnesses: the Defence will attempt to disprove the Crown case, or at the very least, cast doubt on it. It's up to the jury, after they've considered all the evidence, to decide whether the Prosecution has proved their case beyond reasonable doubt, that is, whether the accused is guilty as charged, or not.

The judge will sum up the respective cases for the jury at the end of the trial and direct the jurors as to the law they must apply. The judge will also pronounce sentence if the accused is found guilty.

Mr Davis applied to have Andy sit out of the dock but permission was denied so Andy is confined to a space even smaller than a caravan or a prison cell. A Corrective Services officer stands beside the dock. Who knows why? Mr Davis asks for the officer to sit away from the accused but the application is refused. Andy is no security risk.

Sitting in the raised box on a hard seat feels akin to a medieval pillory. Andy half-expects to be pelted with rotten fruit and eggs. For a person presumed innocent, as are all accused till a verdict of guilty is delivered, the scrutiny of so many people is enervating. He's been told not to squirm because the seat will squeak, and restless unease is a sign of guilt. But he's uncomfortable to the point of muscle spasms, and so many sets of searching eyes unnerve him.

First things first. The jury must be empanelled. When Andy is in the dock, legal counsel are in place, and court staff have taken up positions, forty potential jurors enter the room and shuffle into seats in the public area at the back of the court. There's a single row of seats empty behind them, then a few members of the public.

Andy sees Jason Lemesurier among them and the journalist offers an affirming nod. There's also a sprinkling of people unknown to Andy. They're the regulars at murder trials: ghouls and retirees who view court activity as free entertainment, and perhaps conscientious citizens who like to see the legal system in action. Others Andy might hope to see are not present: Esther, Bert, Clara and Lola are to be called as witnesses so they're not permitted in the court because they might come into contact with prospective jurors.

'All rise!' announces a court officer and everyone who is seated does so, turning to watch Her Honour, Justice Yvonne Fairwether enter. Even bewigged and gowned, she's a diminutive figure who, at less than five feet tall and with mouse-like features, lacks presence. She mounts a few steps to the bench and trips along to her chair. There's either a stack of pillows on the seat or it's wound up to its maximum height or both, because once seated she is visible over the bench. From how she struggled up, there must also be a footstool to help her climb. Her appearance is no surprise to the court staff and counsel, but there's a flurry of whispered comments from the jury candidates.

Before jurors can be selected, the nature of the case is

explained and the opportunity given to request exemption from service. This is likely to be granted by the judge if arising from professed bias, familiarity with a witness, or substantial personal reasons. The process begins.

Andy stands while the Judge's Associate reads the indictment: 'That Andreas Phillipas Contopoulos on the fourteenth day of January 2001 at Greta in the State of New South Wales you did murder Leopold Schwartz.' She asks, 'How do you plead, Guilty or Not Guilty?'

'Not Guilty,' says Andy. It's difficult to get out any sound, and when he does, he has trouble modulating his voice between shouting and clear announcement.

The Prosecutor gives a brief description of the allegation and the witnesses she intends to call. They include Detective Crossley, Lola Montgomery, Esther Schönburg and a number of experts. The potential jurors listen intently. One applies to be excused because her sister died in a house fire, and two others because they're caring for elderly parents or a sick child. They are excused and depart.

The process continues. The selection of jurors is strategically important—Andy's fate hangs in their hands. They're his peers, but who is equal to whom? How can twelve people with no knowledge of his life judge what he's alleged to have done? They'll be offered insight into his life and character but how can they understand experiences so different from their own?

Mr Davis earlier discussed with Andy how the next step works. Twelve candidates are randomly called to take a seat in the jury box. Andy is to signal if he knows any of them or has other insights. Adverse auras don't count. The Prosecution and the Defence each has the right to reject a fixed number of candidates. The Defence might object to a person not of the gender or age likely to empathise with a young man like Andy, or to an apparent prude who could be tough on a young person. They'll be rejected. The Prosecution may not favour a person they deem like-minded to the accused, or even potentially so. For every person rejected, another will be called from the pool. A new candidate may be worse than the previous rejection so counsel must try to keep a rejection in reserve.

Andy rests his hands on the rail in the dock. Part of him is still treating the trial as if it's a play. It will end however the play ends and everyone will go home. Another part of him can barely deal with what he knows is happening—that he's on trial for murder and if he's found guilty he'll go to prison for a long time. *But I was helping* he tells himself again. He remembers what Mr Davis told him: *Just because you're innocent, it doesn't mean you'll be found not guilty. We have to refute the Crown allegations by disproving their evidence or by introducing significant doubt. We will use forensic and circumstantial evidence and witnesses to do so.* Andy accepts this is no play. He tries to sit still on the creaky wooden bench.

The selection process drags on. When the empanelled jurors have taken the oath, twelve pairs of eyes dart around the room following exchanges between court officers, staff and legal representatives. At quiet moments they inspect Andy who strives to appear normal and relaxed. He, in turn, scans the jurors: eight women and four men, ranging in age from about thirty to seventy. Some have auras and some do not. They sit so close together it's impossible to read any of it. They're as confused as he is.

The Prosecution and the Defence are invited to each make an opening address.

Ms Kemble goes first for the DPP. 'Your Honour, the Prosecution will attempt to show that Mr Contopoulos did set fire to the caravan with the knowledge that Mr Schwartz and Miss Schönburg were inside and that he had a motivation for doing so. There is evidence that Mr Contopoulos had a primary role in planning the confrontation with Mr Schwartz, and that this confrontation led to the fire which caused the death of Mr Schwartz. We are aware evidence might be led concerning the accused's diminished physical capacity, but we maintain he was capable of starting the fire and that he did so either intentionally or recklessly.

'Our witnesses include Detective Crossley, Ms Esther Schönburg and Mrs Lola Montgomery. We will also call expert witnesses, including one who will give evidence as to the cause and seat of the fire. Thank you.'

Mr Davis doesn't always make an opening address, but today he wants to sow seeds of doubt about the Prosecution from the outset. He stands up at the bar table and grips the sides of his gown. He acknowledges Justice Fairwether with a slight nod and turns to the jury.

'My colleague in the Prosecution presents an interesting summary but many of her assertions are incomplete or incorrect. The Defence will readily refute the charges. Primarily, Mr Contopoulos was not responsible for organising the confrontation with Mr Schwartz that led to the fire, nor did he light the fire that caused the death of Mr Schwartz. We will show that, on the contrary, the accused showed extraordinary courage in rescuing Miss Schönburg from the fire. We will also show that Mr Contopoulos is a young man of strong moral fibre and great compassion.

'As well as cross-examining the Prosecution witnesses, we will call Mr Herbert Foster and Mrs Clara McGregor.'

The Prosecution calls their first witness. Detective Crossley takes the stand. Yes, he attended the scene of the fire on the morning after. Yes, he took statements in Greta from witnesses but there weren't many. The caravan park had eighteen permanent residents but only three came forward.

Andy's long statement from the morning after is tendered by agreement, and read to the jury. Detective Crossley recounts parts of it in response to questions: Andy was in the vicinity of Mr Schwartz's van when the fire started. No, he did not try to put the fire out and nor did he call the fire brigade. Yes, Miss Schönburg, the woman the accused is described as 'having feelings for', was in the van with Mr Schwartz and did not come out when called, even when the fire started and Mr Schwartz was seen to collapse inside the van.

The detective gave evidence to the effect that the

accused did not appear to be distressed over the death of Mr Schwartz and his associate. In the course of Ms Kemble's examination, he gave evidence from which the question of motive could arise.

Mr Davis steps forward. In cross-examination the Defence should ask only questions to which they already know the response, and believe the answers will favour their client. Detective Crossley is a seasoned witness who believes in Andy's guilt so he resorts to unresponsive answers to point in that direction. He's dedicated to having charges proven. It's nothing to do with liking or disliking the accused: it looks good on his own service record to have convictions recorded when he's conducted the investigation.

Mr Davis tries to draw answers that favour Andy. It's akin to pulling teeth. The detective also manages to infuse speculation into his answers. 'No,' he says. 'The accused did not express hostility to Mr Schwartz—but obviously did not like him.'

'Objection,' says Mr Davis. 'I ask for that response to be struck out. That answer was not responsive to the question. I ask Your Honour to warn the witness.'

The judge obliges but the jury has already heard the remark.

Detective Crossley agrees that the accused claimed to see unidentified men leaving from the back of Leo's van, but he's skilled at nuancing his answers without overstepping the mark, and manages to infer animosity between the gang and Andy, as well as between the gang and the deceased.

Mr Davis wants to substantiate the bikies' presence at the van park and their potential contribution to the fire. Before the trial he subpoenaed the list of items in the box retrieved by Andy and Bert from the drum. The judge, the DPP and Mr Davis have been through a process already, in the absence of the jury, to have the list and the contents admitted in evidence.

He refreshes Detective Crossley's memory with the list, and in due course the list and the gun are formally tendered. The presence in the box of a gun, since linked to the murder of a police officer several years ago, is established. It is also established that suspicion has hung over the chapter of bikies in the Greta area, where the officer died, and that Spider Dragovic is a member of that chapter.

Mr Davis is dogged. It's been made apparent to the court that Leo had enemies amongst people with a reputation for taking the law into their own hands. Detective Crossley leaves the witness box less cockily than when he entered it.

•————————•

TWELVE DAYS HAVE been set aside for the trial. Andy hasn't mentioned his parents for weeks but Bert and Clara believe his mum and dad deserve the opportunity to support Andy if they're inclined to do so.

At the end of the first day in court, Bert says, 'I've run this by Scarpers, and he's spoken to Mr Davis, and they agree, Andy, it will do your case no harm to have your parents in the gallery. Clara and I think they wouldn't like you to be going through this on your own. And you're not, you've got us. Anyway, we rang them today and they'll get here tomorrow afternoon. Clara told them you've got a good group behind you, and truth will out.'

Andy is apprehensive. 'How did Dad sound?' he asks.

Clara answers. 'I only spoke to your mum. She was upset to hear what's been going on. She thought when there was no news after the committal that the charges had been dropped. She was hoping you were sorting things out and finding your feet. She wants to know if the money she puts into your account is enough. She's upset you haven't answered her letters and she wants you to write back to your Aunty Zoe's house. She puts that address on every letter.'

Andy hangs his head and says, 'I don't know what to write. I don't want to tell lies, but I can't think what else to say.'

Chapter Twenty-nine

Day two of the trial. Andy is keen to get going. He's buoyant this morning because yesterday a letter came from Esther. His heart quickened when he saw it, and it soared when he read it.

Dearest Andy she began. 'I'm her *dearest*, I'm her *dearest*,' he repeated to himself. He would have been happy with just that, but he read the rest, again and again.

I am most sad we are apart during the horrible process of your trial. I cannot understand why it is happening. I miss you every day and dream of you at night. I pray you are in good health. Mama and I are both well.

We have had excellent news. We have each been granted a visa. It gives us permission to stay while official papers are created for us. Clara has been of great assistance and accompanies us to interviews with officials. She is personally of the opinion that we will be given 'residency' status.

I am writing to tell you this good news and to give you courage. I know you did only brave and good things at Mr Leo's. We must have faith that you will not be blamed for his death. I wish you also to understand why I was not more outspoken in the months before your trial. Because I was at that time a person of no consequence, and possibly considered by the state as a troublemaker or political agitator, I feared that anything I said would be suspected. Your reputation might have been diminished by association with a suspicious person and my words may have worked against you. I could not have borne that. Now that Mother and I are allowed to be here, my words will be respected, I am sure. I will happily tell the world how you saved my life, and the other brave things you have done.

There's more good news. A community refugee support group has undertaken to find suitable housing for them. Esther tells of Adeline's surprise at being described as a refugee rather than the criminal or illegal person Mr Leo said she was. The kindness with which mother and daughter have been treated has reduced Adeline to tears, but they're tears of happiness.

———————

THE CROWN CALLS their next witness. It's Lola. When the court officer calls her name in the foyer she all but pushes him aside and totters urgently to the witness box. She takes the oath with unlikely fervour.

Ms Kemble, the prosecutor, advances. 'Now, Mrs Montgomery,...'

'Miss, it's *Miss* Montgomery,' Lola corrects. 'I went back to me maiden name after me husband died in the fire.'

'Which fire would that have been, Miss Montgomery?'

'In the boarding 'ouse where we lived back in the sixties.'

'What sort of landlord was Mr Schwartz at Leo's Hunter Holiday Park, Miss Montgomery?'

Ms Kemble asks questions about other residents and what Lola had seen of the relationship between Esther and Andy. She's establishing a motive for Andy to take revenge on Leo.

'On the night of the fire, Miss Montgomery, did you...?' Ms Kemble steers Lola through events, trying to establish Andy as the leader, the instigator, the one who started the fire.

'Oh, no,' says Lola. 'Was me what started the fire in the drum. Leo used to have a fire there whenever them bikie mongrels came round. It was all ready to go. There's nothin' like a good fire!'

'Miss Montgomery, how big was the fire in the drum?'

'It was about this big,' Lola makes a circle with her arms, 'until the good fire got going.'

'What do you mean by the *good* fire?'

'The big one, course. The one what took the whole van.'

'Did you see how the fire spread from the drum to the tarpaulin, and then to Mr Schwartz's caravan?'

'No. We was all dancing round the place with firebrands and some sparks coulda jumped onto the tarp. One minute there was a little thing in the drum and next moment the tarp and some bits and pieces took off. That weren't much. Then, sudden like, the whole van went up. What a sight! 'cept for the people inside, a course,' she adds apologetically.

'So, in the firelight, you could see the people gathered?'

'Sort of.'

'And what they were doing?'

'They were criss-crossing like ants on fairy floss. Couldn't say who was doin' what, but.'

'Did you see the accused dancing?'

'The who?'

'The accused, Mr Contopoulos, whom you know as Andy.' Ms Kemble points out Andy in the dock.

'Oh, Andy, me mate. No. He can't shift that fast. He stayed pretty still. Him and Adeline.'

'But he can walk, can't he?'

'Yeah.'

'So, is it possible, because there was not enough light to see what everyone was doing, that he could have walked to the caravan?'

'S'pose so,' Lola concludes reluctantly. She knows she's been tricked but isn't sure how. She twitches and casts around for an escape route.

'Thank you, Miss Montgomery. That's all I wish to ask you.'

Lola rises but is asked to stay seated. Mr Davis will cross-examine.

He asks first why she made a second statement to the police.

'Me memory came back better and I thought I should say what 'appened.'

'So, Miss Montgomery, was the protagonist...? Sorry, who started the idea of the residents gathering in front of Mr Schwartz's van?'

'Oh, deftly me,' Lola emphasises. 'I went round all the

vans and told 'em they gotta come out. It was their only chance.'

'Their only chance for what?'

'Why, to make 'is Lordship stop being such an... bully.' Lola glances at the judge.

'What did you say to the accused when you went to his van?'

'I told him he had to be there too if he wanted to see his ladylove again—he's sweet on 'er. I told him he had to talk to Fatso, I mean Leo, 'cos he knew all the words better than the rest of us. I said I'd round everyone up but he said he'd get Adeline. So it was mostly me. Andy just went along with what I poposed. We needed Andy to do the talking 'cause he was the cleverest 'dult there.'

'The cleverest dolt? Ah, adult?'

'Yeah, the cleverest 'dult.'

Lola estimates there were at least twelve people dancing with flaming torches under the tarp. It could have been any one of them, even her, she admits, that spread the fire to the tarp. They clarify that although Andy can walk, Lola definitely did not see him with a firebrand in his hand, or see him move away from Adeline until he took himself, as quickly as he could, around the back of the van to rescue Esther.

'Thank you, Miss Montgomery. Who else did you see at other times visit the caravan park?'

'The bikies. Pretty often and always at night. That's why Leo had the drum set up for a fire.'

Mr Davis cuts her off before she can launch into

another rhapsodic description. 'Do you know what happened during those visits?'

'Piss and pot, mainly.'

'Miss Montgomery, could you please tell us in words everyone present will understand.'

'Righto. Booze and drugs. I used to sneak up just outa sight in the dark and could hear most of what they said. It was all about deals and who was doing what and who owed who what. They were pretty aggro shindigs. Never wanted to get in there meself.'

Mr Davis is happy with Lola's answers. He's established the potential involvement of the bikies: grudges and get-evens over sour business dealings would give them a motive, and they were familiar with the park at night. Lola is discharged.

They move on to the forensic evidence.

The Prosecution tenders, by agreement with the Defence, a statement from a Fire Investigation Officer, and another from a forensic expert. The authors take the stand in turn and describe evidence of accelerants and toxic fumes and lack of fire extinguishers. There's conjecture on the volume of flammable material that was in the vicinity, and how the risk must have been obvious to any person of average capacity.

Mr Davis cross-examines. He gets confirmation of accelerants at the rear of the van, and a discarded jerry can with no cap but still with petrol fumes inside.

Mr Davis has another forensic report that's been prepared for the Defence and he'll call its expert author in due course. The report states that except for the tarpaulin and some cardboard boxes, the flammables at the front would not have been easy to ignite, and they would have been slow burning. On the other hand, if an accelerant such as petrol had been poured at the back and some of it had run under the van to the front, a spark from the burning tarpaulin could have easily ignited a fire that tracked back to the rest of the accelerant and caused fire to erupt. The reports differ little but Mr Davis elects to call the author of the Defence forensic report for emphasis.

⸺•⸺

MUM AND DAD arrive during the lunch break and are brought up to speed by Bert and Clara. They warn Mum not to be upset at the proceedings. Andy is busy with Tommo and Mr Davis so it's not until they're all back in court that he glimpses them in the gallery. He knows the whole trial is not his fault but he feels ashamed to have brought such humiliation upon them. He's embarrassed to be on display in the dock and cannot accustom himself to it, and relaxes only slightly when all eyes in the courtroom focus on someone else, but now his parents are here, he registers their scrutiny.

⸺•⸺

ESTHER IS THE next Prosecution witness. She is bewitching—even more so than when Andy first talked to her among the wrecks at Leo's. Dark hair hangs past her shoulders but the face is that of a mature woman. She's girlishly slender in a demure outfit, and her poise and dignified bearing draw all eyes.

Esther confidently responds to questions about how she and her mother came to be living at Leo's. It's no secret—they've had to tell it all to Immigration and Social Security officers. Her whole face smiles when asked about Andy, so Ms Kemble doesn't pursue that line.

Esther goes so far as to say 'Mr Leo,' as she still calls him, misled her mother to keep them on his premises. At times they thought he was protecting them because he said that if they came to the attention of authorities in Australia they would be deported to Germany and treated harshly. Sometimes in the early days he was kind to them and they believed they were in his debt.

The Prosecutor presses Esther on the details of hers and Adeline's relationship with Leo: how did they pay their rent? They had no Social Security income so what else had they to offer? Ms Kemble and Esther agree on the term *personal favours*.

'From you and your mother? Ms Kemble probes.

'Mr Leo was pressuring me to work at an undesirable establishment in Maitland. I refused.'

Ms Kemble asks if the accused knew what was going on and gets confirmation. It's what she's after as a reason for Andy to detest Leo, and substantiates a motive for Andy to harm him.

She takes Esther back to the van.

'Did you know people were gathering outside that night?'

'No. I was dozing, seated on a chair with my hands tied to a rail.'

'Could you see outside? Could you see who started the fire in the drum?'

'No. When the fire was burning, I could see people moving around, but only a little.'

'Did Mr Schwartz say anything when he came back inside?'

'Only some bad words. Then he fell over. He groaned while he lay on the floor.'

'Did Andy offer to help Mr Schwartz out of the van?'

'Yes. He did attempt to re-enter the van after helping me escape but flames blocked hid entrance.'

'Thank you, Ms Schönburg.' Ms Kemble cuts Esther off because she doesn't want the jury to hear good things about Andy.

But Esther keeps talking to Ms Kemble's back. 'Mr Leo was a very big man and too heavy to carry or drag. Andy knew that but he wanted to try: he was very brave.'

Mr Davis cross-examines in tiny steps and allows Esther's own words to tell the story.

'Yes. Mr Leo knew of the friendship between Andy and me. I heard him tell Andy that I would be released when Andy paid Mr Leo's debt.'

'Had you ever been into Mr Schwartz's van before?'

'No, I had never previously been there.'

'Did you go to Mr Schwartz's van willingly?'

'Definitely not! He took me there by violent force. It was a great shock to my mother to see Mr Leo drag me away. I can never forgive him for that. She has a weak heart and such a sight could have had grave consequences.'

'Why didn't you simply leave the van?'

'Mr Schwartz tied my hands together and tied the rope to a rail so I could not go out.'

'Did Andy come back with the money?'

'He could not get real money so he made a clever trick to seem the debt was paid but Mr Leo was suspicious and did not release me.'

'How did you get out of the van?'

'The fire was already fierce when Andy bravely entered the van and cut the ropes. He guided me out through a hidden door. If he had not come in I would have perished.'

'Did anyone else come in to help, or to save Mr Schwartz?'

'Someone else, I believe it to be the Goob man, came in but he made no attempt to help me and Andy, or Mr Leo. Instead, he took something from a shelf and fled.'

With a few more questions, Mr Davis builds up a picture of Andy as a gentle person who is opposed to violence.

'Had you, Ms Schönburg, ever heard Andy express a desire to harm Mr Schwartz?'

'No.'

'Have you ever heard the accused plan, or seen him commit, any violent act for self-defence or any other reason?'

'No.'

'Do you believe he is capable of starting a fire that would harm people?'

'Never. He was in training to become a doctor. He wishes only to help people.'

Esther is the last Prosecution witness. The Crown closes its case.

Chapter Thirty

Day three. It's time for the Defence to respond to the Crown case. Andy sits in the dock but he won't be there long this morning. He's agreed to take the stand and will be the first defence witness called. The slight familiarity Andy has with courtroom procedure has taken the edge off his nerves. Mum and Dad are in the gallery. Their eyes are glued on Andy as he leaves the dock, enters the witness box and takes the oath. At least he can speak from there.

In preparation, Andy and Mr Davis previewed questions and there'll be no surprises in the answers. They cover how Andy came to be at Leo's and the course of events since then: what he saw the night of the fire; where he was standing when the tarpaulin ignited; his feelings for Esther, and that even if she had chosen to go into Leo's van, Andy would never have endangered her, or sought revenge.

Mr Davis asks Andy what association he had with the bikies. The point is made that Leo compelled Andy to ride with Spider to attend to the dog. Andy had no friendship with Spider but did his best for the dog. As for getting River to hospital, Andy acted solely out of concern for the boy—he was not trying to ingratiate himself with River's parents. Mr Davis asks Andy to describe the shadowy figures behind Leo's van on the night of the fire, and whether or not he recognised them.

'I clearly saw their backs because the fire was strong by then. They had jackets on like the bikies wear and I could see beards sticking out past the sides of their faces. And one of them was the same shape as Spider Dragovic.'

'Did you hear anything?'

'Yes, I heard one of them say, "C'mon, Spide, she's gone up. If it's in there, the fire will wreck it. That's all we need. Let's get outa here."'

'Did you smell anything?'

'Yes, there was a strong smell of petrol.'

Again, Mr Davis raises the contents of the box in the drum to establish a possible motive for the bikies to start the fire. The box and its contents, and the list of contents, have earlier been tendered by consent, and Andy agrees it's the same list that was given to him at Maitland Police Station after he and Bert witnessed officers force the box open and examine its contents. Mr Davis asks Andy to look at the list.

He asks, 'Is there a gun on that list?'

'Yes, there is,' Andy replies.

Mr Davis establishes with his questions and Andy's answers how the box came to light, and the likelihood that if Goob risked his life to retrieve it from the fire, he most likely knew it contained something of great value.

'Andy, did you see evidence of friendship between Mr Schwartz and Spider Dragovic? Did they appear to be on good terms?'

'Hell, no!' says Andy.

'Why do you think that?'

'Leo kept a gun hidden under pillows on his outside seat when the bikies came around. He showed it to me once and it was different to the one in the box. I don't think he was afraid of them but he didn't trust them at all. He probably knew a lot of bad things they'd done and they knew the same about him. Maybe there was a balance.'

The Prosecution objects, of course—it's speculation. Upheld.

Mr Davis had subpoenaed Hippo Jack's record of interview in Queensland and now has it authenticated, and uses the interview to put Spider and Hippo at the scene of the fire with a jerry can of petrol.

Ms Kemble objects again. Overruled.

By getting upright citizens such as Bert and Clara onto the witness stand in support of Andy, his credibility will be increased. Mr Davis introduces them in his questioning.

He asks, 'Andy, did you get help or advice from anyone in handling the difficult circumstances at the caravan park?'

'Yes. Bert Foster who lives near the shops in Greta gave me food and I could stay at his place if I had to get away from Leo's. Bert went with me to get the box out of the drum. And Clara McGregor, who's a friend of his, helped me, too. Clara took me to the Disability Advisory Committee in Maitland and to doctors and stuff like that. She also helped get me into TAFE and helped Esther and Adeline.'

Mr Davis concludes with, 'No further questions, Your Honour.' He smiles at Andy before sitting down. Andy feels he's done well.

Mr Davis has subpoenaed Hippo Jack's deathbed statement. Unfortunately, it doesn't mention the fire, so he doesn't introduce it in evidence.

———————

Ms Kemble, the Prosecutor rises. From her aura and the look on her face, Andy can see she doesn't like him at all. Her attitude is more than that of a professional opponent—she really doesn't like him. It occurs to Andy that her slightly turned left arm and weak left leg could be evidence of cerebral palsy. Can she see in him what she would hate to be seen as herself, let alone become, a person who sends primary visual signals that they are less than perfect? That could be the source of her aggression. Andy can't change how she sees him, but understanding her motive eases him. Given the opportunity, he would console her. He would let her know that despite his physical awkwardness, he's happy in his head, and a contented mind in a damaged body is easier to live with than a distressed mind in a standard form.

I have accepted my new physical self. I accept the person I have become. It seems a strange time and place to arrive at that conclusion, but Andy recognises the realisation for what it is.

———————

In the lead-up to the trial Mr Davis gave Andy advice on how to behave while being cross-examined. He put practice questions that the Prosecutor might ask, and told him, 'Just answer the question. Answer it the same way if it is asked more than once. Don't elaborate. Ms Kemble might ask questions to stir you up and make you say something more, so be alert to that. And she's not your pal, even if she pretends to be, so don't let her draw anything out of you with friendly words.'

Ms Kemble asks questions about his family and the need to meet his father's expectations. Then come the questions about Esther. Did he like her? *Yes*. Did he like her very much? *Yes*. Did he believe she liked him? *Yes, he did believe that*. Did Andy think that because Esther was vulnerable, she was more likely to react positively to him? Andy doesn't understand the question. Do you think, says Ms Kemble, that because Ms Schönburg had no opportunities to meet young men, that she welcomed your attention? *She's not like that*, says Andy. *She's intelligent and kind and sensible.*

Did he dislike Leo? *Yes*. Did he think Leo was a bad person? *Yes*. What would he do to get Esther out of Leo's van, even if she had gone there voluntarily? *Anything*. It's the wrong answer.

'Mr Contopoulos,' Ms Kemble continues, 'did you rush to the back of the caravan to rescue Ms Schönburg?'

'Yes.'

'So you moved quickly?'

'As quickly as I could.'

'I put it to you that whether or not you lit the original fire in the drum, you were quite capable of moving fast enough with a firebrand to join the other dancing protestors and set fire to the tarpaulin at the front of the caravan.'

'No. I didn't do that. I can't dance.'

'Mr Contopoulos, did you know Mr Schwartz stored petrol at the caravan park?'

'Not really.'

'Yes or no, Mr Contopoulos.'

'Not really.'

'Were you free to wander everywhere in the caravan park?'

'We weren't supposed to.'

'In the several weeks you had been at the caravan park, had you explored the grounds?'

'Pretty much.'

'So you could well have come across stored petrol?'

'I suppose so. If it was there, I might have passed it.'

'Mr Contopoulos, is it correct that early in the evening of the night of the fire, you and Miss Montgomery agreed to meet in front of Mr Schwartz's van at 10.00 p.m?'

'Could you say that again, please? It was too long.'

Ms Kemble labours through the repetition.

'Yes.'

'And did you, in the several hours up till 10.00 p.m., convey small quantities of petrol in several trips from the storage area to the back of the caravan, and there place it in a single larger container? Or with that much time, did you drag in short stages a jerry can over the distance?'

Ms Kemble realises her error and without being asked, breaks the question into smaller segments.

'No. None of that.' Andy is intensely alert.

'Mr Contopoulos, once the fire took hold, you were able, despite your physical impairment, to get to the secret entrance at the back of the caravan to rescue Ms Schönburg. Is that true?'

'Yes.'

'Would you not have also been able, just a little earlier, to get there while other people were dancing, and tip over the container of petrol so that it ran under the van and around items stored there?'

'No, no. I wouldn't do that.'

'I put it to you, Mr Contopoulos, that by whatever means you put the petrol there, you did tip it out to run under and around Mr Schwartz's van knowing there were people inside. Is that true?'

'No! Never!'

'Do you agree it would have been one way to have revenge on Mr Schwartz for his treatment of Ms Schönburg. What do you say?'

'I wouldn't do that.' Andy frets at the accusation. The questions keep coming despite his denials. His voice has weakened and his answer is not convincing. He adlibs. 'Goob was always spying on us and he would have seen me doing lots of short trips. And no way could I carry or drag a whole can.'

Ms Kemble asks about the two men Andy claims to have seen leaving the scene. Again, he says he believes they belonged to the local motor bike riders group.

'Didn't you accompany one member of that group, a Spider Dragovic, to his house to treat his injured dog?'

'Yes, but...'

'Didn't you also accompany that man's son to hospital when he needed treatment?'

'Yes, but...'

'Mr Contopoulos, I suggest you were in league with that group of bikers to either extract information from Mr Schwartz on the whereabouts of something Mr Dragovic had an interest in, or you wanted revenge on Mr Schwartz regarding Ms Schönburg.'

'No, it's not like that.'

'No further questions.'

———•———

DAY FOUR. MR Davis calls an orthopaedic specialist to give an opinion based on prior association as to Andy's physical capacity to commit the offence as claimed. He tenders the medical reports of Andy's accident and treatment. They confirm his impaired mobility and reduced strength: he would definitely not be able to carry a full jerry can.

The Crown accepts the reports and declines to cross-examine their authors.

The police officer who was on duty in Maitland when Bert and Andy surrendered the box from the drum at Leo's is called. The officer gives evidence the gun in the box is the same type used to kill a police officer several years ago. That is an unsolved crime.

'Does this match the item surrendered by the defendant and Mr Foster at Maitland Police Station?'

'Yes, it does.'

'And do you accept the way it has been recorded that it came into their possession?'

'Yes, I do.'

Mr Davis has confirmed an important point: that the box was not a concoction by Andy, but was linked to Goob and Leo. If its contents relate to criminal activity by Leo or the bikies, then it gives the bikies motive to be after it, and perhaps to recover it at any cost.

It's not a dramatic round of questions, but as Mr Davis takes his seat beside Mr Scarpetta they exchange a look that says they're satisfied to have confirmed the origins of the box and its contents.

Ms Kemble cross-examines the officer in an attempt to establish that sort of gun is not rare. The officer agrees there are a few around.

Mr Davis calls the Defence's forensic expert. His responses emphasise the contents of his report—a burning tarpaulin would not have been enough to cause the flare-up of fire that consumed the caravan but if an accelerant such as petrol had been poured at the back of the van and had run underneath to the front, a spark from the burning tarpaulin could have started a fire that tracked back and erupted. And there was evidence of an accelerant.

Ms Kemble cross-examines about how small an amount could have had the same outcome but she fails to make inroads.

Mr Davis calls Bert Foster. He's there to substantiate Andy's character as a person who would not retaliate aggressively. Bert is asked to recount how he met Andy and what they discussed in relation to the caravan park: he describes how Andy planned to address issues constructively, never vengefully. Bert recounts his and

Andy's secretive retrieval of the box. Bert insists they didn't do it for gain but to ensure the bikies didn't get their hands on it.

'We thought whatever was inside might explain what was going on between Leo and the bikies,' Bert says.

It's speculation and Ms Kemble objects. Upheld.

She cross-examines Bert but gets nothing.

Mr Davis calls Clara McGregor. Clara confirms she took Andy to the Disability Advisory Committee meeting at the council chambers and that she saw him come out of the mayor's office. Andy has already given evidence that's when he found out the impending sale of the caravan park. It's an excuse to get her on the stand to describe the positive, community minded activities Andy has undertaken since she's known him.

Ms Kemble has no questions for Clara.

———•———

THE TRIAL HAS taken fewer days than set aside, and now it's time to sum up. The Prosecution and the Defence barristers will each address the jury.

Ms Kemble reviews all the evidence against Andy, and everything that could be slanted against him. Facts pile up and Andy had a motive: Leo mistreated him and abducted Andy's love interest; Andy associated with criminal types, the bikies, and joined in activities with them, knowing there was hostility between them and Leo; and so it goes on. Did he align himself with them to get revenge on Leo, and Esther, too, for that matter, by burning the van with both of them inside, only thinking to mask his involvement at the end by rescuing Esther? As for the gun in the box and Spider's connection to it, Ms Kemble struggles to find a plausible alternative explanation.

Ms Kemble depicts Andy in the worst possible light and if he was on the jury, he would convict the person she describes. He knows he's innocent of the charges but her address is persuasive.

Mr Davis is an experienced campaigner and takes his time. He addresses the jury on Andy's background, character and why he was at Leo's. He underscores the relationship between Esther and Andy, and the extreme danger, as attested by an expert from the fire service, that Andy put himself in to rescue Esther—far more danger than if someone wanted only to exonerate himself from starting a fire.

Much hangs on Andy's credibility. Did he really see bikies, or anyone, at the back of the caravan? 'You must,' Mr Davis tells the jury, 'assess this young man's character for yourselves, based on the evidence of the witnesses. Not one person who knows him has been critical of his honesty, his actions or his attitudes. Indeed, two people of excellent standing in the community have given unreserved high praise of his character. There has been no contradictory evidence, and we heard from Detective Crossley that the accused denied the allegation from the start, as he did before you in evidence, and he has never wavered.

'There are also matters of fact presented by expert witnesses that must be considered: the ferocious fire that consumed the caravan was undoubtedly caused by an accelerant at the rear, and not only has it been shown that the defendant did not start the fire at the front, but that he was incapable of carrying the jerry can of petrol to the back.'

The judge gives her instructions to the jury, including pointing out matters of law they must take into account. The jury retires to consider its verdict. It's late in the day, so all the players are sent home but told to be available at ten o'clock in the morning in case the jury reaches its verdict by then.

Mr Davis hopes the jury is not out for long. *Not Guilty* verdicts are usually returned in short order, and the longer the jury is out, the more likely a guilty verdict will be returned.

———•———

AFTER THE JURY retires, the accused and witnesses are permitted to associate again. Bert leads the way to a Chinese restaurant—he thinks it more diplomatic than Greek or German or Australian—where they fill a large booth. Dr and Mrs Contopoulos sit opposite Andy and Esther, while Bert and Clara, with Adeline who had to be entreated to come, sit at the top of the U-shaped cubicle. Adeline and Esther are rigidly decorous as Clara introduces them to Dr and Mrs Contopoulos. The eyes of the two mothers meet as they politely shake hands and there's recognition of the most important thing in each of their lives—their child.

There's no light-hearted banter. On the day they arrived, Mum managed to give Andy a hug outside the court and there was a brief handshake between father and son, but no words. The circles under Mum's eyes are dark and large, and her lips have lost their firm set. Dad's face is drawn and he's smaller inside his suit.

Bert tries to strike up conversation with Dr Contopoulos who listens but stares at his son. Andy looks at the menu or runs his eyes along the table to Clara—anything but meet his father's glower. While Esther reassures her mother, she slips her hand around Andy's and with a gentle squeeze brings it to rest on her lap. It has the effect of a press-button start motor that projects resolution through him. Andy raises his head to meet his father's glare and their eyes lock. Neither flinches and icy tension immobilises everyone. The only sound is Mrs Contopoulos's rapid, shallow inhalations.

'I did nothing wrong, Dad.' Andy maintains the eye contact and speaks in a gritty monotone no one has heard before. 'I was helping people. I still am helping people. Isn't that what you wanted me to do? If I can't be a doctor like *you* planned, I can still do good things. There were bad people doing bad things round here and I've helped change that. If you don't believe me, go home. I have Esther and I have good friends who believe in me.'

Mrs Contopoulos's eyes roll sideways to gauge her husband's response. Bert purses his lips, sits back, crosses his arms and transfers his gaze to Andy's dad. Game on. Esther tightens her grip on Andy's hand.

Dad's eyes get watery but he refuses to blink. No tears fall. 'I do not like to see my son on trial for murder. It is a disgrace. Your mother threatened me with further disgrace, in fact a divorce, if we did not come. So, we are here. I accept that you believe you committed no crime and that you were attempting to help. We'll see how the law interprets what you have done.'

Bert sits forward and speaks in a gently instructive tone. 'Dr Contopoulos, it's up to you and Andy to sort things out between you, but you don't need to wait for the jury. Those charges are a load of codswallop. You should know that. I wouldn't be surprised if Andy was nominated for a bravery award and what's more, if things turn out as I think they will, he will receive a reward for helping to solve an old murder. Just thought you should know all that.'

Esther sits taller and says, 'Dr Contopoulos, all that Bert says is true. Andy did save my life and he saved my mother's life by making sure she saw doctors. Also, a boy who was injured he saved. Andy bravely made a bad person drive to the hospital with the boy. We are most proud of him. He has saved lives as a doctor would, but by different means.'

In a challenge to Dr Contopoulos to doubt what she says, Esther leans over and gives Andy a lingering kiss on the cheek. He and Esther squeeze hands again under the table.

Andy is fortified with self-belief. That's just as well because he has no confidence in the jury.

Chapter Thirty-one

Day five. Mum and Dad wait in a café across the road. As soon as Tommo hears the jury is ready to return a verdict, he'll ring and they'll come over. Andy's group lingers around the foyer of the courthouse.

Andy and Esther sit holding hands: their faces show hopeful apprehension. They ignore Bert who hides his nerves by launching a broadside against a state government issue aired on the radio this morning. They do all care about people whose homes are resumed to build tollways, but none of them can commiserate right now. Bert finger taps the bench beside him. Clara tries to hold them together with suggestions on work Andy might apply for. There's no enthusiasm for that topic either, so she diverts to something light-hearted: she's heard that Lola is organising some women at the refuge to put on a concert at a nursing home, and describes the planned acts.

Late in the morning the jury sends word to the judge via a court officer that they've reached a verdict. The court assembles. Andy's stomach churns as he makes his way to the dock, and it spasms as the judge enters and takes her seat. He's told to stand and it feels like play-acting again. He knows he could disappear down the hole in the floor to the cells below if the foreman of the jury says one word rather than two. The disasters he's had so far in his life were unexpected. Could another one be unfolding?

When everyone is in place the jury files in. Their faces give nothing away.

The Judge's Associate asks the Foreman of the jury, 'Do you have a verdict?'

'We do.'

'How find you regarding the charge, that on the fourteenth day of January 2001 the defendant did murder Leopold Schwartz?'

'We find the defendant *Not Guilty*.'

There's a great exhalation behind Andy and a gulping yelp that sounds like his mother.

'So says your foreman. So say you all?' the officer enquires of the jury. They signal agreement.

'You have been found not guilty, Mr Contopoulos. Is there any reason Mr Contopoulos should remain? No? You may leave the court.' It's the judge's final input.

Andy shuts his eyes and sees himself as a giant balloon filled with a heavy gas: he's rolling and bouncing along the ground, ready to take off in a strong wind, but still weighed down by this awful experience. He's apprehensive of more processes, more questions to answer, and more bumps in the road. He doesn't move.

Tommo comes to help him from the dock. 'Come on, Andy. Let's get you out of here. It's time to go, mate.'

———•———

A WEEK AFTER the verdict, numbness gives way to relief and to the realisation that decisions must be made, and even better, that he's free to make them. Andy is getting his breath back after being squashed by a massive weight for a long time. Bert is pleased to have Andy, and Casper of course, stay with him until the *young fella* gets on his feet. That suits Andy because he can't move away from Esther. Most days he goes by bus to see her and it's only a block to where she lives with her mother from the stop where he gets off.

The bus driver smiles at him as he boards and it's great to be out and about in this perfect weather. He has news for Esther and although it's nothing momentous, it is evidence of progress in his life. To him it's proof that he can regain control.

Mrs Edwards, the owner of the Federation cottage where Esther and Adeline rent a flat, is in the front garden—a square of grass on each side of the path with an hydrangea on either side of three steps leading up to the front porch, and a garden bed against the front wall on one side. She's kneeling on a hessian sack to plant seedlings in the well-turned earth. When Andy opens the gate to the path that leads along the side of the house, Mrs Edwards swivels to greet him.

'Hello there, Andy m' boy. And how are you? Beautiful day. Go right round. I'm sure they're in.'

Andy smiles and thanks her as he carefully closes the gate. The flat was a lucky find by Clara. Esther and Adeline have their own facilities, their own entrance and the use of the yard. They can walk to shops, the library and a park.

Andy reaches the compact back yard and sees Adeline inspecting a shrub. Bushes and small trees around the fence line enclose the patch of grass into a private space. Mrs Edwards' cat, Methuselah, sashays around Adeline's legs, and as soon as she sits on a bench, the cat jumps onto her lap. Adeline pats Methuselah fondly while the cat drools and pushes himself against her.

'Good morning, Andy,' Adeline says. 'Cats are my favourite animal. I had pet cats when I was a child and they were my best friends.'

Esther emerges from the house and dances a couple of steps before she reaches him. They hold hands and touch cheeks. Esther smiles at her mother as she leads Andy inside.

'I will make tea, Mama, and bring it back.'

Andy and Esther catch up while she prepares a tray.

He says, 'I have an allowance now, from the government. Clara helped with the forms and she came with me to an interview. Bert said I could live at his house anyway, but now I can pay rent without getting a job. I still want to get a job, but I can't decide whether to get a job or do a training course. I don't like the small business course I'm doing: some of it's too hard for me, and it's not interesting. I'll keep going till I find something better, or get a job. And I know I'm not up to finishing Medicine. Even if I did manage to finish it, I'd be so limited in what I could do—I can't stand up for a long time, or use both hands easily, or work long hours. I might get fitter but I'll never have stamina. Bert and I talked about it yesterday.'

Esther lets Andy talk. He has to find his own path.

'Bert and I watch the news and he says I should read the papers every day. He says it will broaden my horizons. Get this, Esther. I remember exactly something Bert said because it made so much sense. He said that because my life has changed so much, I need to be able to see it all from a hilltop to decide which valley I want to go down into. We can't stay on hilltops because the air is rarefied—we have to get down and amongst whatever is going on.'

Esther says, 'I think Bert is a wise man. Many fine people do not have much schooling, let alone a university degree. We do not make friendships based on the level of another person's education. There is no training anywhere that teaches people how to be worthy. It is the course of life that brings out the strength and goodness inside each of us.'

Andy tries not to gape at Esther. How is she so wise so young?

'I've decided to go to Sydney to see my mum and dad. Just a visit to see how they are. And I need to know I can travel on my own. It would help if I was a pigeon with a homing instinct.' Andy's humour surprises them both.

After her smile, Esther's *Oh* is ambivalent. Respect and being dutiful are qualities she understands, but what if Andy's parents prevail and keep him in Sydney? There's a faint frown on Esther's brow as she pours tea.

•———————•

AFTER THE ACQUITTAL, Andy parted on good terms with his mum and cordial ones with his dad, but there was no invitation from them, or offer by Andy to go home. He's talked with Mum a few times, and said he'd come down one day this week, so he knows she'll be there. Bert agrees it's a good idea to go, and helps Andy plan the trip.

They go to Maitland Station to catch the Sydney train. It terminates at Central Station, which is past where Andy wants to get off, but it means there's no risk of overshooting and ending up in Melbourne. If Andy does miss his station, Strathfield, he's to get off at Central, ask for the urban trains, and consult the indicator board for the correct platform and time. Bert writes out the name of five stations before Strathfield, from each direction, so Andy will have plenty of warning as his stop approaches. He must check the name of every station as the train stops, and be ready to get off. Andy is positive he knows the way from Strathfield Station.

Bert assures Andy as they wait. 'Piece of cake, mate, piece of cake. If you're not sure, just ask someone.'

Andy gets off at Strathfield on the way down as if it's a daily commute. There's a moment of disorientation because pedestrian routes out onto the streets have been redirected due to maintenance. He's relieved to emerge on the correct side of the station to a familiar streetscape. Walking with the crowd of dispersing passengers is reassuring because it's a scene from his former life, even if they do impatiently brush past him to get where they're going one minute earlier. The only difference between him and the other bodies is his faltering pace.

He passes familiar landmarks: the neo-classical pile with turrets and a widow's walk; the row of Federation mansions; the bulging sandstone garden walls with sweet alyssum plunging over the edge. He'd forgotten home was so far from the station. He turns a corner and sucks in his breath as he starts along *Greek Street,* so-called because of its many houses with columns and statues and fountains.

His front yard is exactly the same: concrete, pots and statues—all so very neat and controlled. The curtains are unchanged and the blinds are raised to exactly the same level as they always were. Nostalgia threatens to swamp him. There's a brief moment when Andy believes he's the old Andy coming home on any day from uni. Mum will be inside to hug and feed him and life is good. It's a brief moment. He still has a key in his wallet but he rings the bell.

Mum opens the door and drags him in before she flings her arms around him. They topple back against a wall, laughing. She looks down and sees there's no bag in his hands.

'My son! My son!' There's more hugging and her strong hands rub the sides of his face. 'Where is your bag?'

Of course, she's hoping he's come home for good, or at least to stay a while, so Andy is candid from the start.

'This is just a visit, Mum. I wanted to see you and Dad... to make sure you're both okay, and to tell you I'm all right, too.'

'But you cannot travel back today. Two trips in one day is too much for you. Stay tonight, please, Andy. Your room is ready. It has always been ready. And I have made your favourite foods, all of them!'

It's hard watching her elation subside. Andy weakens. 'Maybe one night,' he says.

Mrs Contopoulos makes coffee and puts food in

front of him. They sit in the kitchen at the breakfast bar and talk. Andy reassures his mother, again, that he's happy and well, apart from the obvious, and that he has a future. He tells no lies, but nor is it prepared patter.

'Mum, none of us wanted our lives to turn out this way. We didn't want to lose Lydia and I didn't want to have the accident. But I'm alive, I have a life and I'm still your son. It won't be the life you and me and Dad thought, but it might even be better. You know, I was a bit of an arsehole before. Some of the things I did weren't so nice. I'd rather be the person I am now, and disabled, than be like I was.'

Andy forces the words out. 'I think I'm a nicer person now, I do. You didn't always see it. It would have been a waste of a life to stay like that.'

Mum takes his hand, murmuring, 'No, no, you were a good boy.'

Andy rubs her shoulder and gives a quiet hug. Then he breaks the big news, and happily, because it feels so right. 'I can't go back to uni—it's just not for me and I'm not up to it, no matter what Dad says about hard work. But there's lots of other things I can do. Bert says I can live with him while I get organised. And don't dislike Bert because you think he's taking me away from Sydney. I have to stay up there because I love Esther and I'm going to ask her to marry me. You might even get some grandchildren. You could be a Yiayia.'

Mum is lost for words. Maybe Andy could do better—a Greek girl perhaps, but who would have him as he is? Disabled and unqualified? She leans over and kisses his cheek.

'I'm happy for you. She is a nice girl. Make sure you invite us to the wedding.'

They sit and talk till Dad comes home. Mum greets him in the garage and he comes calmly into the kitchen.

Andy has a similar conversation with his father to what he had with his mother, and contrary to Andy's expectation, it's not traumatic. Dad's a beaten man: the drive has gone out of him. The auras are of sadness and bitterness. While there have been successes for himself, he's been denied the crowning glory of brilliant, successful children. He's failed them, his wife and himself.

Conversation is subdued at dinner. Looking at his depleted parents, Andy perceives how much heartache he's caused. He wants to give something back if he can, to rebuild their spirits. Having been the cause, he seeks to become the cure.

Andy can't catch his father's eye, but says to his bent head, 'Dad, I want to say I'm sorry for all the grief I've caused you. I wasn't being a good son when I had the accident, but you were a great father then. And you still are. I love you and Mum, and I want to be a better son than I was before. I was always going to move out of home, away from you, at some stage. I've done it at a different time and in a different way than any of us planned. I'm still your son, just not the one you expected to have. I can still have a worthwhile life, Dad, and we can still share the parts of our lives that we want to.'

Dad finally looks up. There's no anger on his face, or hurt or denial, just sadness and maybe, Andy hopes, a hint of acceptance. Dad pushes his chair back and leaves the table. Mum waits till he's left the room.

'Thank you, Andy. They were good things to say and your father needed to hear them. He is all right. He has come to understand how you are and he knows the future will not be what he thought it would be. I am so much better, too, for having you come home, if only for a visit.'

'I can visit often. There's no reason why not.'

Mrs Contopoulos softens and smiles.

'Please, Andy, stay tonight. It is too late for you to travel. It's no matter you didn't bring a bag.'

She turns away and speaks boldly but self-consciously when she says, 'All your things are still there, as they were, when you drove away with your friends.

'I will ring Bert so he doesn't worry about you.'

Andy is too tired to argue, and can see the point. His mum wants to mollycoddle him: get out pyjamas, run a bath and turn back the bed, but he won't have it. Andy kisses her on the forehead and shuts the bedroom door. He finds everything he needs by instinct.

Andy is up early enough to have breakfast with his dad. There's no conversation. Every few minutes Andy throws in an opener. 'I'm going back to Newcastle today.' Dad nods. And then, 'Clara found a nice flat for Esther and Adeline. They love it.' Another nod. 'I'm looking for a job,' is his last attempt to engage his father, and it doesn't work. Dr Contopoulos gets up from the table, kisses his wife on the cheek then comes to where Andy is seated. He says nothing but shakes Andy's hand with both of his own, and leaves the house immediately.

'That was good. He will be all right,' says Mrs Contopoulos.

Andy's trip back to Newcastle is without incident. At Bert's he's blasé about the trip. He makes out it was no big deal, when in fact, it's the first normal thing he's done independently in more than two years.

Chapter Thirty-two

Bert orchestrated a six a.m. get away from Maitland to allow time to find their way, and for train delays and taxi shortages, but there were no problems, so Andy, Esther and Bert are among the first to arrive. They have time to relax before the big event instead of getting there stressed. Esther has never been to Sydney and Bert hasn't been to the 'big smoke' for years, so it's been non-stop chatter along the way: tall buildings, so many people, such vehicles... and as for the Harbour Bridge, it's a marvel!

Andy has come to Government House today to receive an award from the Royal Humane Society for bravery in rescuing Esther. He was acquitted nine months ago of the murder charge, and the memory of those shocking events — the fire and the trial, is so chilling as to believe they happened in another universe. But Esther also emerged from that tumult, and here she is, fondly stroking his shoulder, aglow on his behalf at the honour he will receive.

A cab brings them up from Wynyard Station through the first set of stone-pillared, iron gates into the Botanic Gardens, then through the more elegant entrance into the grounds of Government House. The Gothic Revival residence and offices of the Governor of New South

Wales sit comfortably on a hill overlooking the harbour. It's a setting for ceremonies and formal occasions, yet welcoming to all visitors. The pale sandstone building does not dominate the hill or the city, but occupies the site with dignified serenity.

They alight from the taxi under the grey portico and are ushered into the Main Hall with its grand ascending wooden staircase. The trio is mute in the regal atmosphere: rows of flags and portraits of notables bedeck the walls. The room is a composition in mood; soft lighting, red carpets, warm wood tones, gilt finishes on wood and picture frames. It signals establishment, solidarity, confidence.

Andy could invite three guests to share the event. Bert offered to accompany him and Esther and then stand aside so both of his parents could attend. Andy's mother tried to persuade Dr Contopoulos but he would not come. She, however, promised to be here. If Mount Olympus were to fall across her path, she would tunnel underneath it, scramble over it or simply demand it get out of her way.

Andy looks for her now and here she is, reaching out to hug him. So good! Mrs Contopoulos takes Esther's offered hand and kisses her on each cheek, then shakes Bert's hand. They smile at each other. And keep smiling: no words can increase the pleasure of the moment.

Bert takes Esther's arm. 'Come, my dear. I believe this is how a gentleman escorted a lady to the dancefloor in former times. I can't cut the rug anymore, so let's peruse the artwork.' Bert explains the slang as they move away.

Mrs Contopoulos says, 'I tried for your father to come but you know what he is like. So stubborn! He will never admit that he is wrong, even though the words are choking him. He brought me here and he will pick me up afterwards. I would not be surprised if he is hiding behind a tree and will peer through a window. Believe me, Andy, he is proud of you for this. Our whole family is proud of you. Of course, they love to have a doctor in the family, but a hero... that is even better to the Greeks!'

Warrant Officers guide Andy and other awardees to their places in the adjacent State Drawing Room where adjutant staff sort the recipients into order: the highest awards are made first. Andy is pleased he's not amongst the first few: that way he'll see how it's done. He's not nervous because it's not a trial—just excited, and he wants to conduct himself with manly composure.

Huge open double doors join the room to the State Ballroom where rows of seats are set out for guests. A covered colonnade is outside. Andy can see lawns that are as green and smooth as the synthetic surface of a tennis court, and garden beds coloured with late flowers. Moreton Bay fig trees loom graciously: any one of them, with their far-reaching branches almost horizontal to the ground, would accommodate a treehouse home for the Swiss Family Robinson. Through gaps in the foliage, the blue-grey harbour appears to have a million tiny mirror balls floating on it.

A small band plays while people settle, then the Governor, Her Excellency, Lady Stephanie Marquet, arrives and takes her seat. Someone steps up to the lectern to read the citations. The first recipients have been shepherded from the Drawing Room to the outside colonnade and along to the door leading back inside the Ballroom. As each name is announced the person moves inside, their citation is read, the Governor offers congratulations and attaches the award. A photo is taken, and the recipient, with all eyes upon him or her, progresses down the centre aisle and exits into the Main Hall for another commemorative photo before taking their seat back in the Drawing Room.

Andy's gut contracts: he will look a fool walking down the centre of the room with a swinging arm and a dragging leg. He prays no one will laugh. As the ceremony proceeds Andy hears descriptions of exemplary service and heroic action: he's one of these people and physical impairment does not seem important in the grand scheme of human interaction.

Now it's his turn and he's ushered forward—feels like he's floating—and stands before the gathering while his citation is read:... *despite the caravan being well alight and the flames increasing rapidly, Mr Contopolous risked his life to break in through the rear of the caravan and battle through thick smoke and poisonous fumes to locate Ms Schönburg whom he found to be bound and unable to leave with him. Mr Contopoulos groped around for a knife, cut the ropes by which Ms Schönburg was bound and escorted her from the caravan which was shortly enveloped in flame. Mr Contopoulos completed the rescue despite his own significant physical incapacity, the result of an accident approximately two years before the rescue.*

Andy is not aware of reluctant legs or a wavering arm. If his body is misbehaving, he doesn't care. His life today is in the heart and the head, and his clear, bright eyes search the crowd for Esther. He moves toward Lady Marquet, receives her congratulations and she pins the award to his chest. Andy can't imagine that a Vice-Chancellor's salutation at a university graduation could be any better.

Now for the walk. He sets off, feeling ten feet tall, just the way he did leaving the field as a fifteen-year-old when his team won a soccer grand-final against the odds. He's cruising! Sees Bert, sees his mother, finds Esther and their gaze locks. How different this is from the time their eyes first glued to each other through the caravan window less than eighteen months ago when he stood on a car battery and saw her and Leo! On that day, through nothing more than a line of sight, they communicated need and longing. Today, once more it is their eyes that say it all. Andy glides the length of the room.

The band plays again at the conclusion of the ceremony and refreshments are served. Everyone wanders into the garden to chat, stroll and enjoy the drinks and nibbles on offer. Mrs Contopoulos checks out the warm savouries sniffily, but is impressed and takes another. Bert tries some but holds back as he prefers plainer fare. He watches Andy heap a pile of food onto a serviette. 'Hungry work being a hero, eh?' he laughs. Esther has to be encouraged. She's wary lest they get a bill on the way out. Andy tells her it's all included. 'It's on the house! It's free.'

'How amazing a government would do such a thing,' she says. 'How many governments give such happiness to their people?'

The foursome stroll across lawn and look back. The building's blond sandstone dazzles in bright light and the cloisters beckon, offering shade or shelter or discreet seclusion. Further down toward the harbour they can see more water and the Opera House. Esther lingers, entranced.

'We'll go there soon,' Andy promises. 'And we'll bring your mother. We'll see an opera that she chooses. Would you like that?'

Tears well in Esther's eyes. 'I love you so much, Andy. You are a good and kind man, and you are a hero. What more could a girl want?'

'How about I ask Mum to send you her recipes for my favourite dishes?'

Chapter Thirty-three

It's another big day. Since the accident there have been a few: the fire, a trial, and an investiture at Government House. This morning, a month after he received his award, Andy sits alone in his kitchen sipping tea. The day is unfolding like the petals of a huge and luxurious jungle bloom—the Queen of the Night flower that his mother used to nurture: each petal a masterpiece unfurling at an inexorable, steady pace; stamens like flags at a royal wedding; and a tsunami of fragrance. By dawn the miracle bloom was a drooping mass of fleshy, cream petals.

He and Esther will marry this afternoon in the yard of his... their, new home. The wedding is today, but the flowering, their marriage, will go on and on. Andy strolls up and down the hallway, smiles into each room, leans on the windowsill of the sunroom and inhales the satisfaction of ownership.

He received a reward for information leading to the conviction of the person responsible for the death of Detective McMaster. Since Andy's own trial, Spider Dragovic has been tried and found guilty of that murder. Hippo Jack was a likely accomplice but he's already paid the price. The reward was large, almost $300 000, because it was an old case and the victim was a police officer.

It was enough to buy this house—a weatherboard cottage on the outskirts of Maitland above the one-in-one-hundred-year flood level, and protected by a levy. It has three bedrooms, an updated kitchen and a new bathroom. There's a lounge room with a fireplace where a gas heater has been installed, and a spacious sunroom-cum-living area at the back, facing north for winter warmth. A timber veranda has been added off the living room, and gives a pleasing view down the sloping block over the floodplains and across to creeks that thread the hilly edges of the flatlands and wander on to the great Hunter River. In a backwater at the bottom of his yard there are ducks, eels and tortoises, and there's no weldmesh fence between the house and the ponds.

Andy is at peace in the Lower Hunter with its alternating brown and green alluvial fields, the vulnerability to flooding, whatever mitigation is in place, occasional frosts in winter and hot muggy days in summer. It's halfway between town and country, and between tropical and temperate zones, with the benefits of both.

Bert and Clara helped organise the wedding, and Clara has been shopping with Esther and Adeline for bridal finery. The two helpers arrive mid-morning and while Bert checks the marquee and chairs, Clara asks Andy to sit at the table.

'Have you bought Esther a wedding present?' she asks.

'No. I didn't know I should. I thought a ring was all I needed.' Andy still panics with little provocation.

Clara soothes him. 'Of course a ring is all you need. And you've bought a house. But,' she emphasises and draws breath, 'I do have something you might like to give her, and Adeline, to make it an even more wonderful day. After the wedding though, so as not to divert attention from you two beautiful young folk.'

Clara pulls a thick letter from her bag and hands it to Andy. It's addressed to Clara and bears German stamps.

'Explanation,' Clara says. 'I got to know Adeline pretty well when I spent time with her at the hospital, and while getting their affairs sorted. She told me about the bundle of letters the woman who looked after her in Queensland—you couldn't call her a mother by any stretch of the imagination—gave her when they threw her out. It's been a great sorrow to Adeline for years that her parents most likely felt she'd rejected them for leaving her here, when in fact she understands they would have thought they were giving her a new life, perhaps even saving her life. She was not given their letters as they arrived so had neither an address nor evidence they were alive.

When she got to Leo's he wouldn't sanction her contacting them because, he said, it would put her at risk of deportation, and him at risk of prosecution for harbouring an illegal immigrant. He wouldn't even post a letter for her.

'I calculated that if Adeline's parents had her when they were in their twenties, they could still be alive. Life was tough in East Germany before the wall came down, and if they survived those conditions, they'd only be in their sixties now, so not too old. They might have had more children when they returned to Europe, who would be siblings for Adeline and aunts or uncles for Esther. The ladies might not be as bereft of family as they think.

'Anyway, I got cracking with enquiries, and guess what? They are still alive, there was another child, and he has children too! I didn't tell Bert what was going on as I didn't want anyone to get their hopes up. It's been hard to keep it to myself.

'This letter is a reply to me in English from the son, and the other one enclosed is from his parents to pass on to Adeline. They are all so thrilled to find her. Why don't you give it to Esther right after the wedding? For her mother. You can read it tonight before you two leave. Bert and I will stay around to make sure Adeline copes with the surprise. It's all good news but it could be a shock to her.'

Andy hugs Clara and says, 'That was a wonderful thing to do. It will make them so happy. Thank you.' He puts the envelope into an inner pocket.

Bert comes in breathless but it's from nerves rather than exertion.

'Have a break, Bert,' says Andy. 'Don't wear yourself out before we get started. If it's too much I can get Jason or Tommo to be best man.'

'Not on your nelly! I'm good for both. I'll be Esther's Pop and walk her down the stairs like I was her dad giving her away, then I'll stand right next to you to be best man. Wouldn't miss any of it for quids.'

Clara quizzes, 'And who's going to look after you when you fall in a heap, Bert?'

Bert doesn't hear her. 'Andy, where's the ring? Have you got the ring?'

'I saw you put it in your pocket,' Andy smiles.

'Have the caterers arrived?'

'Long ago. They're under control in the kitchen.'

'Crikey! Is the celebrant here?'

'Yes. I've spoken to her. She's sorted.'

'I've booked the cab, Andy. I know I booked the cab to take you into Newcastle afterwards. To the Novatel. To the honeymoon suite, mate. Mate,' Bert plonks a hand on Andy's shoulder, 'You're like a son to me,' he says. 'I know you love your dad, but you're like a son to me.'

Andy places his hand over Bert's. 'And you're like a second father to me, and a great mate—certainly better than any of those bastards that dumped me in Greta. But they were better friends than they knew: I met Esther and you and a heap of other good people, and I met the new me. That would never have happened if I'd gone back to Sydney.

'Ooh. There's people arriving. I'd better go and say hello. Come on, Cas, let's see who's here.'

Casper pads beside Andy. He's had a bath and is wearing a black bowtie on his collar. Although Andy has moved into his house, Casper stays with Bert until Andy's yard is fully fenced. Andy stipulated a fence that would not block the view, so it will be post and rail with dog wire covering, and it must have a gate so they can easily reach the water. It will be done by the time they're back from the honeymoon. When Andy went to Bert's yesterday, he found dog hair on the lounge.

'What's this, Bert?' Andy queried, holding a strand in the air. 'I thought Casper was an outside dog again.'

Bert coughed. 'Must have come in on my clothes.'

Andy had visited Bert to rehearse his speech. Clara suggested to Andy weeks ago that he might have a future as a public speaker. Andy was incredulous, but when Clara pointed out that his life had thrown up huge challenges, and not everyone who encountered such obstacles got over them as well as he had, Andy began to think the idea was not so crazy.

Bert and Clara had made suggestions to the draft of his wedding speech, and Andy had been practising. As long as he remembers the main flow, which isn't hard because it's chronological, he can make a fist of it—so much, in fact, that he can do it without prompts, and with dramatic input. Never had he thought such a thing possible for himself, not even pre-accident.

Between Andy and Esther, they don't know many people in Greta and Maitland and Newcastle, but enough for a party. Mrs Edwards arrives, then Lola and Jason and Tommo. Bert's daughter and her husband come in, then two friends Andy made at TAFE. Andy knows his mother will come because she promised, but he's still wondering about his dad. Thirty-five minutes to go. And Esther, well, he's sure she'll be there.

He asked her, 'Are you sure you're not marrying me because I'm the only man you know, or because you think you owe me for saving you from the fire? That's not enough for marriage.

'You don't know what I was like before the accident.

I think not very nice. What will happen if I keep recovering and go back to what I was like before?'

'I will beat you on the head again,' Esther laughed. 'You must stay as nice as you are. And don't think you are the only man I know. Some men in Maitland look at me and smile. I could become acquainted with them, if you wish, in order to make a comparison. Mmm?'

She teased more when he scowled.

At a quarter to the wedding hour, Andy hears cars pull up in front of the house and he goes to the open front door. Wow! Mum and Dad get out of the first car, then his Aunty Zoe and her husband and their son and daughter, his cousins, emerge from the second car. Wow, all over again!

Andy hungers for more faces from his past and scans the arrivals for Chris, his mate from uni. He wants a brother there, or the closest he had to that. At the same instant he remembers Chris is dead, and died saving him. If Esther and I have a child, Andy resolves, we will call him or her Chris.

Mum reaches Andy first. She hugs him and holds his face. 'My handsome boy! What a day!' Aunty Zoe is crying and laughing at the same time. It's a Greek reunion: ebullient and heart-felt, except for Dad, of course, who is reserved and sheepish, but not sullen. He hangs back till last, shakes Andy's hand and offers a muted, embarrassed congratulation.

'Thanks, Dad.' So much relief comes out with two words. What the heck, Andy thinks, and throws his arms around his father. Dr Contopoulos doesn't resist the embrace, and gives Andy one quick squeeze.

The family group bobs through the door into the depths of the house. Bert and Clara have been taking turns to peer through the front window, and on the dot of the appointed wedding hour Bert barks back over his shoulder for Andy and everyone to get to the marquee in the yard. A limo pulls up and Bert hops more than limps to meet it. He helps Adeline out and Clara conducts her through the house. Adeline knows the place well already and has selected the furnishings for her room. She will move in from the flat she and Esther have been renting after the newlyweds return from their honeymoon.

Esther emerges from the car, her hand in Bert's as she lets the bridal gown right itself around her. It's a simple, full-length, cream satin dress with a deep, square neckline and tiny, fitted sleeves. From the hips down, it flares and has a single deep ruffle that spirals around the dress to the hemline. Her hair is gathered softly at the back of her head but is allowed to drop to its full length in light coils.

'Oh, darling, you've been let out of Paradise,' Bert says.

He escorts her to the back veranda where they stand arm in arm in full view of the gathering. Spontaneous clapping breaks out: Esther is as poised as an ornamental bridal figurine on a wedding cake, except that she laughs at the applause. Adeline almost dissolves with joy. Andy can barely make Esther out for the dazzling glow she emanates.

Esther and Bert head for the stairs. 'Please, Bert, hold me firmly. I am shaking so much.'

'You and me both, sweetheart,' he replies, 'but we'll get there.'

With Esther's hand on the rail, and Bert's against the side of the house, they manage an elegant descent to the marquee. Esther and Andy stand face to face in front of the celebrant. They've written their own vows and there's nothing about *obeying* or *till parted by death,* but there are words about love and trust, about helping others, about being thankful for what they have been given, and about making the most of each day. They are declared married and sign the documents.

Accompanied by rowdy acclamation, the couple circulates then moves to a table. Their plan is to complete the toasts early so the rest of day can flow, so Jason, as M.C., calls on Bert to propose a toast to the bride, which he does, then extends it to all the women present, with a noticeable tilt of his head to Clara. Jason calls on Andy to speak. He stands and places the cue cards on the table before him, then slides them to one side.

'My wife—that feels great to say—and I welcome you to our home on this wonderful day. It's the happiest day of my life so far and you have all made it perfect by sharing it with us. Earlier today Clara asked me did I have a gift for Esther.'

Bert and Clara murmur to each other as Andy departs from his rehearsed speech.

'Apart from my love, a ring and everything I own, I said, no, I did not. But I've come to see I do have a gift. It's something that has grown in me since I had the accident. Please don't think that because I can make this speech,

I've recovered enough to go back to uni. I can say these things to you because the thoughts are in my head and want to come out. I don't have to search for them.

'You all know who I am but you do not all know me. I am not who I used to be. I believe I have become someone better because of what happened. I once had the life of a privileged son, and parents who provided me with everything I needed, and more than I needed, but through no fault of theirs I had no self-knowledge. Yet they sowed the seeds in me of what I have become, so there is credit due to them. I propose a toast to my parents, Dr and Mrs Contopoulos, Mum and Dad, who have never let me down.'

Andy continues. 'If I had not been injured, I would never have been so concerned with why people act as they do. I have learnt to understand and accept how they are, starting with myself. Because so much was stripped away from who I was, I have no preconceptions or expectations of people's behaviour. I don't understand innuendo or sarcasm, and even humour goes over my head most of the time.

'Most people don't have an easy life. Obstacles stop them doing what they want to, and terrible things happen, sometimes through bad luck and sometimes because of stupid choices. My life was easy till I made a dumb decision to play a game on the road, and it has been hard since then.

'Esther and her mother, Adeline, found themselves in an impossible place. They had no one to turn to and nowhere to go. They didn't have much to be happy about but they found joy in many places in the mind. I propose a toast to Adeline for the amazing way she raised my beautiful Esther to be well-educated and thoughtful, despite their hardships.

'People have different ways of dealing with problems: sometimes they get angry or act crazy to give themselves time and space to figure out what to do, or they just go quiet and stay confused. I was in despair and unwell, then a wonderful thing happened—I fell in love. Even better, that love was returned. Truly, it was as if a door did close on all the terrible things I had been through, and another opened onto the rest of my life.

'Through these ups and downs, I have developed insight into behaviour: what makes us strong or weak, and what we need to make ourselves and each other whole. But today is not about what I have learnt, it is about Esther's and my marriage.'

Andy places an arm around Esther.

'The gift I give you, Esther, is my insight of who you are—a perfect woman and the most wonderful human being I have ever known. You have my love and devotion forever.'

Andy surveys the gazing faces and is nonplussed by their tears, including Esther's.

Clara is no exception and punctuates her thoughts with exclamations of *Yes, Andy!* and *You hit the mark!* She can certainly see a role for him as a motivational speaker at schools and rehabilitation centres and venues for troubled youth.

Andy finishes with an invitation to anyone who wants to speak.

Dr Contopoulos stands. There's a tense wait till he raises his glass and says in a measured voice, 'Na Zisete—long life and happiness to my son, Andreas, and his wife, Esther, our new daughter. My wife and I welcome you, Esther, and your family, into ours.'

He scans the guests to see how his words are received, and sinks to his chair with relief as they whistle and clap and cheer. Mrs Contopoulos turns her head into his shoulder, to conceal a happy sob.

The guests party as daylight fades, and continue eating, dancing and chatting under lanterns in the garden.

Andy takes Esther aside and gives her the letter. She reads the one to Clara.

'This is amazing! How did this happen? Mama must be told but I hope it is not too much for her. Too much happiness can shock the heart as much as a burden of sadness... yet she must know.'

Esther brings her mother into the lounge room and seats her.

'Mama,' she says, 'There is a special present for you... something quite wonderful. We must thank Andy and Clara for it.' Esther hands her the envelope addressed simply *Adeline*. Adeline stares at the writing, uncomprehending. She lifts the barely adhering flap and removes the letter, sees the German language, turns a page to see the signature, and clasps her throat.

'It cannot be true! They are still alive! I dared not

dream of this. Esther, who has found them for us?'

'It was Clara, Mama, who found them. We will write back, and Andy says we can ring them on a telephone. You can speak to them. If you get strong, perhaps we can visit them.'

Adeline reads her letter again and Esther, who has learnt German from her mother, translates it for Andy. Clara comes in and Esther re-reads the letter for her. Adeline retreats to a bedroom but emerges in half an hour red-eyed and limp with happiness.

Andy and Esther sit on the veranda holding hands and murmuring endearments. Esther promises not to snore at night if Andy doesn't, and she laughs when he takes her seriously. He tells her about room service in hotels and they decide that's how they'll have their first breakfast together.

Nothing is said, because they don't yet know, about how they will spend summer evenings dawdling from the house to the water at the bottom of the yard, sitting on the grass and dangling their feet in the coolness, and of how Casper will be told not to chase ducks although he'll be allowed to swim and retrieve sticks from the pond. Andy and Esther have yet to learn how much water a large dog can shake on his stick-throwers.